TWO LIVES WITH YOU

OTHER TITLES BY LAUREN HO

Last Tang Standing

Lucie Yi Is Not a Romantic

Bite Me, Royce Taslim

PRAISE FOR *TWO LIVES WITH YOU*

"A fascinating and compelling look at one couple's chance to fall in love again after life has pushed them apart. You'll be reevaluating your own relationships when you turn the last page."

—Jodi Picoult, #1 *New York Times* bestselling author

"Who knew flirting with your husband who doesn't know he's your husband could be this romantic?"

—Mindy Kaling

"Lauren Ho has the rare gift of being hilarious and devastating on the same page. *Two Lives with You* is a smart, unflinching, deeply human look at love, resentment, desire, and the quiet choices that shape a life. It's messy, insightful, and wildly entertaining—proof that Ho is operating at the absolute top of her game. Read this if you like your fiction sharp, honest, and just a little bit dangerous."

—Justinian Huang, bestselling author of *Lucky Seed* and *The Emperor and the Endless Palace*

"*Two Lives with You* is an unputdownable exploration of marriage and the road not taken. It's the perfect read for anyone who has ever secretly thought, *Is this it for me?* I truly loved every page!"

—Amy Lea, international bestselling author

TWO LIVES WITH YOU

a Novel

Lauren Ho

MINDY'S BOOK STUDIO

This is a work of fiction. Names, characters, organizations, places, events, and incidents are either products of the author's imagination or are used fictitiously. Otherwise, any resemblance to actual persons, living or dead, is purely coincidental.

Published by Mindy's Book Studio, New York

www.apub.com

EU product safety contact:
Amazon Media EU S. à r.l.
38, avenue John F. Kennedy, L-1855 Luxembourg
amazonpublishing-gpsr@amazon.com

ISBN-13: 9781662541469 (hardcover)
ISBN-13: 9781662528064 (paperback)
ISBN-13: 9781662528071 (digital)

Cover design and illustration by Philip Pascuzzo

Printed in the United States of America

First edition

To my siblings—yes, it's your turn now

A NOTE FROM MINDY KALING

As a self-proclaimed ball of anxiety, I spend an unhealthy amount of time thinking about alternate versions of my life. What if I'd taken that job. What if I'd dated that person. What if I'd moved to that city. What if I actually left the oven on that one time. So when a book comes along that lets me explore parallel realities with zero real-world consequences, I'm immediately in.

That's the question that drives *Two Lives with You,* which follows Dana, a burned-out ER nurse, and her husband Nigel, a stay-at-home dad. They love each other but they're stretched thin and stuck in that stage of adulthood where everything feels harder than it used to. As the stress builds, they both start wondering what their lives might look like if they hadn't chosen each other. Then one day, as luck would have it, they wake up in a universe where they never got married. In fact, they never even met.

In this new reality, their lives look much better on paper—Dana is a wildly successful public speaker, Nigel is thriving in advertising... it's almost like this is the reality that was actually meant for them. And yet, they keep crossing paths. Their chemistry is off the charts. They sense some sort of cosmic bond. You start to wonder if maybe some people just can't stay out of each other's lives.

Ho knows exactly how to keep the story grounded without draining the magic out of it. This book is about marriage, second chances, and the uncomfortable possibility that sometimes getting everything you wanted won't always make you happier.

Read *Two Lives with You,* then spiral about all the minor decisions that may have potentially changed your life trajectory. At least that's what I did.

Prologue

Our House

Dana Smiley didn't believe in signs, and she certainly didn't believe in fate. She believed in cold hard facts, and the cold hard facts were telling her that the house she and her husband were in was haunted.

Consider the listing: two-story colonial, four bedrooms, granite countertops, hardwood floors, big yard, good school district—all this, under market price?

There was no other explanation: It was a murder house.

"It's not a murder house," Nigel whispered as they climbed the stairs a few paces behind the smiling forty-something bottle-blond real estate agent in heels. Everyone was sweating—they were in the middle of a heat wave—but Nigel glistened. "Trust me, I checked. I also ducked out to speak to the neighbors while you guys were in the walk-in closet, and they were *so* friendly."

"Everyone's friendly to you," Dana said, somewhat accusatorily.

He gave her a crooked, boyish grin. "That's because I like people."

She scoffed, wiping her sweating brow with a hand. "I *like* people too. May I remind you that I'm a nurse?"

"How could I forget my luck in marrying a medical professional?" Nigel said, grabbing her sticky hand and giving it a lingering kiss. The real estate agent—Jessica—who'd stopped to allow them to catch up, cooed at the sight, and even Dana's stone heart fluttered.

"How long have you lovebirds been together?" Jessica asked.

Dana and Nigel exchanged glances before chorusing, a tad guiltily, "Ten months."

The "ah" that the agent responded with, coupled with the darting glance at Dana's belly, told them everything. *Ah, it's that kind of relationship.*

Only Dana knew it wasn't. Sure, she got pregnant barely two months into dating the man she'd met in her ER, and now she was carrying his unbelievably big-boned progeny, but this was the real deal, and no, it had nothing to do with his accent or his crooked smile or his soulful brown eyes, those superficial nice-to-haves that reel you in at the beginning, and everything to do with the need-to-haves that keep you with someone: how he could lift her with his words after a long day at work, how he listened with his heart and mind, and how he was so, so blisteringly smart. He never failed to be kind to those who sometimes didn't deserve it, people Dana would have told off (Dana dearly liked the act of telling people off when they were wrong). And he was patient, let's not forget that—she'd been wading through pregnancy brain fog recently, and her temper was shorter than usual. She felt like Muncher in *Ghostbusters*, gassy and snarly and full of rolls. Yet he endured, *yes dear*–ing his way through the occasional tantrum, even when *she* didn't deserve his patience or kindness (case in point: last weekend, when the pregnancy cravings hit and she sent him out for pickles and then forgot she had requested pickles and got upset because he brought home pickles and not the salted caramel ice cream she *remembered* requesting).

Dana shot Nigel a covert look of fondness. He was almost too good to be true.

The bowling ball inside her kicked her bladder, and she winced, brought back to earth. People like Dana weren't built to daydream. That's why it surprised her that she and Nigel—a dreamer of the first degree, someone whose career as an adman was entirely about inspiring others with words and images—seemed to be working out. She kept waiting for the other shoe to drop. When would he realize she was hopelessly dull?

"Are you OK? Do you want to sit down?" Nigel asked, catching her reaction to the bladder kick. Dana waved him away with a wan smile—he'd been hovering with a capital *H* for the last few months, a mixture of golden retriever–level exuberance and concern, which normally she found very attractive, but now she mostly wanted to be left alone to wilt in some fridge.

"I'm good," she said. She glanced around the bright-pink kitchen, the one major flaw of the place. She directed her question to the real estate agent. "So tell me, what's the catch?"

There it was, Dana in essence: the problem spotter. If Nigel was sunshine and positivity, Dana was pragmatic fatalism. That's why they worked so well together.

Nigel turned and gave her a wink and a thumbs-up behind the agent's back.

"There, um . . . there isn't one," Jessica said, the smallest twitch of one eyelid giving away her discomfort at Dana's dead-eyed stare.

"The house has just been renovated with full Italian granite and hardwood floors. The walls are spotless, like no one's been living in it," Dana said, pacing around the kitchen, her No-Nonsense Nurse voice on. She stopped and pivoted slowly toward Jessica. "Someone died in it?"

Jessica's smile grew fixed. "No. The owners renovated three years ago but then moved away soon after, when their daughter, who's living in Indiana, got pregnant. And now they figured they should make the move permanent. That's all."

"But no one died in here?" Dana repeated, wanting to hear the actual words. You always had to hear the words; her lawyer friend—fine, somebody she saw on *Law and Order*—had taught her that.

"No," Jessica said. She added, somewhat apologetically, "I mean, as far as I know."

Dana and the agent eyed each other like gunslingers in a Western. Finally Dana's demeanor relaxed and she nodded. "OK."

"Dana, just forget the price and its possibly messed-up history for a second and tell me: Do you like this place?" Nigel asked.

"I do, it's . . . it's just . . . I don't know," Dana murmured. Her lips wobbled and her eyes prickled with tears—she wasn't one to wear her emotions on her sleeve, but the hormones had destroyed her defenses and her poker face, honed through eight years of nursing. She felt all of them, every day: terror, overwhelming joy, anticipation, anxiety, anguish, and excitement, just to name a few. "The house is great, Nigel. I just—it's all moving so fast." Her voice cracked on the last word.

"I'll give you both some space and wait on the patio," Jessica said.

Nigel walked up to Dana and hugged her close. She sagged against him, feeling the tension ebb from her with every breath. "Don't second-guess yourself, Dana. You like the place. I see you casing it like you're already interior designing the space and planning trips to Pottery Barn and IKEA."

"I am," Dana admitted. "But even at this price, it's at the high end of our budget. The very tippy top."

"You let me worry about that," Nigel said. He'd just gotten a job at a boutique ad agency in Baltimore—a step down from his career trajectory in New York, but an internal transfer had never been an option since his agency didn't have offices outside of LA and New York. He pulled away and paced the kitchen. "Let's run through the positives: It's move-in ready, meaning we don't have to spend a dime on unnecessary renovations; the community is diverse; the backyard is big enough for the four kids we'll have—if you're on board—and it's in the neighborhood of a great public school. Your dad's literally two miles away in the care facility and we can visit him every weekend. It's perfect."

She hated when he made sense. Especially in that warm, grinning, forever-boyish way that made her believe life could be one long adventure if you just leaned into it hard enough. She walked back into his arms again. "I don't know if I'm up for visiting him every weekend," she mumbled into his chest. "It breaks my heart seeing him like that, no matter what's happened between us." Her father, her sole living parent, had advanced Alzheimer's—more often than not, he did not recognize her.

"The option's there," he said quietly. "That's all."

Sensible, reasonable, but imaginative. Add all those qualities to the secret sauce that made Nigel . . . Nigel. That made Dana sure this wasn't just *that* kind of marriage—even if she was pregnant—because he was unlike anyone she'd ever been with, in that she couldn't envisage a world, her life, without him.

"Well," she said, brushing imaginary lint off her belly, "if the baby likes it, I guess we're good."

Nigel regarded her with those eyes. "And does the baby approve?"

The bowling ball stayed still—typical. Dana met his questioning gaze with a kiss. "She says she's happy if I'm happy, and I am, so . . ." She exhaled shakily. "Yup, lucky house number twenty-three! I guess we're getting a mortgage!"

"Great," Nigel said, eyes shining (possibly with relief). He waved Jessica back in and told her the good news.

She clapped her hands together. "That's wonderful news! Shall we go back to the car and sign the paperwork?"

As they walked down the flagstone path, Nigel waved at their soon-to-be neighbor from across the street, a white-haired woman with electric-blue eyeglasses and a toy poodle that might've just been stuffed, and Dana tucked her hand into the crook of Nigel's arm.

"We're definitely doing this, huh." Dana tried to sound matter-of-fact when her heart was racing with anticipation and anxiety—her two most familiar states of mind these days. "Homeowners—and parents. All at once!" Maybe it was more anxiety than anticipation she was feeling.

No matter how far she'd come from her beginnings, Dana always felt like she was only a couple of steps ahead of disaster. She couldn't explain why she was wired like this—maybe the financial stressors of her childhood and her parents' constant bickering had something to do with it—but the fear was always there, lurking in the back of her mind. An imagined sword of Damocles hanging over her at all times.

When she first got together with Nigel, she kept telling herself, *It's a fluke, it's a dream, he'll leave me when he's done having his fun.* But then she got pregnant and Nigel kept staying, kept choosing her. She'd never had anything like that.

What's the catch?

She shook her head. *I really got to stop doing that.*

He paused on the path, probably picking up on something she hadn't meant to show. He turned to face her and put his hands on her arms, squeezed them, and told her, "I know this is moving really fast for you and you're worried. I get it. It's all new to me, and I'm scared too, Dana. This is a lot for anyone to take in all at once. But it'll be all right, you'll see. We'll be all right."

"How do you know?" Nobody knew. Anyone who claimed otherwise was setting themselves up for failure.

He patted his chest. "Because it's normal to be afraid of changes, but my heart and my head are aligned on this, so I know this will pass." He nodded in the direction of the house with its gently sloping front lawn. "In fact, I'm already imagining us eating toast in that sunroom while the baby throws mashed avocado at the cat we don't own yet."

"I'm a dog person," she said, eyebrow raised.

Nigel smacked his forehead. "Oh, crap, how did we miss this discussion? *That's* my deal-breaker."

They laughed. "The backsplash is pink; so are the tiles in the guest bathroom," she said, half laughing, half crying.

"So we'll renovate. It's just tiles, Dana."

They reached the agent's car—a spotless white Range Rover with enough bottled water to hydrate a football team—and slid into the back seat while Jessica cranked up the air-conditioning for Dana and pulled out the contracts.

Nigel didn't even read any of it. He initialed and signed away his freedom without a second thought, using his usual messy, sprawling script; meanwhile, Dana's handwriting was neat and almost apologetic, taking only just enough space as to be legible. And yes, she read the contract. Every last word. In their relationship, she was the one who dotted the i's and crossed the t's—which was a good thing, because Nigel was very much a big-picture guy.

"Congratulations." Jessica beamed, handing them their copies when they were done. "You're homeowners! Well, pending a few more niggling steps, of course. But you did it! Whoop whoop!"

Dana felt her last meal—or maybe it was the baby—somersault in her belly. "Oh my God."

Nigel chuckled and laced his fingers through hers. "Breathe, Dana. The most difficult part is over: We've got each other. Things can only get better for us."

"Famous last words," Dana said as his lips met hers. But then the baby kicked, as if in agreement or in blessing, and for once Dana Smiley, chronic overthinker that she was, let herself be swept away by the moment. She could do this, she decided. This man was the beginning of a brand-new life, one they got to build together. She should be so lucky.

Dana

2023: The Hour Approaches

It was the hour of the Maintenance Shag, and Dana had to hurry home. In spite of her best efforts, the morning was getting away from her, and she had much work to do in the house before she could flop down in front of her husband in choice underwear (i.e., those that hadn't gotten gray and saggy in the wash), the door to their bedroom carefully bolted, and say, *Ravish me, honey*.

People in their forties—in her case, thirty-nine, but she was close enough—were supposed to ravish their partners still, after sixteen years of marriage, weren't they? Popular media didn't shed much light on such bedroom maneuvers; it was more interested in people in their twenties and early thirties, tops. But they had to, surely? And, more important, how often should they endeavor toward such ravishment? Their gimlet-eyed marriage counselor—or rather, the IG marriage therapist whose advice they could access for free (all they could afford given their household's straitened purse strings)—had suggested that for couples in their age bracket (old, beaten-down millennials) who'd "been together for some time," once every two weeks would be appropriate to "maintain the fire"—although *fire* was certainly optimistic phrasing at this stage, at least in Dana's unbiased, unprofessional opinion.

So here they were, headed for their third scheduled biweekly ravishment.

But first, tomatoes. Dana stood blinking in the ugly white light of the big-box retailer in front of shelves of jarred and canned tomatoes: paste, whole, pureed, stewed, diced. Which type of tomato went in Bolognese? Her phone was dead and she couldn't check. She wasn't a cook; almost everything she made came from a box. And the food *had* to be home-cooked today, because Shobana, her daughter Bex's close friend and possible love interest, was coming over for dinner—a first for Bex, who so far had preferred to keep her friends confined to the Cheng-Smileys' gaming den / basement, and out of the house before 6 p.m.

It was deeply destabilizing to her that sixteen-year-old Bex might have a *love interest*—Bex was a child. It felt like only yesterday they had been watching cartoons together on Saturdays and discussing the merits of being a mermaid versus a fairy princess (Bex was firmly Camp Mermaid—she was part nautical, that one), and not too long ago she'd been a sweet toddler who called Dana "Mummy," which always made Dana think, somewhat incongruously, of Prince Harry. The adorable way Bex had puckered her lips around the consonants made her heart ache with nostalgia.

The simple joy gave way to something else, something dimmer. For reasons she couldn't quite articulate, everything was shot through with anxiety these days, even the good emotions and memories. *Or maybe the truth is, you're anxious because you've forgotten how to be around them.*

Her fingers flickered back and forth between the diced and pureed options, the varietals:

Napoli, Roma
DOP San Marzano
Santorini, too

Just words in a haiku to Dana, albeit ones with real-world consequences that, to Bex at least, were life and death. Her mother *had* to impress Shobana, whose mother, Selvi, was some fancy litigator and amateur chef on top of being a single mom, *or else*. Bex only used italics when it was a matter of life and death (i.e., her mother's).

If Bex killed Dana—Dana closed her eyes and sighed. She couldn't begin to imagine the chaos that would unravel. Not that she actually thought her daughter would murder her, but hypothetically speaking, if she did decide to off Dana, where would that leave Nigel? How would he cope? Just yesterday morning, she'd caught him—when he thought she wasn't looking—eating *around* a piece of bread she *knew* was moldy. She hadn't had the chance to toss it out before he put it in his maw, probably because Bex was screaming and Emmie had jammed a fork into Gill's curls and Dana was coming in to break up that fight after a dreadful night shift, but should it really be on her to make sure he took care of himself? What happened to Old Nigel, her can-do-anything man? Or was Nigel, in his infinite stubbornness, trying to prove a point—to himself and, by extension, to her? That he would endure. That he was a *survivor*, by eating moldy bread in spite of his allergies. Or was it because they were at the end of the month and money was tight? Even so, there was no need for such frugality, such stoicism, such acts of false heroism, really—not yet, even though they flirted with the danger of financial ruin on the daily these days. All they needed was a major accident, to be honest. He should not have been so cavalier around *mold*—unless this was some kind of statement, a slow, passive-aggressive flirtation with death?

Maybe this was on her for marrying a man named Nigel. Nigel: a name one either grew into or dragged through adulthood like roadkill. And to think, back in the early days of their courtship, she had cried that name out in passion—heat in every syllable. *Nigel.* It was almost unthinkable now. Because there was nothing about the name that should inflame one's loins. Yet, somehow, once upon a time in Dana's life, "Nigel" had been spicy.

Once upon a time, Nigel had been her everything. They had been so happy. So close. So in sync. But now—

Dana grabbed two cans of each type of tomato on offer, threw them in her cart, and started making her way home. The kids would be home from soccer practice in exactly two and a half hours, and the small window of opportunity to maintain matrimonial status quo in the Cheng-Smiley household would be over for the weekend. She had to hurry; her ravishment awaited.

Nigel

Radioactive Dad

Nigel Bradshaw-Cheng did not think he was in any way a violent person. Yet here he was, hunkered down in the room with his son as they frantically plotted how to take down an army of subterranean monsters in the most merciless, painful way possible.

"You have to maximize sun damage or there's a chance the mole rat heretic will regenerate," Gill advised as the two of them batted at a five-foot-tall mole rat / human recombinant, who flailed at their advances. "We have to corral it and force it to its death in the UV antechamber. Throw the switch as soon as it's in there. Flambé the crap out of it. Show no mercy!"

He was eleven.

"Sure I can't just fry it with a flamethrower?" Nigel said. He was turning forty-three in a few months, and his butt and back were starting to hurt. Beanbags were not meant for anyone above the age of twenty—there was no dignity in these things.

"No, Dad!" Gill shouted, pushing the screeching mole rat into the corner of the lab with a spiked shield—they were playing this new game called *HellFire: Nuclear Bottomfeeder Maxxx*. "Only UV rays kill mole rats! OMG, Dad, this is not the time to deviate from the *plan*! We *talked* about this!"

"OK, OK!" Nigel said quickly. Per usual, he shied away from confrontation, even from his offspring. Dana was the disciplinarian of their household, whereas Nigel was . . . Nigel was the Good Cop. Yeah. That's what he was. The Good Cop.

The mole rat's radial howls filled the room, but Nigel's attuned hearing picked up the beeping that indicated Dana was entering the code to open the front door. Shit. Gill was *not* supposed to be home, and he, Nigel, was definitely not supposed to be playing computer games. Nigel threw the controller into a corner of Gill's things and flopped down on his son's bed, placidly thumbing through a sports magazine that he only managed to flip upright as his wife entered the room.

"Tottenham Hotspurs, I say," he said, apropos of nothing. The article was about tennis.

"Gill!" she said, very loudly, ignoring Nigel, which was immediately a red flag. "Why are you home? You're supposed to be at soccer practice."

Her glance slid to Nigel, who shrugged. "He told me he wasn't feeling well," Nigel supplied.

Dana seemed to grow before his eyes. "Does he look sick to you?" she said in her Quiet Voice—another red flag—gesturing at Gill, who despite having his eyes trained meekly at the floor, was also taking the opportunity to save his game under "Dadbro mashup March29."

"You guys were gaming?" Dana said. A rhetorical question. Oh, how slim Nigel's chances were of getting laid now. How very slim.

He'd gravely miscalculated how quick Dana's grocery run was—earlier she'd told him she was going to the larger Aldi in Rosedale, which would have necessitated a longer drive, but she must have given up and gone to the smaller one closest to them. Which meant she'd come home almost forty minutes earlier than expected and before Nigel could legitimately have neglected to mention that Gill had not gone to soccer practice at all.

Gill ventured a sickly cough. "I have a cough," he said. "Dad said I could stay home."

Gill was not fond of group sports—he was also not fond of sports, or groups. Nigel sympathized and identified with his son. He found that as he'd entered his forties, he'd begun to retreat from all activities in which more than three persons, including him, would be involved. Even weekly pickleball with the Fosters had become a challenge. (Incidentally, what was up with the millennial pickleball craze? It used to be that fit middle-agers played tennis, but now it was pickleball this, pickleball that; Nigel figured it was because pickleball was easier on the knees and millennials were a generation raised to pursue ease.) It might have been exacerbated by the fact that he was recently—well, almost eleven months ago—laid off. That could kill a guy's going-out mojo, fast.

"If you're staying home, you better have a ruptured spleen at least," Dana muttered.

"But that would mean I'd be dead by now," Gill pointed out.

"Gill, I paid good money for those soccer lessons," Dana said, her voice tight. "The least you can do is attend them."

"But Dad said—"

Nigel jumped into the fray. "Gill, your mother's right. You should have gone to soccer lessons if your spleen is intact."

Gill snapped his mouth shut and shot his father a hurt look of betrayal. "I have a social responsibility not to spread my cold germs around. You're in health care, Mom, you know that."

"Did you say you had a cough or a cold again?" Dana asked, an eyebrow raised.

Gill sighed. The jig was up.

Nigel struggled to a sitting position—Gill's mattress had far too much give for his back and gut. "I have to, ah, go change," he said. That was their code for sex.

Dana shot him a glacial look. "That won't be necessary."

Nigel started to stand before giving up and sinking back down. There was no point in leaving the sanctuary of his son's musty-smelling room then. Letting Gill skip practice had been risky, yet Nigel's heart had softened when Gill begged to skip out on soccer practice. It hadn't even been Gill's idea to go for those lessons in the first place—it'd been Dana's. One of the vestigial after-school activities that they hadn't pruned completely. Dana thought it would be good for Gill's general health to be outdoors from time to time, since he didn't get much exercise or sunlight as it was.

Nigel found it hard to say no to his kids these days—it felt like Dana was already doing a lot of that when she was around.

Dana exhaled sharply. Her shoulders sagged and she dragged her palm across her face. "Sorry, Nigel," she muttered. "It's been a long night."

Nigel bit his tongue. If he was being truthful, the past three years had been one long, sleepless night shift that Dana never really got off, even with the vaccine. He forced himself to relax, to project encouragement; Dana was exhausted, and he knew he was partly to blame, starting with the slip-up that had led to Emmie's conception—not that Emmie was a mistake, of course! She was a happy surprise, but it was undeniable that having three kids was expensive. Then last year, he'd been laid off from the small ad agency in Baltimore, where he'd spent over a decade of his life—the AI wave had been the last straw that broke the camel's back. That, on top of a few bad investments, only deepened the financial squeeze.

Everything felt tangled in the moment, and the light at the end of the tunnel seemed impossibly far. Yet shoulder on they must.

"The groceries are in the car. Everything's ready for your dinner," she said to Nigel.

"Do you need help, Mommy dearest?" Gill said, doe eyes on full display.

"No need," she said curtly. "I've got other plans for you." Gill's face fell.

Dana stalked out of the room, barking instructions to Gill, who trailed behind her like a defeated mole rat. *The thing about computer games that makes sense*, Nigel thought as he scurried to the car to get the groceries, a looming feeling of dread building in his stomach, *is that you can always start again.*

Dana

Time's Up

Dana ordered Gill to vacuum the house and rake the yard—Bex's chores.

"But I am sick," he cried when Dana pronounced her punishment. "My throat tickles."

"If it's only a tickle, you can clean. I vacuumed and ironed right up till my last week of pregnancy with Emmie," Dana said, unmoved, her expression suggesting she'd have kept at it if she hadn't been busy birthing a human.

"You're so hard on your own spawn," Gill moaned. Dana pointed wordlessly in the direction of the living room. The clock was ticking.

As soon as the vacuum was running, she turned to Nigel. "Get changed," she said. Nigel made his way upstairs and washed up before sliding under the fresh sheets, after which Dana got under the covers and proceeded to give him a stoic, efficient blow job that really was mostly hand. Then he clambered over her, squishing parts of her as he went, and did his best. It was all over in seventeen tight minutes.

Oh, how things had changed, Dana thought, watching Nigel place a hand towel over a wet spot in a totally useless gesture (paper towels would have been better for the job). Once, in a fit of lust while vacationing in France one spring, they had pulled over in a field of lavender and had a good go at outdoor sex at Nigel's behest, even though he was (mildly) allergic to pollen and had to pull out his spare inhaler at a critical moment. Still, it had been wildly erotic. Or just spontaneous morning sex in the haven of their bedroom before it was time to wake the kids for school, back in the early days of parenthood. Nowadays, she was lucky if she didn't think about dinner midway through those twenty or so minutes of conjugal merging, penciled in so neatly between soccer practice and snack time.

Scheduling was Dana's favorite thing. Or rather, it had become her favorite thing, because that's what she told herself it had to be—it was, after all, a large part of what she did, aside from the scary stuff. No one else could run the household the way she, a trauma nurse, could, because she was used to much, much more: People found very creative ways to get injured on a daily basis, and she had front-row seats to the entire shit show. In contrast, Nigel worked—*used to work,* she corrected herself—in a job with a personal assistant who curated his day for him so that he didn't have to think.

Since life was so unpredictable with its many disasters, Dana craved the normalcy of routine, the clarity of a well-planned schedule, segmented into beautiful blocks of minutes. Life, boxed and unboxed, laid out in its flat-pack harmlessness: A typical Saturday, for example, was basketball (Bex); coding (Gill); playdate (Emmie); debate (Bex); soccer (Gill); guitar (Bex). Lovely, uncomplicated lines of text, instructions for getting through a day, a week, a month, a year—a life. The easy high of crossing items off a to-do list. Dana sometimes found herself adding forgotten items onto her lists just so she could cross them off right after. She craved these little hits of dopamine.

She found it harder and harder to get excited about things these days. She would show up, do what was needed, then leave. It wasn't that she didn't care—she did, she just sometimes felt like feeling nothing, doing nothing, was safer in her case. She understood, dimly, that her emotions were like atoms heading toward an inevitable collision, yet she was trying in vain to prevent that from happening even as she hurtled toward an electrical field. Even when she did nothing, she could feel herself being pulled in opposing directions. She often felt confused by how she could hold contradictory opinions and feelings about the same thing. She knew, deep down, she should feel guilty about how little time she spent with Emmie, her sweet, bubbly two-year-old, but she also didn't want to spend time with Emmie because Emmie needed more from her than just showing up, and she had nothing left to give. She wouldn't crack. Couldn't. She had no time to. If there was no money coming in, they were all doomed.

She needed to be a well-oiled machine—literally—so they could survive.

She took her phone out and noticed a stream of text notifications. Dana squinted. (Her vision might be going, too, another fun new change wrought by aging.)

Ahhhhhh babylyve call me? I've got something to ask you!

Followed ten seconds later by: OK fine you're busy but CAN YOU COME TO GREESE in 9 days?

And: I INSIIIISSSSTTTTTTTTTTTTTTT!!!

Given the familiarity and typos, it could only be Pia, her best friend since high school, reaching out from yet another new number.

We'd hv SO Much FUUUUUUUUUUUUNNN

Out of the corner of her eye, she saw Nigel emerge from the bathroom, his short, rust-brown hair damp, wearing an old, graying robe and a careful expression. Something about the combination made Dana's heart constrict. She could sense that he had more words to share, but she didn't want to hear them. Couldn't. The elephant in the room, the one that had been there since Nigel lost his job, was back. The jack that had gotten out of its box and wouldn't allow itself to be banished to where it came from. She threw him an offhand smile and went back to her screen, pretending to be immersed in a Reel someone had posted. It was about growing potatoes in one's backyard. Dana hated gardening, but she had a poker face, and as long as Nigel didn't watch the content, she could get away with pretending to be engrossed.

"I love you," Nigel said. She could tell from the faux-careless way he said it that he'd been carrying it around like a wet booger at the end of a pinkie, desperately waiting to drop those words ever since she'd gotten home, a type of belated peace offering for Gill skipping soccer. Otherwise, it'd been a while since he'd said that to her—they were past such niceties. She grunted in reciprocation, keeping her eyes fixed firmly on her phone.

She could sense him opening his mouth again, more words bubbling beneath the surface—grittier words. Barbed words. She clenched up.

Nigel cleared his throat and said, "I'm going to check on Gill to see if he's actually cleaning."

"Yeah," Dana said. A pang of guilt hit her—these days, it felt like all she ever issued to her husband and children, aside from Emmie, were orders. Instructions. "Maybe . . . maybe let him know he's excused from yard work. Bex was supposed to handle that anyway. He just needs to have vacuumed the living room and kitchen and he's off the hook."

"Gotcha." Nigel shuffled to the door. He stopped and turned. "So, for dinner tonight, are you in or out? I vaguely recall you mentioning last week when Bex asked if she could invite Shobana over that you'd cook? I didn't want to presume even though you bought, like, a ton of tomatoes." He paused. "A literal ton. Enough to feed an army."

Another notification, a voice note this time. Dana pressed the phone against her ear and Pia's nasally voice blasted into her ears: *"Babe, I mean Greece! Our No.1 European dream destination when we were teenagers, remember? Sure, I've been a couple of times to Mykonos for work—can you imagine, some shipping company's annual dinner or something—but it's not the same when it's for fun, am I right? Anyway, it's my fortieth in two weeks and I was planning on a WILD, FLIRTY celebration on a booze cruise. I know it's pretty spontaneous, but I finally managed to free up some time so I thought, why not? Anyway, an all-inclusive ten days on a cruise ship with the best people! The girls from LSE and UMD are coming and you must! You're my closest, oldest friend! YOU MUST!"*

"Dana?" Nigel prodded.

"It's only $9,300 for nine nights, a bargain for all the alcohol and islands we'll be visiting!"

"Dana, the dinner tonight."

Dana herself would be turning forty in a month, and she had nothing planned. Nothing. She would be lucky if she and Nigel could afford the local Italian restaurant.

"I can't," Dana lied impulsively, her thoughts spinning with the text and Pia's invitation. The idea of spending an evening with Selvi, Shobana's polished, beautiful, *rich* lawyer mom, felt like a special kind of torture tonight—even if she did like Shobana and was glad her daughter had found such a lovely friend and/or romantic match. "Sorry, it's a last-minute thing. One of the nurses is down with mono, so I have to sub in his shift."

"Oh." There's a long silence. "I didn't know people got mono anymore," Nigel wondered. He scratched his belly, the soft fuzz of it visible through the gaping robe. There was a weighted pause. "I guess I'll break the news to Bex before rescuing our son."

"Good luck," Dana said. She cleared her throat. "I'm sorry. I know I did promise to cook, but I guess you can always get food delivered?"

Nigel's face was impassive. "It's OK, hon, it happens. We know you can't really plan around your shifts."

"Yes."

"Bolognese, you said?"

"Yup, that was the plan." It was going to be a disaster. Nigel was an even worse cook than she was. "Just . . . just look online for a no-fuss recipe."

"All right, hon." He hesitated before pressing a quick kiss to the top of her head—something he used to do when they first started dating, something she'd once loved—then left the room. Dana looked up from the Reel of a professional parkour athlete vaulting across cityscapes, and then a clip of her famous former schoolmate—fine, former crush—Yomi Owope playing a jazz trombone solo at a world music festival, and wondered, not for the first time this year, how much longer she could pretend this life was enough. If there wasn't something else—some relief—out there that could make her feel like she wasn't dissolving into the ether.

Who was she to her family these days? She wondered if they even saw her anymore, beyond a cash machine. Her teenagers didn't return her hugs when she remembered to dispense them, and her toddler . . . well, her toddler preferred the neighbors, she was sure of that. The Foos played with her, at least.

Her phone buzzed: Mom remember I asked you about this last week? Can you pls buy me these sneakers mine are falling apart I swear

Bex, sending her a link to a pair of fancy new kicks, not even checking whether Dana would be home tonight. Probably because Super Dad Nigel would be, and that was enough for her. A hard, knotty feeling lodged in Dana's chest. She bit her lip and did what was expected—she bought her daughter a brand-new pair of guilt sneakers. Then she grabbed her things and got ready for her shift—the one that didn't exist.

Tonight, she just wanted time alone. Away from everything and everyone.

Nigel

Prep

The late-spring afternoon sun broke through the cloud cover and offered some relief from the gloom of Nigel's thoughts as he bustled around the kitchen, solo, as per usual, preparing for the big dinner. Dana had left an hour ago, muttering about shifts. But she wouldn't meet his eyes when she said this—not that she often did these days, anyway.

In response, Nigel had cranked out a "No problem, honey," even though he very much thought it was problematic how easily she lied to him these days, and how easily he accepted her lies.

Nigel cracked open two cans of tinned tomatoes and set them aside, chopped a few cloves of garlic and half a sickly onion, then began sautéing the aromatics in a generous glug of extra virgin olive oil. After a couple of minutes, he added diced celery and carrot, stirring them while he checked his messages, before tossing in the ground beef and lamb he had preseasoned with salt, pepper, and a dash of paprika. He poured in half a shot glass of red wine and let it cook before adding in tomato paste, tomato puree, and a single bay leaf and covering the pot—the sauce was to simmer for the next hour and a half on low heat—not nearly as long as he'd like, but good enough.

As the kitchen warmed with the comforting smell of his childhood, he wondered how it would feel to run into the wall in front of him hard enough so he could sleep for a very long time. Thank God it was a Saturday. Emmie was at the Foos' across the street (the old lady had passed on and the Foos moved in soon after, maybe a year and a half ago)—they had a girl Emmie's age, Rena, and loved having Emmie around, so they claimed. Or maybe they felt pity for him for coming to drop-offs and pickups in the same rumpled plaid shirts, unshaven and slightly damp with perspiration, dark eye circles de rigueur. Maybe they could sense he needed a hand.

Trouble was, the Foos and the Cheng-Smileys weren't friends—not really—so their silent offer of help wasn't appreciated. Not when it was laced with judgment.

A few days ago, Tommy had said it with a smile: "Anytime you need a hand with Emmie, *buddy*, we'll look after her." He probably meant it as kindness, but to Nigel, it landed like a verdict.

You're not doing a good enough job with your life.

There was some truth in that—not when it came to Emmie, or the other children, of course. He lavished them with love and care, was the model parent. Showed up for all the PTA meetings. Helped with homework when the older two deigned to ask for his help. Ensure Emmie had all the support she needed to hit her developmental milestones. It was vis-à-vis Nigel that the standard of care was slipping, and men like Tommy Foo, who noticed everything, could see that. In under a year, Nigel had gained around fourteen pounds, and none of that was muscle.

You're not good enough. You need help.

Nigel winced at the thought—he didn't want to be Tommy Foo's charity case. The man was younger, better-looking, richer—everything Nigel feared he no longer was. To be pitied by Tommy Foo struck something raw in Nigel: his pride, or maybe something more intrinsic, something closer to his identity. With Nigel the two were hopelessly intertwined. It was easy enough to dismiss and condemn a man for being proud, especially with all the biblical baggage that word carried, but Nigel's pride was also the spark that fueled everything good in him: his devotion to his work, his quiet joy in his children's successes, his refusal to fade into the background of his own life. It was also, undeniably, part of that ineffable quality that had first drawn Dana to him, the thing that made her fall in love.

These days, he wasn't sure if he had much pride in anything anymore, and that worried him. A sharp bark of laughter from across the street, filtering through the open kitchen windows, snapped Nigel's train of thought in two. It sounded like it had come from the Foos' backyard. Probably where they had installed a hot tub. Gill had excitedly asked if they could have one after going over to pick up Emmie last week, and for days afterward, Nigel found himself scrolling through hot tub ads, wondering which model the Foos had picked out.

Nigel recognized the green-eyed monster in him rearing its ugly head whenever he caught wind of some new gadget or home improvement at the Foos'—it didn't help that the Foos were so humble, so discreet about their discretionary spending. He wished they would just come out and brag about it already so he could resent them with all his being. He needed a new target.

"Dad," Gill said behind him, making him jump in surprise—his son had the maddening ability to move as silently as a shadow in the night. "Is Mom working tonight?"

"Yes," Nigel said evenly. "Why?"

"Because she left her scrubs at home." He pointed at the clothes bag on the chair—the one that held Dana's spare pressed uniform, forgotten in her hurry to leave the house for her supposed shift. Dana had this thing about not wearing her uniform outside the hospital, not since the pandemic, when medical staff were the focus of some people's ire. She always brought them from home and changed into them quickly before her shift.

"She probably has another stored in the locker at the hospital," Nigel said. Sometimes he marveled at himself, how smoothly he lied.

Back in the early days of Nigel and Dana Versus the World, he had been the guy who couldn't keep a straight face when he wasn't telling the truth. He'd telegraphed everything; he was soft and gooey, all heart. A big cinnamon roll, as the kids these days said.

Maybe she's cheating on you.

Nigel stabbed the knife into a bystander potato. He was now also a person prone to hurting vegetables. Potatoes were his favorite. They had the right amount of give in their flesh, unlike pumpkins (too much), or onions (too slippery or mushy). He once tried to Fruit Ninja a watermelon and nearly broke a finger. Watermelons were deceptively hard, like wives.

Gill sighed. His phone made a series of alarming beeps—they'd caved and given him a smartphone last week, one of Nigel's old work phones that he had "forgotten" to turn in on the last day. "Dad . . . don't you think Mom's acting a bit weird these days? Like, a little bit, I don't know, more distracted than usual?"

"Is she?" Nigel said, forcing himself to sound neutral.

"Yup," Gill said, scratching his cheek while he scrolled through his phone. "Like last week, she told me she was going to pick me up from soccer at one, but she came at two thirty. Said she forgot."

Nigel's heart thudded dully in his chest. Dana had, or used to have, the memory bank of a murderous alpha dolphin—she stored information and facts with ease and deployed them just as easily. "That does sound unusual." He had follow-up questions, but they were probably the kind of questions you asked your therapist, not your eleven-year-old son. Complicated questions like *Should I bring your mom, who looks at me like I'm a plateful of old rice, to the romantic weekend getaway on occasion of her fortieth I planned on surprising her with on a private farm, just the two of us, putting Bex and you in charge of Ems, if she won't even enjoy it?* and *How do you know if a relationship is over?* "You know, she's had a lot on her mind." That part, at least, was mercifully true.

Gill slid him a long look, and not for the first time, Nigel wondered how much his children knew about how closely they were orbiting a collapsing star.

"Maybe Mom needs a vacation," Gill suggested.

A vacation—or a divorce?

Nigel twisted his knife in the potato. "Maybe we could all use one." He should cancel the weekend. He'd lose the small deposit, but it was fine. Better that than see her looking for escape routes from their staycation.

"Disneyland!" Gill said, forgetting about erratically behaving moms in the face of cotton candy and strangers dressed as anthropomorphic mice. "I want to go to Disneyland!"

Nigel made a noncommittal noise and bustled off to tend to his sauce, even though it was simmering along nicely. If he hemmed and hawed long enough, Gill would finally turn twelve, the tide of hormones that had been threatening all spring would finally come in, and then he'd be too busy masturbating into socks and other receptacles, Disneyland forgotten, because there would be no family vacation. Nigel knew this intuitively. Dana was hiding something, maybe someone, from him, yet he couldn't bring himself to confront her.

Nigel knew his inability to meet things head-on these days was one of the reasons Dana's lips curled when other mothers praised Nigel for being such a patient father, especially with Emmie, the toddler. He knew *patience* was not the word she would have chosen, at least not after the layoff last April. The word she might have been looking for was *loser*. He couldn't blame her if that was what she felt about him—there was a side of him that sneered at his unemployment. Growing up in a financially stable upper-middle-class family with two earners—his father serving in the military, his mom a pharmacist—where his interests and dreams had always been nurtured, meant Nigel had grown up thinking a career he enjoyed would be a given, almost a birthright—it was certainly expected of him. Losing that stability chipped away at more than just their household income; it took a wrecking ball to Nigel's identity as a provider, however evolved he was about a lot of issues.

The doorbell rang and Gill ran to the living room window and shrieked "Emmie!" like he'd won the lottery. Emmie was back from her playdate at the Foos'. Nigel put down the potato he'd massacred and walked to the door, smiling widely even before they saw him. "Tommy!" he said, greeting his least favorite male neighbor faux-cheerfully as he tried to extricate a red-faced Emmie from Tommy's right leg, Gill skulking behind Nigel in wait. "Thanks for having Emmie over for a playdate. She give you any trouble today?"

"Trouble?" Tommy said, laughing affectionately as he ruffled Emmie's wispy caramel hair. "Lil' Emsterdam here?" (Nigel cringed at the nickname.) "Never. A bucketful of sunshine and wit, this one, and she and Rena had so much fun playing tea party with their stuffies, didn't you, Emmie, my dear?"

"Don't wanna go home, Uncle Tommy," Emmie shrieked, still latching on to Tommy, who, Nigel noted with irritation, was wearing a pair of this season's moss-gray Acne Studios jeans he coveted. "Wanna stay with you! Papa go away! Papa's *mean*!"

"Ha ha ha ha ha," Nigel said, trying not to show how much the comment stung. He tried to prize Emmie—who *struggled*—off Tommy's leg without success. "She's hilarious, this one. She clearly doesn't mean that."

Tommy pursed his lips. "I don't want to overstep, Nigel, we all know kids exaggerate, *of course*, but I try not to minimize their emotions when they are expressing themselves." *Oh, you little self-righteous prick.* Chuckling, Tommy took a knee and gazed into Emmie's tearful eyes with practiced ease. "Emmie, I hear you. I know sometimes we can have preferences, but no matter how you feel in this moment—and I want to *assure* you, they are valid emotions!—I'm sure you want to spend time with your dad and Gill, don't you?"

It was like he'd said the magic word. "Gill!" she exclaimed. She unlatched from Tommy without protest and tumbled past Nigel into

Gill's waiting arms. Tommy grinned fondly at her back and straightened up. He was taller than Nigel, Nigel realized with dismay. "How are you, Nigel?"

"I'm good," Nigel said through gritted teeth. "We're hosting a dinner party with friends." Not entirely the truth, but hey, he didn't need to explain himself.

Tommy nodded. "Smells good. Well, Valerie and I would love to have you over for dinner! We've been trying for some time now, and yet it's been almost eighteen months since we've moved into this neighborhood and nothing has materialized." He chuckled. "If I didn't know better, I'd say you weren't interested." He looked straight into Nigel's eyes, presumably to suss out Nigel's true feelings.

Can't you take a damn hint? was what Nigel wanted to say. But he needed Tommy Foo and Valerie Foo and their adorable child, Rena, who spoke Mandarin and was *taking to the piano like a born natural* and was already fully potty-trained. He needed them and their free childcare.

Nigel injected the tiniest bit of apology into his tone. "We've been wanting to—it's just, well, Dana's schedule is so unpredictable, you know? Shifts popping up like teenage zits! And I'm so busy with the kids and freelance work."

If Tommy didn't believe him, he certainly tried hard to validate *Nigel's* feelings. "Well, I hear you, man. Work can take over one's life. But if you feel like you lack balance in one aspect of your life, you got to rectify the imbalance, figure out the root cause instead of pretending all is well. Otherwise every other area will suffer. Life, after all, is very much about the unsexy work of finding balance in every aspect of our lives, not just pursuing the false ideal of excellence, or abundance, in plain consumer-speak. We need to set our priorities right."

Tommy Foo was a life coach and a Pilates instructor *on the side*. That's why he spoke like a shrink and looked like a dream. Nigel bade him good day and shut the door a little louder than he should have, cutting the exchange short when a long time ago, he would have invited

Tommy in for a coffee, maybe even a beer. *He'll understand,* Nigel thought as he watched his kids play on the kitchen floor while the Bolognese sauce simmered. *He's always talking about knowing when to draw your boundaries, preserving your safe spaces.* Well, Nigel was drawing his boundaries and avoiding his triggers, Tommy being one of them.

Nigel watched as Valerie opened the front door a heartbeat before Tommy could knock, and the delighted laugh of surprise and the goofy kiss on his lips she gave him. He remembered when Dana used to greet him like that—when *he* used to greet her like that, the brightest bit of his day at the end of any tunnel—as soon as he got home. "Always with a joke and a kiss, this one," she'd say, uncomplaining. The small things that threaded a marriage together.

His heart panged and he pulled the windows shut almost viciously. He knew why he was acting like a petulant kid with Tommy in spite of his better intentions. Because the hard grain of truth was this: Nigel would have given just about anything to be in Tommy's position—working and having a wife who loved him. A man who had it all.

Nigel

Dinner Begins

Bex's friend Shobana arrived at exactly 7 p.m. with her mother, Selvi Selvaraju—a woman who always gave Nigel the impression that laughter and general enjoyment of life were distant, inconvenient concepts—in tow. Too bad their children's budding love story made her presence today *his* inconvenience, Nigel thought morosely.

Shobana and Bex's friendship began when he dented the bumper of Selvi's ridiculously large sedan—a BMW, which told you something about the person driving it—in his haste to make some meeting almost a year and a half ago while driving Bex to some class or other. Bex instantly recognized Shobana and began chatting while Selvi and Nigel sorted out the admin of accidents. The teenagers would not have necessarily crossed paths otherwise, since Belmont High was large and they weren't in the same cliques, but then Bex started going to the local Krav Maga beginner classes at Shobana's suggestion, and then both parents would see texts from Shobana on Bex's locked-screen notifications, and then the study sessions at the Cheng-Smileys' became a weekly thing, and now it appeared as though the omelet was made, platonic or not.

Two weeks ago Bex had announced that she'd officially invited Shobana to dinner with the parents, the first such invitation Nigel and Dana's famously private daughter had ever issued. She had gatekept her friends even before Nigel was . . . disemployed. Shobana was important to Bex, that much was clear. So Nigel had asked Selvi, quite reluctantly, over text if she would join them, and she had agreed almost immediately.

And now here she was, dressed in some sleek DVF wrap dress in a geometric print, looking too chic for the chaos of the Cheng-Smileys' home and his own casual non-iron polo and khaki shorts (why, oh, why hadn't he put on long pants?).

"Nigel," Selvi said.

"Selvi," Nigel said, reflecting her clipped tone. Turning to Shobana, he smiled. "Hey, Shobana." Shobana was radiant in a flamingo-pink long-sleeved top and black bell-bottom jeans (when had the seventies come back?), her short inky bob spliced with gold barrettes.

"Hi, Mr. Cheng!" she chirped, blushing.

The sound of Bex's frantic blow-drying upstairs drifted down. "Well, um, come on in," Nigel said, wishing he didn't have to include Selvi in his invitation. His small-talk skills had atrophied and wouldn't stand up well to scrutiny. He and Dana had not hosted adults in a long, long time.

Selvi and Shobana trailed him down the hallway to the living room, where only Shobana perched on the edge of the two-seater at Nigel's entreaty to *make yourselves at home*. Selvi stood stiffly beside Nigel, definitely eyeing—and cataloging—everything, while Nigel prattled on.

For once, the bubbly Shobana was deadly silent—not surprising, considering her mother's condor-like stare. Nigel's train of small talk arrived at its terminus and stayed there, underscored by the whine of the hair dryer. *Hurry up,* Nigel begged his daughter.

After another minute of solid silence, Nigel broke down. "Bex should be down in a bit," he said. "You know her! Always running ten minutes behind schedule." Shit, should he have highlighted this less-than-desirable trait to his daughter's possible love interest's mom? "But she's very, um, kind to animals," Nigel added, before mentally kicking himself.

"Right," Selvi said. The silence came back. "Oh, I almost forgot," she said in a faux-nonchalant voice. There was nothing nonchalant about this woman. "I got you guys a little gift." She fished out a golden wine bag from the depths of her tote bag. "Champagne," she said. "For having us over for dinner."

"That's so kind of you, thank you, you shouldn't have," Nigel said automatically. His fingers grazed hers and a jolt of electricity he was not prepared for raced up his arm. Nigel almost fumbled the bottle, but thankfully Selvi didn't notice. She was looking around the house, a pinched look on her face.

"Is Dana home?"

"Um, she had a shift she couldn't turn down," Nigel said. He winced internally at the second *um* of the day.

"Oh," Selvi said without further comment. The room's air thickened with new silence.

Shobana cleared her throat. "Could I go upstairs and hang with Bex while she gets ready?"

Selvi pressed her lips together, then said, "I prefer if you stayed down here, please."

"Yes, Mom," Shobana said bleakly.

The clock ticked. Nigel forced himself not to fidget. He let his gaze wander around the room, desperate for an interruption. Relief swept over him as Gill slouched in from the den, trailed by Emmie, his human remora fish. Nigel had confiscated Gill's phone earlier to ensure he'd show up for dinner. He mumbled a half-hearted "Hi," then skulked around the living room, picking things up only to drop them again—aimless, restless, like someone coming down from a high. Behind him, Emmie followed happily, warbling the *Bluey* theme song.

An alarm on Selvi's phone beeped. Nigel started—did this woman actually set a ten-minute alarm? But wait! Here came Bex, running down the stairs, saying, "Oh hi, Shobs, hi, Mrs. Selvaraju, I'm so sorry I took longer than expected but I'm here now!" without a single pause in that sentence and at maximum volume.

"Hello, Bex," Selvi said, but Nigel's firstborn barely acknowledged her. She was shining at her friend, who in turn was shining back at Bex, the two of them acting like they were long-lost Care Bears separated at birth. It was nauseatingly cute, kind of like Xena and her "bard," Gabrielle. It made Nigel sentimental for Dana again. God, he was a romantic fool, wasn't he? He blamed his genes and a steady diet of K-dramas.

"Madam, shall we dine?" he said to Shobana, gallantly offering his arm.

"We shall," the girl said solemnly. She reached out and took his arm, then Bex's, and at the visible shiver of happiness that skated down his firstborn's body, a little piece of Nigel's heart broke—what was left of it, anyway. His children were growing up so fast.

He caught Selvi's eye then, the little flicker of emotion that showed before she shuttered it. Nigel knew single parents led tough lives. They were exhausted—always everything to everyone, never a moment to themselves, so consumed by their children's needs that they forgot to leave room for their own. For a working woman like Selvi, it must have been even more unrelenting.

Before he could talk himself out of it, Nigel cleared his throat and offered his other arm to Selvi, saying, "Madam, if you please," expecting her to shoot him down with the small curl of her lip he had already seen her dole out to other irritants; instead, she surprised him by unhesitatingly taking his arm and giving it the tiniest squeeze, something like gratitude in her eyes. "Why not," she said.

Dana

Catalyst

Dana had, against her better judgment, decided to call Pia back after all, even though she couldn't remember the last time they'd had a conversation. Most times, Pia would send her voice notes or texts, and Dana would respond monosyllabically. But today, a restlessness prompted her to reach out, to hear Pia's nasally voice—that is, if her best friend would just pick up.

At a flicker of movement near the corner of her eye, Dana shrank back down in the front seat of her SUV, not wanting to be made by colleagues or anyone she knew in the parking lot in front of Brightstar Harbor Hospital, where she worked. Given her position, someone would have a question or a request on her time, and she really should make Nancy Padua's birthday drinks in an hour—she'd somehow missed the email inviting her, which she was kicking herself over, because the birthday drinks would have been a legitimate excuse to leave the house instead of a made-up shift. (Plus, she could have had some actual fun.) Instead, she'd cocked everything up by lying. Hence here she was, pretending to be needed at work, while simultaneously hiding from work. Could she catch a break?

The line clicked, and then—

"Dana?" Pia's voice was bright but tinged with uncertainty and surprise, and Dana's heart scrunched with guilt. She hadn't been keeping in touch as much as she'd like with her oldest, closest friend. *Another area of my life where I'm not up to par.*

"Hey," Dana said. "Sorry for the late call." It was 8:30 p.m., but Pia was supposed to be in London—or was it Amsterdam? "I figured I'd skip the messages and chat."

"Don't worry about it," Pia said breezily. "I'm in Tokyo, it's the afternoon, and I'm in my hotel room working on my, uh, speech for later." Someone coughed in the background, and there was a series of intimate rustling noises as that person left the room. Suddenly Dana felt a wave of self-pity for the life she was missing out on. Whatever was happening over in Tokyo in Pia's hotel room was definitely unscheduled, not another item on a checklist. "Is everything . . . as it should be?" Pia was definitely worried—Dana could hear it in the careful way she phrased this oh so neutrally.

"Yup, just sparkling," Dana says. She wouldn't be the friend who dived into the personal-update train immediately. "But I've got not-so-great news about Greece—"

"Oh no," Pia said, before sighing. "All right, hit me."

Dana steeled herself. "Look, I'm really sorry, but I can't make Greece, even if I would have loved to."

"But you *must*," Pia wheedled over the phone. "Everyone we know will be there! From high school to college! And you can meet my London and speaker friends, all the new ones." Her tone became serious. "But you know you're my main boo. It won't be the same without you."

"I can't, Pia," Dana said. She cleared her throat and fought against the closing-up sensation. "I would love to join you and the girls—"

"And Yomi," Pia clarified. Yummy Yomi, or Yomi Owope, had been the best-looking guy in their high school. A year Dana's senior, he was a former band geek (trombonist) turned gifted jazz musician who toured internationally and was a published poet to boot. They used to hang out when they were volunteer peer counselors. Dana was trying not to think about him in an objectifying way and failing spectacularly. The nickname might or might not have come from her.

"Are you and Yomi—"

"Nope," Pia said slyly. "The man's all yours, so please go for it. Are you interested?"

"I'm married," Dana reminded her best friend. "Remember Nigel?"

"Married schmarried," Pia said. Dana could almost hear the *pfffff!* of her raspberry blowing. Pia had always been more open-minded about relationships, whereas Dana always thought of herself as a one-and-done kind of person—although lately she wondered if her "done" had been "the one" in the first place.

"How's Nigel?" Pia said, a little bitingly—Pia couldn't understand why Nigel wasn't doing more to help Dana out financially. Dana couldn't blame her friend for having that impression; she was aware of how Nigel's unemployment looked to the outside world—like a choice, when Dana knew it spoke of darker, more complicated truths. "How are things between you both?"

"Where do I begin?" Dana said. "Look, I don't really want to bring down your and Tokyo's mood."

"Don't worry about Tokyo," Pia said. "Tokyo is on some mood-enhancing drugs." She chuckled. "As am I."

"That's nice," Dana said awkwardly. Friendships were weird, a time capsule of the era in which they'd flourished. Pia and Dana had met in high school, when they were both "oddballs": Dana was frequently distracted by her unstable homelife—their financial woes and cultural differences often led her parents into screaming matches right in front of her, their only child—and took refuge in sculpting dramatic plaster of paris figures and theater, where she met free-spirited Pia, who even then talked incessantly about leaving Baltimore to be a world-famous person before social media as such was invented. Pia was the only one who seriously entertained Dana's fantasies of being a notable sculptor who would exhibit in galleries around the world. Everyone Dana knew after high school, when she started getting serious about her academics, knew her only as Responsible, Nurturing Nurse Dana. She needed some time to warm up before she could access that past carefree self while talking to Pia because it had been buried for so long. Young Dana would not have found Pia's casual pill-popping uncomfortable, even if she didn't partake herself.

"You don't worry about Tokyo, is what I'm trying to say," Pia added. "Are you OK, Dee?"

Dana let out a strangled laugh. "That's the question, isn't it?" Her mind drifted to earlier that afternoon, after their Maintenance Shag, when she happened to go to the study to retrieve a book and saw Nigel's open laptop. His résumé was still up on the screen, and Dana's heart panged again. Where was he in his job search? Was he getting any hits? She wished she could ask. It felt like a long time since they'd asked each other real things like that.

How are you, really? Where are you?

Instead, it was always, *Have you seen my last message? Have you done this/that? Will you please go do XYZ?*

Pia was silent for a few beats before she ventured, "Is this call about Nigel?"

Dana sank lower in her car seat. "It is and it isn't."

"Dee, it's me—you can tell me anything."

She didn't need more prompting. "Nigel and I are going through a rough patch," she admitted. "Things have changed since he lost his job about a year ago."

"I'm sure he's struggling. That's a big hit to take, for him," Pia said carefully.

"I'm sure it is." Then she forced out, "I don't think I am . . . fine either."

"What do you mean?"

It rushed out of her in a jumbled torrent. "It's *all* of it. Ever since he lost his job, he's become the main parent, I've become the sole breadwinner, and the dynamics between us have become . . . twisted. I mean, not that he wasn't already the main parent during the pandemic—you know, I was in the hospital all the time—I suppose that's when the kids got much closer to him over me . . . but at least I kind of felt like we didn't really have a choice and we all had to soldier on, you know? He could work remotely back then, so the energy at home, even on the rare occasions I could spend an evening out of the hospital, were still positive . . . like we still laughed, we still made love. We . . . we *fucked*." Pia and Dana shared a surprised laugh at Dana's rare openness about their bedroom antics. "But then Emmie happened, and then almost a year after her birth, he lost his job, and things . . . Oh my God, I don't even know how to explain it to myself, but things are *different* . . . He's changed in the last year, although h-he looks the same to everyone else outside the family. To everyone else, he's doing what he's been doing since the pandemic, he's still the consummate dad, he never complains, but I can tell he looks at family life—at us!—different. Now he doesn't say it, but I *know* he thinks I'm the toxic one, I'm the one who's resentful and bringing that energy home. I have too much work, and I can't tell him, because at least I have a job, you know? In this economy? And as a creative director, he's not getting more relevant with AI and technology. I think he's hanging by a thread. Like he's so good at masking it but I just know. But I feel so uncomfortable broaching the subject. God, Pia. Nigel's become like . . . like a stranger." Her voice broke and she drew several ragged breaths. She was literally out of it.

"Shit, babe, wow . . . Honestly, I had no idea the situation had gotten so bad. I'm so, so sorry," Pia said softly.

"Maybe I'm just overthinking things. Maybe I'm spiraling because I'm just so tired," Dana said. She rubbed her temples. "I—I just feel like everything's on me now. The bills, the house, keeping everything from falling apart. I don't see the kids as often as I'd like, but when I see them, I'm angry. And I don't even know why. Some of it is fatigue, sure, but if I'm being honest, I just feel, like, guilty. So guilty. Especially with Emmie, not being able to be there for her physically . . . and emotionally, I think." She let out a huff of frustration. "And if I'm perfectly honest, I'm especially angry at Nigel. He's just . . . he's so loved by the kids. He's Super Dad. I . . . I'm jealous. I don't want to resent him, Pia, but I do. Just a little."

"Wow." Pia exhaled noisily. "Have you told him that?"

Dana mirrored her. "I don't know how. We're a house of cards as it is, Pia."

Pia was quiet again, then said, "Maybe you start by telling him how *you* feel. Not about him. About you."

Dana leaned back, staring at the roof of her car. "I don't even know what I feel anymore. I have everything. But I also feel I have nothing of my own. Don't get me wrong, I love my kids. I do. I just . . . I just had them so young, you know? And then on top of it we got pregnant on accident again, just as the pandemic restrictions were lifting, and you know—bam!"

"You don't have to justify yourself to me, Dana. You know I don't care about kids, and I know you love yours."

"I just feel like I'm suffocating, and I don't know how much of it is because of the work stress and how much of it is from dissatisfaction with my life choices," Dana finally admitted. "Because I've never really . . . I've never really made any decisions for myself. Just me."

Pia's voice softened. "Then maybe that's what you should be figuring out first."

Dana shut her eyes, letting those words settle. Because the truth was, she'd spent so much time worrying about Nigel and the kids, about money, about keeping everything together, that she hadn't stopped to ask herself the one thing that mattered: With all the changes in her household, where did everything that had happened to her, everything that she had done in response, leave *her*?

What do you want?

After a few beats, Pia spoke up. "This might be out of turn, but you and Nigel have been co-parenting with meager benefits for quite some time now. Maybe it's time to explore greener pastures. Press the reset button on your love life. Leave your marriage. Burn it all down and go."

Leave Nigel? Dana scoffed internally, fighting down a surge of irritation. In spite of Pia's commiserations, the contrast between their lives couldn't have been starker: What did her single, carefree, successful, and happily childfree friend know about commitments? Dana would never leave Nigel. Couldn't, for multiple reasons. Some of it was the collected detritus of their shared history, sure—try untangling the mutual friends you've collectively amassed over the years, or even splitting existing shared accounts. The admin! The logistics! Dana shook her head at the sheer sprawl of what disengaging from Nigel would entail. It was undeniably easier to plod along, maintaining the status quo. A classic example of the sunk-cost fallacy, maybe—you'd put in the money, time, and monogamy, so surely you should stick it out; surely your shared history meant something and was, in itself, worth fighting for.

But what if this was just irrational persistence? It was undeniable that these days he felt like another item on her to-do list and nothing more. "A co-parent without many benefits" was an accurate—if depressing—description. What if something—someone—better was waiting for her out there, and her inaction was costing her a chance at real happiness, even if it meant a do-over? Could she really live like this for the next two, three decades, ticking along like life was an increasingly bland series of obligations?

Ah, the internal monologue of a true romantic, she thought wryly. But the truth was, romance was for the young and unjaded—and Dana was neither. She had to be pragmatic and weigh the pros and cons, and Dana was nothing if not pragmatic by nature. Maybe that's why she'd had such a negative reaction to Pia's suggestion, because if she was being truthful, there was a part of her that had considered it—and that was the part Dana was trying to ignore. She was afraid of opening that door and finding her answer.

"Come to Greece," Pia said, reverting to type. "Please! It's just ten days. *Ten!* When was the last time you had a vacation? You deserve it."

"I'd love to come, you and Yomi notwithstanding, but I've got commitments." *Large financial ones,* she didn't add. She couldn't just spend their money on a frivolous trip.

But of course Pia knew. They weren't old friends for nothing. "I know you do, so why don't I pay for your flights at least, if money is a bit, you know, tight? Or all of it, if you'd let me? I know you're prickly about these things, but what's a few g's between old friends? Nothing." Pia grew businesslike. "Listen, hon, this has been the best financial year for me. I've just gotten this massive speaking engagement with a tech company and my calendar is booked solid for the next two years, and I have no children to spend my money on, just me and my independently wealthy parents and older sister."

It's not just about the money, though, Dana thought, a surge of despair threatening to overwhelm her.

"Pia, that is so generous of you, and I love you for it, but . . . but I can't accept," she said. "Expenses aside, I don't have that much leave." Despite her cynicism, Dana had been hoarding her days off, hoping that Nigel would surprise her with a romantic trip somewhere for her fortieth. But with each passing week, that possibility was looking more and more remote. She wasn't expecting a fancy shindig, just something sweet and thoughtful. A weekend in the woods, maybe somewhere in Carroll County. Nigel had broached the subject of them doing something for her fortieth—just the two of them—a couple of months ago, in the midst of one of their weekly sit-downs, and she'd been a little lukewarm at the idea for multiple reasons—turning forty, in particular, scared her. She was so far from what she thought she'd be at this age, and maybe some of that had come off as reluctance, but they'd agreed they would do something. Had he forgotten?

"You must have enough leave. You don't *do anything*," Pia responded, pressing on with her agenda. There was a brief pause when she heard herself and backpedaled. "Ah, shit, that sounded super dismissive, I'm so sorry."

"It's OK," Dana said, although privately she was smarting. It wasn't OK—and once again, she was reminded of the vast gulf between Pia's enviable life of "me firsts" and her own. "Also, I need to give people adequate heads-up, not just a week before—the hospital staff is swamped after recent budget cuts. Not to mention I'd need to arrange childcare to support

Nigel." By *childcare*, she meant her aunt Florence, who lived close by and wouldn't charge her an arm and a leg—that was, if Florence was still alive and/or mobile. She was seventy-eight, after all. It was too bad Nigel's parents lived in Peterborough in the UK and had six other grandchildren to occupy themselves with; her mother, long separated from her father, had passed sometime during the pandemic in Austin, with her second family.

"Babe, you're killing me," Pia moaned. "Why won't you take a few days off if I'm paying for everything? You are the cornerstone of my *life*! You've been there for all the important milestones, all of them! Seven measly workdays, Dee! Don't you want to come?"

Dana shut her eyes. She imagined saying yes and actually going to Greece. Hugging her best friend, whom she hadn't seen in the flesh in years. Seeing Yomi Owope for the first time in almost twenty years and hearing him call her Sweet Dee, her high school nickname, again. Dancing like she didn't know what time meant. Wearing clothes that didn't smell like the hospital and talking about shows they'd binge-watched while inhaling cocktails instead of patient stats and DNRs. And traveling to new places, even if it wasn't the backpacking, low-impact, and sustainable way she would have preferred. Being spontaneous for once.

She could almost taste the coarse salt of the frozen margarita, feel the sun on her shoulders.

Of course she wanted to go. Who in their right mind wouldn't want to go on a vacation and not think about real life for a bit?

Then the guilt came rushing back. Her punishing inner voice spoke up: *Great. You want to leave, to have fun and come back with debt? How responsible, Dee. If you're not even there for the kids emotionally, you could at least be fiscally responsible. What kind of parent are you?*

"I'm not coming, Pia, and that's final. There's just no way, what with work being what it is. I'm sorry."

Dana spent the next fifteen minutes of her precious time off consoling Pia, who couldn't fathom the concept of needing to adhere to company policy when it came to requesting time off.

When Pia finally hung up, Dana got out of the car and headed to the waterfront to clear her head before Nancy's birthday shindig. The hospital, a brown bear of a building, stood by the Patapsco River. A scarf of cool breeze wound itself around the building and ruffled the surface of the spangled water. There were distant flashes of lightning over the water; a thunderstorm was coming. It had been a faltering start to spring, with stretches of warm, sunny days broken up by biting, rain-soaked ones. Spring always seemed indecisive in her hometown. *How apt.* Her beige slacks and lightweight woolen turtleneck were sensible choices given the weather, but Dana wished she had put on something a little less *her* today, something more daring, something insouciant with lace and satin and peeks of skin. Her head ached. She started to walk toward the waterfront, barely registering the harbor lights and the brine-scented breeze that always comforted her when she felt unmoored. *Is this the entire breadth of my universe?*

She stayed by the water for almost twenty minutes, lost in her thoughts, until a diving gull alerted her that it was time to head to her colleague's birthday drinks. She started her car, a hot stone of complicated emotion weighing down her gut. It just felt like every decision she made brought her no joy these days.

Maybe because you don't really want to go to drinks either, because you're so fucking tired and your hair is greasy and your eyes itch in fluorescent lighting. Let me ask you something, Dana: When was the last time you did something just for yourself?

Family is sacrifice, Dana reminded herself. *It's not just me now. I have other people to care for. I won't give up the way my parents did on their marriage and their family.*

The words felt hollow, even if she believed them. *Had* to believe them. The foundation of her world depended on it.

But the call with Pia had unearthed old questions, and the biggest one was ringing through her mind, unwilling to be silenced:

Is this all?

Nigel

Dinner Is Going Well . . . ish

Nigel felt more optimistic as the evening went on. Dinner was going well, all things considered. Dana's absence wasn't a hindrance, wasn't even remarked upon by Selvi beyond the initial observation. Selvi liked his food; he could tell by the way she relaxed the moment she bit into it, like she held herself aloft from enjoyment until it was assured. She ate the pasta in neat but wolfish bites. She even took two portions. Success.

She glanced up after the first couple of bites, an eyebrow raised in surprise, and said, "This is really good, Nigel," and Nigel's heart soared. Nigel wasn't sure if anyone else other than Gill had ever complimented his cooking. Dana didn't even *know* how much his cooking had improved since Emmie's birth; it was something he'd picked up in the last year (there was only so much one could take of boxed or microwavable meals)—at first it had been out of necessity, when they decided to cut day care and Emmie had to be fed real food, but he'd kept learning out of curiosity, then joy.

Selvi took another generous bite and made more appreciative noises. "Seriously, no one told me you could cook, Nigel."

Something in his chest loosened at her words. He realized part of the reason he'd hesitated in asking her to dine in the first place was because he'd been sure that she, a hotshot litigator, would sneer at his homespun food. This was a modified Jamie Oliver recipe, rustic at best, but here she was, putting his food into her mouth with gusto. Nigel gripped his knife, cleared his throat to release the words threatening to pile up in there, and said, with much more emotion than the situation warranted, "Thank you."

Bex shot her father a look while Emmie and Gill traded food across the table. Nigel had made a sweet potato–and-carrot mash for Emmie, which, predictably, she had given to Gill in exchange for his pasta. Emmie hated mashed anything, while Gill loved mashed everything. Gill also loved making Emmie happy, so even if he hadn't wanted the mash, he would have given her everything on his plate for the pleasure of her babyish chuckle. Meanwhile, Bex treated both of her siblings with determined indifference, her eyes fixed on Shobana, whose attention was split chiefly between her mom and Bex, and sometimes, as an afterthought, him.

Shobana and Bex disappeared upstairs around 8:30 p.m., about ten minutes after Nigel served dessert—a lovely peach cobbler, a TikTok recipe. Gill excused himself and beckoned for Emmie to join him; earlier that day, Nigel had asked Gill for his help to put Emmie to bed while he had a chat with Selvi post-dinner. Now Gill knelt and let Emmie climb onto his back; the adults watched as he wore her upstairs like a human backpack.

"Your kids are so well behaved, you're fabulous with them," Selvi observed, and Nigel felt that irrational swell of gratitude again.

They were doing dishes side by side, in spite of Nigel's insistence that he'd handle it himself. (*You're the guest!* Nigel had said. *Your dishwasher is down,* Selvi had said simply, pulling her long waves into a girlish ponytail.) She wouldn't take no for an answer. Nigel was glad. The truth was, the dishwasher hadn't just recently broken down—it had been out of commission for so long they were using it as storage space. Dishes were a pain in the ass, Nigel's least favorite chore. He had dry skin, and the cheap dishwashing liquid always left his hands raw and red. It was nice having company while doing something as basic as dishwashing. The quaint, shared domesticity of the act thrilled him. Nigel liked having her stand next to him at their cramped kitchen sink, him scrubbing and soaking the dishes in the warm soapy water before rinsing them off and handing them to her to dry and stack; he liked the idle chatter and the comforting closeness of another human being as they went about fulfilling their duties in the small scheme of things.

He could smell her, the fresh, saline tang of her skin, the nutty sweetness of her shampoo. He had always thought that Selvi would smell more masculine, like the interior of an upscale boutique hotel, plush vanillic florals dipped in musk. The kitchen was quiet except for the rustle of the dishrag, the soft clink of stacking porcelain and their steady breaths.

She was so soft tonight, the hard edges gone. He wondered how many people were like this, wearing the hard armor of their past as they hurtled through the day, pausing every so often to let a handful of people into the secret garden that lay behind their walls.

She was beautiful, Nigel realized with a start. And he was *attracted* to her.

Nigel made himself leave the kitchen then, blurting that he needed the restroom.

He climbed the stairs to his room and hid there for a full ten minutes, psyching himself out from whatever madness had befallen him. *She's Shobana's mom. She's Shobana's mom* (rinse and repeat). *What's come over you?* Selvi was good-looking, sure, but he was acting like a lovestruck teenager; he suspected it was because she was the first woman he'd hung out with, alone, in over a year, who'd paid him genuine attention and a compliment, and he'd been so deprived of any kind of words of affirmation—his love language!—that he'd almost forgotten himself.

When he had sufficiently gathered his wits, he came back down and saw that Selvi was standing silhouetted in the light coming in from the yard. She had turned off the kitchen light and was staring at something only she could see, so that her regal profile was limned by moonlight.

He cleared his throat and tried for levity. "Hey, ready to ruin the girls' alone time?"

She turned and smiled, armor back on. "Sure."

—~—

Shobana and Bex were innocently playing computer games on two different chairs when Nigel knocked and entered, nothing rumpled on them bodily or bed-wise. They were like two sleek meerkats who happened to run into each other on the savanna and decided to watch the sunrise together. They turned and faced Nigel with identically innocent smiles, the kind of smile that Nigel hadn't seen on his daughter since she was eight. *OK, player,* he thought, lifting an eyebrow. He knew when he was in the presence of greatness.

"We're heading back," Selvi said crisply. "It's almost nine."

"OK!" Shobana said without resistance. "It *is* a school night, after all."

"Definitely," Bex said, nodding sagely. "I guess I'll take the opportunity to read a couple of chapters for AP Lit before I turn in."

Nigel stared at Bex. Who was this person?

Bex and Shobana hugged chastely, zero lingering, and Shobana trailed Selvi and Nigel down the stairs without protest. At the door, Selvi handed Shobana the keys and told her to wait in the car.

Selvi turned to Nigel. "Well, this was . . . pleasant," she said, old Selvi back except for the look in her eyes.

Nigel stuck his hand out, not realizing the danger.

She took his hand and a frisson of heat raced up his arm at her touch. Their hands clasped and stayed there without progressing to the perfunctory shaking that usually followed. Nigel heard Sixpence None the Richer's "Kiss Me," his goddamn prom song, playing in the movie theater of his head. His problem, as his wife loved to remind him, was that he was a goddamn romantic, a goddamn sentimental fool. He didn't love easily per se, but the part of him that needed the romance of a yearning gaze, a tentative touch, had not been fed in over a year, and it was stirring, no longer content to lie dormant. He jerked his hand back and her brow creased before smoothing out.

"Good night," Nigel said curtly, almost desperate for her to leave.

She stared at him and gave a hard nod before leaving. Nigel felt a deep sense of relief. He loved his wife—he *loved* his wife.

But then, her car wouldn't start.

Nigel

Recruitment Drive

Nigel went up to tell the kids he was taking Selvi and Shobana home. Emmie and Gill were already asleep when he checked on them, while Bex was reading one of her romantasy novels "for a class assignment."

"Sure, Dad, have fun," Bex said, distracted. It was a careless comment, but it struck Nigel hard. *Have fun—I haven't had fun in ages.*

In fact, it felt like he'd not really been living his life, but that his life was living him, if that made sense.

What happened to me?

"I really don't understand. I just sent the BMW for servicing two weeks ago," Selvi murmured as they got in the clunky Civic. Nigel knew it was directed at him: an explanation and an apology.

"It's fine," he said, distracted. How could he have reached this stage of his life, when he could no longer remember the last time he'd had fun? With friends, with his wife, on his own (unless you counted binge-watching stuff on streaming, but that was more passive distraction than fun).

"The car smells funny," Shobana said suddenly, in a rare break from her Model Friend character.

"Shobana!" Selvi chastised.

"It's OK," Nigel said. "I spilled coffee in it last week and the baking soda in the heat has somehow made it worse."

"That's not it, though," Shobana said, sniffing.

Then it hit Nigel: The car smelled like someone had slept in it—that was what it was. The upholstery held the grease and sweat of prolonged skin contact on synthetic material: Dana. Nigel knew she slept in the car sometimes, typically after she'd taken a night shift with overtime—too tired to make the twenty-minute drive back home. (The SUV had been acting up in the past few months, so on the days Nigel didn't need the car, Dana favored the Civic for the longer drive to work.) His heart panged. How to explain the rage and helplessness that threatened him sometimes when he thought of her sleeping in their car, broken by her shift? How to explain how frustrated he felt, week after week of getting told they didn't need copywriters anymore. That the world didn't need what he could provide, didn't need *him* anymore.

"Crack the windows then," Selvi said, more harshly than the situation warranted.

"Jeez, Mom, chill," Shobana said. The window descended and the night breeze rushed in, lifting the tired-person smell. But it did nothing to dissipate what was brewing in Nigel's chest.

They arrived in front of Selvi and Shobana's redbrick town house on Charles Street.

"Would you have time to come up for a quick drink?" Selvi said nonchalantly.

Nigel's face flushed. "Oh, I, um, I don't know, it's getting late."

"It'd be great if you could. I want to ask your professional advice on something. A"—she hesitated—"recruitment brochure."

Professional advice. Nigel's mouth went dry. Was she flirting with him? She had to know that her choice of words would have an effect on him. And then the other giveaway to her intentions, that hitch in her voice, that had been clear as day—or was Nigel out of touch? *Why are you even thinking of* . . . *What is wrong with you?* But a gut feeling was a gut feeling. Nigel *knew* something was up.

Wrinkling her nose, Shobana said, "Mom, Mr. Cheng isn't your corporate lackey. If you want his professional advice, you have to pay him."

"Oh, I'll pay him," Selvi said, and Nigel had to close his eyes and mentally take a deep breath at the sudden, inappropriate image of Selvi in lingerie that beamed into his consciousness. "You can park in our garage," she said, indicating where he should go.

"Well, I'm going to bed," Shobana said. She got out of the car and slammed the door. She hurried to the town house, her keys out, Selvi following with terse admonitions for her to wait up. They got in and Selvi shut the front door behind them, no doubt in order to have a private word with her daughter about the latter's rudeness. Nigel swung the car forward, nosed it into the narrow garage beneath the house, and jogged up the steps to the front door. There he lingered, fidgeting, waiting to be invited in by Selvi. *Like a vampire,* he thought randomly, as though there was something illicit in what he was about to do.

The door opened with a burst of light. "Come in," Selvi said. Nigel walked in, his heart hammering, feeling more alive than he'd been in months.

Nigel knew that Selvi, a woman at the pinnacle of her profession and who he intuited would have good taste, would have a gorgeous house, and she did not disappoint. The house, a two-story glass-fronted designer bauble, was as elegantly minimalist as he had hoped. Tasteful artwork in a blend of traditional Indian folk art and abstract washes of paint complemented the austere, contemporary furnishings. Coffee-book tales of sumptuous fashion and art that actually looked like they'd been read (noting the little Post-it tabs in some of them in dutiful blue). The house exuded the blessed calm of an owner without young children and with enough money to hire help.

She showed him around and asked him if he'd like a drink. "I have sparkling water, juice, and tea if you're not drinking, wine and other spirits if you are."

"What are you having?" Nigel said.

She laughed. "I'll have a glass of red wine. Care to join me?"

Yes, yes, he would.

The wine in question was a Châteauneuf-du-Pape, ruby-red fruity seduction. Nigel settled on the couch next to Selvi, who pulled up an iPad and showed him what she wanted him to give his *professional opinion* on.

"The thing is, we'd like something that showcases the firm's commitment to diverse hiring without being too . . . on the nose about it." Selvi's elegantly curved nose had the tiniest gold stud, discreet yet unmistakable. Nigel's eyes roved over her face. She was the first adult woman, besides his wife, he'd been this close to since he'd been let go from his job.

She was waiting for his input. Nigel gave himself a mental shake and said, "I'd use bold, punchy colors, maybe a bit of neon even, on the firm's navy-blue background for contrast, with testimonials from standout employees, talking about the welcoming culture and your proactive recruitment of talent from underrepresented backgrounds. Something that reflects the reality of America's urban workforce today—" He was rambling. He was not even sure if he was responding to the question anymore. But Selvi's eyes were attentive. Patient. Focused on him.

"All in all," he continued, gathering himself, "a diverse workplace is an asset in an interconnected world. It's something to showcase, not tiptoe around. The younger generation looks for that now. You shouldn't be afraid to emphasize it visually. I'd put you on the front page of the brochure—alongside others who reflect that same story."

A hint of a blush tinted her dark cheeks. "Thank you." She bit her lip and fiddled with the stem of the glass; she had short, cleanly buffed nails in a soft, elegant taupe. "So. I've been meaning to ask you something."

Nigel tensed up, unsure if he felt anxiety or excitement. *She's going to make a move. She's going to kiss me.*

And what's my move if she does?

Maybe he tilted forward as he thought this, because immediately Selvi scooted back on the couch, cleared her throat, and gave an embarrassed laugh.

"I, um, gosh, this is . . . this is unexpected."

Nigel flushed. "I-I'm so sorry, I thought—" Did he really, or was he just projecting? He wasn't sure, but his face must be as red as his Bolognese sauce by now.

Selvi opted to brush the entire situation under the carpet. "Listen, I'm sorry if I was giving off mixed signals."

"You weren't," Nigel muttered, humiliation complete. "You were extremely . . . proper. I—I . . . I'm the one who mistook this . . ."

Selvi cleared her throat and valiantly tried to steer the conversation to safer grounds. "The truth is, I wanted to know how things are going now that you're not . . . you know." Her flush deepened. "I mean, you're a stay-at-home dad after almost two decades of working."

Oh my God, Nigel thought, his stomach churning. So this was an *intervention.* Selvi hadn't invited him over to *seduce him*—she'd merely wanted to ask him how he was getting along now that he was just some pathetic loser.

He radiated inadequacy, apparently, even to acquaintances. "H-how . . . how did you—"

"Bex told Shobana, and Shobana told me." Her expression clouded. "I'm really sorry, Nigel. I know it can't be easy. I thought . . . I thought I'd help your family by giving you freelance work. I know we weren't really friendly before tonight, Nigel, but I always thought . . ." She shook her head. "You always struck me as being really . . . well . . . sure of yourself."

In the past. That was the unspoken part of the sentence. All too well, Nigel saw the hilarity of his delusion—him, dad jeans, slightly worn plaid shirt; Selvi, elegant wrap dress and silk stockings. He had seen her as an equal when she had seen him as—

Selvi sighed and rubbed her brow. "Look. I really do need help with the brochure. I'd be happy to pay your freelance hourly rate. You can redesign our recruitment brochure, then potentially all of our marketing material. What do you say?"

A charity case. The shame. The shame of being offered crumbs of work by a woman he'd flattered himself into believing was into him. This whole evening she had only been thinking of how to broach the subject of his unemployment. So she could save him.

He stood up rather abruptly and said, "I have to go."

"Nigel," Selvi said. "I'm sorry if I crossed a line." How deeply ironic that *she* was now apologizing to *him* for crossing a line, when he'd nearly—

Nigel made himself laugh. It came out choked and pitiful, not too far from how he was feeling, really. He tried to brush it off, his deep, deep mortification. "It's fine, you didn't. I really . . . I really appreciate your kindness, and I'll send you my quote as soon as possible." He still had Bex to think about, still had to *save face*, as his half-Chinese father liked to call it; his parents were all about keeping up appearances and sticking to established norms of their upper-middle-class, relatively traditional upbringing. "Good night."

She got up too. "It really was a beautiful dinner, Nigel. I'm glad our girls are . . . you know. Figuring things out."

Nigel didn't trust himself to speak, so he nodded. He couldn't see a future in which he hosted a dinner for Shobana and her mom again, not unless his life took a 180-degree turn for the better and he became the CEO of a Fortune 500 company.

She sent him to the door with a whispered "Good night," and Nigel forced himself to start the car and pull out of the garage. Truth be told, what he really wanted to do was let the earth open up and swallow him. To disappear.

Dana

What Are You, a Psychopomp?

Dana missed a couple of turnoffs to Nancy Padua's fiftieth birthday drinks at the dive bar on West Mount Royal Avenue and decided she would visit her father instead. She managed to get there only fifteen minutes before the visitation cutoff point, but her favorite receptionist, Sheila, waved her in. Maybe because Dana's eyes radiated end-of-the-road desperation.

"He's had a good day," Gary, the caregiver on rotation, said. "They were in the common room watching *Casablanca* tonight, and Arthur had an extra pudding."

"Dad always did like Humphrey Bogart." She managed to keep the wobble out of her voice. "He thinks they look alike."

Gary chuckled. "He's not wrong."

Gary left her in the room with her dad, who no longer recognized her but seemed to like her enough. Arthur Smiley had always been a reserved man, and in his decline, he'd withdrawn into himself. Since it was 9 p.m., he was already in bed, as per his usual bedtime routine at the care facility. The patients were encouraged to go to bed early, especially when they got to this stage, where even reading became impossible.

She sat next to him and held his hand. "Hi, Dad," she said.

"H-hello," her father rasped. He peered at her, his eyes curious. "Nice to meet you." He didn't say anything else, but he smiled. She squeezed his hand and he returned the pressure. It was almost like he recognized her.

He let her hold his hand as she asked him how his day was ("Good" was all he said—he had trouble retaining short-term memories), then politely dropped it after a couple of minutes. He fell asleep as she recounted her day—just the tolerable, routine bits, not the parts that shook her.

Gary came to get her at 9:40 p.m.

"Sorry, Dana, but we have to—" He motioned at the clock on the wall.

She got up, blinking quickly as though that would dry her tears. "Ah, shit. I totally lost track of time."

"I tried to push it, but you know the rules."

She shook her head, trying for nonchalance even though he must have clocked how swollen her eyes were. "Don't. I get it. I'm sorry for overstaying."

"You're always welcome here," Gary said, and just the way he said it struck her again. She felt the powerful urge to throw herself at him, to press herself into his comforting chest and cry. To feel something—anything, other than this despair.

She waved goodbye at Sheila, her composure rattled.

She barely made it into the open-air parking lot before the tears came. Thank God she was parked in a corner with no one around. She circled her car, opened the trunk, and chucked her purse in, then slid to the asphalt, her chest squeezing. Everything hit her all at once: Her father's hope for recovery was all but over. Her hopes for her future—everything was over. *This is all that's left.*

This is all that's left of me.

She dropped her face into her lap and sobbed quietly, safe in the knowledge that no one could see her. Her whole body, especially her heart, ached. She sat there for what felt like ages, waiting for the courage to go home. It was 10 p.m.; the dinner must've been over by now.

"Are you all right?" a voice said, startling her enough that she stopped and glanced up to see who it was through a fog of tears. An older woman, Asian, face lined, wearing a white uniform. An RN or similar, someone heading in for a shift at the facility. Dana struggled to stand up, but to her surprise, the older woman dropped to a squat beside her and motioned for her to stay where she was. "It's fine, you don't have to get up. I'll join you, if that's fine by you."

"Thank you, yes please," Dana said dully, perfunctorily. "I'm just . . . gathering my strength before I head back." She figured the woman might decide to leave her after a polite amount of time had passed—Dana was calm-looking, and not a threat to herself or others. Yet the older woman didn't leave. In fact, she sank down onto the pavement—in her white slacks and white shirt—and sat with her back against the dusty body of the SUV beside Dana, ignoring the latter's weak protests.

"I would ask if you're OK, but I'd hazard a guess and say no," the woman said dryly, gesturing around them. She had a bell-like voice, skin as translucent as rice paper, and she smelled strongly of woodsmoke. Dana felt a faint prick of unease—the parking lot was beside the rolling landscaped grounds and the entrance to the two-story facility, with only a quiet road leading to it. Dana hadn't heard anyone drive by since she got there, so where had this woman come from?

Almost as though she could hear Dana's thoughts, the woman said, "I was just walking out from the facility for"—she hesitated—"a smoke and was on my way back in when I saw you."

Plausible. "Look, I don't mean to be a jerk, but I kind of want to be alone," Dana mumbled, tucking her car keys in a claw formation behind her, just in case.

"But you're not safe out here," the strange woman said. "Someone could hurt you."

Dana almost laughed at the idea. The only risks were being robbed or kidnapped, and the facility was not exactly in a high-traffic area, and there were many cameras on the grounds. Besides, who would even want to rob a woman as basic as her? The most valuable item of clothing on her was her watch, an ancient Casio no one would ever mistakenly tag as "vintage," and the white Crocs that nurses loved to wear at work. "I'd like to see someone try, more than I'm already hurting."

"Do you want to talk about it?" the woman asked gently, though Dana could sense an eagerness in her mannerisms that came through in spite of her nonchalance.

Dana hesitated. Normally, she wouldn't dream of spilling her personal drama to a stranger. But then there was the fact that it had been so long since she'd had a real, one-on-one conversation—aside from the one she had with Pia. The urge to unload was almost physical, like pressing against a recent bruise just to feel something.

"It's . . . it's kind of embarrassing and trivial. You won't understand," Dana said, flushed.

The woman shrugged, undeterred. "You'd be surprised at how much I get people—even ones that are nothing like me." A flicker of secret amusement passed across her face. "Try me."

"It might take a while, and you're on your way to work," Dana hedged.

"I have time," the woman said. She shot a glance at the doors of the facility. "My client doesn't need me—yet."

Dana didn't need further prompting: Before she could second-guess herself, the words came tumbling out.

"My best friend, Pia, is turning forty," Dana started. "She's celebrating with this ridiculous luxury booze cruise. In Greece, our dream destination when we were teenagers. And it's going to be epic, like everything she touches these days, like, all-inclusive, top-shelf everything, gorgeous people in designer outfits lounging on the deck at sunset—that kind of cruise."

The woman raised an eyebrow. "That sounds . . . expensive."

"Oh, it is," Dana said with a humorless laugh. "She keeps calling it 'her once-in-a-lifetime splurge' and telling me I have to come, that it won't be the same without me. And I want to! God, I *want* to. I haven't had a break in so long. But the cost of the last-minute flight ticket alone is more than my mortgage. And even if I could scrounge that up, there's still the clothes, the special drinks, the tips, the 'let's get matching spa treatments' peer pressure . . ." She let out a sigh. "I can't even afford a weekend staycation without abusing my credit card, let alone a floating five-star hotel."

The woman didn't rush to fill the silence, which made Dana keep talking. "It's not just me missing out on the cruise. It's everything. Work is a nightmare. I feel like I'm barely treading water. I'm physically and emotionally wrung out, but I have to keep going because I'm the sole breadwinner." Her breath quickened just at the thought of underperforming and potentially being let go. "I have three kids. A mortgage. Groceries to get, extracurricular activities to fund. My bank account looks like a crime scene. And so I stay"—she swiped her hand over her face—"and I endure."

"How come you're the sole breadwinner? Are you married?" the woman prompted, her voice careful.

Dana let out another laugh, this one even more bitter. "My husband has been out of a job for almost a year, and he hasn't found anything commensurate with his almost two decades of experience as a creative director. I know he's been trying to find a job—any job—in the same industry, but have you seen what's happening with AI? It's brutal. I . . . I think he's really down about it, so I can't say anything. Especially since he's the best house husband and stay-at-home dad ever. He's so good he and the kids don't even notice when I'm not around anymore. And he doesn't notice me, not as a woman, not romantically. We're just going through the motions."

She rubbed her hands together, as if she could smooth away the embarrassment. "I know I sound pathetic."

The woman was quiet for a beat, then leaned forward slightly. "You don't," she said. "You sound like someone who's been holding their breath for too long."

That made Dana look up. There was no pity in the woman's expression, which somehow made this stranger's kindness worse.

"And now I'm just out here by myself in a parking lot, wondering if . . . wondering if I made the right choices in my life. Don't get me wrong—I *love* my family, I love my kids, absolutely adore them, and my husband . . ." Dana hurried to add, worried that this older woman might judge her. God forbid a woman admitted to feeling anything less than 100 percent certain about her decisions to get married and have a family; they'd eviscerate you, "they" being the pious Never-Put-a-Foot-Wrong internet morality police she had internalized as a child born in the eighties. "But sometimes everything just feels so . . . overwhelming."

"I hear you," the stranger said. "It's funny how many young people don't get—often until it's too late!—how linear time is, how unrelenting it is. How our every little decision when we're young can widen into sinkholes that can swallow and imprison us decades later. And then we're left lamenting what could have been."

"Oh my God, yes!" Dana sputtered. She stabbed the air. "That! That!" Although it was sad to hear it put so starkly. But it was too late for her now. She'd never know any other life.

The woman leaned forward, so close that for a moment Dana held her breath, mesmerized by the woman's curiously bright eyes, until the stranger broke her trance by asking, "Tell me, if you could change anything, anything at all in the world, what would you want?"

"Can you give me back my dignity?" Dana joked, a little uncomfortable with the woman's penetrating stare.

"Don't deflect," the woman said quietly. "There's no one else here. Just tell me: What does *Dana Smiley* want?"

What do you want, Dana Smiley? Dana asked herself. Life was asking her: Was this it? Was this all? What was next? Was there even a Next that would be vastly different from whatever this stasis, this status quo, was? *I'm grateful, I'm so grateful for this, of courseofcourseoffuckingcourse, but am I allowed a better life?* It was like she was a butterfly pinned down in a glass case who, after the pin in her back was removed, found that she was alive, she always had been, and she could leave the case before the lid was popped back on but she had to *hurry*. But those observations felt too personal to be shared with a stranger. "I want a lot of things,"

Dana said offhandedly. "Better job security, better finances, maybe a vacation. For my lower back not to hurt. I don't know."

"Small, small dreams," the woman said. Her eyes were very bright, almost gold, under the streetlight. "Humor me. Let's pretend I'm someone with the power to grant you anything you truly desire. The big stuff. No resurrection of the dead and going back in the past, you understand, but beyond that—the sky's the limit."

The sky might be the limit for another woman, but Dana was realistic. She knew what kind of butterfly she was, the kind who, perched on the edge of her freedom, worried about her babies pinned down next to her, her children who she didn't think her partner could handle without her. She wasn't that kind of butterfly, no. Her escapism could only be taken in half measures, an end date in mind. "I'd like a week," she decided. A break from her life.

"A week?" the woman said, raising her eyebrows. "Be specific, my dear."

"I . . . I'd like some time to myself to live as a single woman, with a different . . . a fun job, just to . . . just to see what that life would look like if I had made different decisions in life." *If I had not married Nigel, essentially,* she finished in her head.

"Like a marriage vacation," the woman said shrewdly.

"Exactly!" When the stranger put it like that, it sounded so harmless. So right. "That's exactly what I want. But of course, at the end of it, I don't want there to be any consequences to my original life, no matter what happens in my alternate one," Dana said decisively. That sounded like a good plan: time off to get in touch with her own thoughts and desires, to know herself and to find herself again. To explore in an unfettered way. Maybe then she'd be able to decide if she wanted to stay in nursing—if she wanted to stay in her marriage.

The woman shook her head. "I've got to be up front with you, love. That's not possible. Even though I *could* take you out of your current timeline and put you in an alternate world without technically altering your original world or timeline too much—time passes differently in your alternate universe—*you* will be affected in one way or another . . . permanently. Because magic doesn't exist in a vacuum. There is a price for every wish." The woman's voice sharpened. "And portals to an alternate timeline are . . . friable. If your actions seem to favor your new timeline, there can be unforeseen, destabilizing consequences to your world."

Choices, decisions, consequences—Dana was sick of thinking about them. It felt like all she had been doing since the pandemic happened was holding back, overanalyzing, waiting and seeing on the big things, till she no longer knew what she truly felt, truly wanted. But she knew this: She wanted a break from her life. To find herself again. She wanted to just live in the moment for a week and worry later about *consequences*. "Then I'll deal with them afterward. Just let me have that week."

The woman held Dana's gaze for several long, unblinking beats. Then she nodded.

Before Dana's astonished eyes, the woman started to whisper under her breath, nonsensical but ominous-sounding gibberish that raised the hairs on Dana's neck and arms. When she finished, the very air around them took on a strange new charge, giving an almost ozone-like smell. The noise around them dimmed; Dana didn't even hear the chirping of crickets anymore. She couldn't quite quell a shiver of disquiet.

The woman's voice had changed, deepened to almost a growl. "I grant you, Dana Smiley, a week in a new universe, to do whatever you want in that world."

Dana's eyes fluttered—she was so *tired*. She blinked hard and tried to bring herself back to the present. Was she hallucinating this? She'd been taking double shifts every week for the past month without breaks. "That sounds heavenly," she said.

"Right. And now, I need something from you to open the path. Hold out your left hand."

Dana felt her hand obey as though she were in a trance. A haze had settled over her, lending a dreamlike quality to the interaction. *This can't be real.* She must have fallen asleep when she sat down on the ground.

Because the woman's eyes were glowing gold. The whole of her was glowing gold.

Dana gasped, wanting to back away, but try as she might, she stayed rooted to the ground.

The woman took Dana's palm and, with her pinkie finger, scratched along the latter's lifeline with the edge of a knifelike fingernail. A single drop of blood appeared before Dana could even process what was happening—although she felt nothing. She shuddered at the sight of her blood, transfixed. The woman swiped her thumb over the drop of blood, smearing Dana's palm with it. A cold, uneasy feeling skittered over Dana's heart, but then she blinked, and the woman stood apart from her, her hands in her pockets.

"It is done," the woman said. "I have put you in a universe where the question you seek answers to can be explored in a sufficiently authentic way, and the relationships forged in it can be replicated in this life should you wish to." She stood up, businesslike and without a backward glance, and started walking away. Dana's blood was coursing slowly in her body and her senses were duller than before, as though she'd been drugged. That whole exchange had happened, right? Dana shook her head to clear the sudden swell of fatigue that threatened to pull her under. It felt like the conversation was anecdotal, something that had happened in a past life or to another person entirely. Only the slight twinge along her lifeline reminded her of the wish she'd made.

Her head spun a little and she closed her eyes. *I don't feel good.* Like she'd had one too many Flaming Sambucas, her go-to drink when she wanted to be drunk. She waited for it to pass, but it took her a good quarter of an hour before she finally felt well enough to drive.

Dana drove home in a daze. Nigel was out by then, headed to Selvi's with her and Shobana in their trusty Honda Civic after Selvi's car refused to start; Bex provided all the details, too hyped to sleep. Dana listened to all of it dimly, glad that the evening had gone well for her daughter. When she went to kiss Emmie good night, she found her youngest in Gill's bed, snuggled up to her favorite sibling, who slept with his arm flung over her small, warm body. *She's almost three,* Dana thought, and was surprised by how emotional it made her feel. She kissed them both, wondering why it felt like a goodbye.

Dana crawled into bed without even bothering with her usual two-step—fine, one-step (facial wipes)—skin care routine. She wondered if she was losing her mind.

It occurred to her in that liminal state between sleep and surrender that she had never told the woman her name, yet the stranger had known it. Said it like an invocation to a deity. *What do you want, Dana Smiley?*

Sometime around eleven, Dana's phone died even though it had been three-quarters charged the minute before. That was when she missed the call from Nigel and, later, the one from the hospital.

Nigel

This Is Not Happening

The Honda Civic was on its last legs. It was a 1996 model, boudoir-burgundy seats, rust-spattered exterior faded to a nothing gray. Whenever the speed went above sixty miles an hour, the engine sputtered. But it never gave them any real trouble—it was reliable in the way machines used to be, *back in the day*, when they weren't meant to be scrapped for metal as soon as they broke down but sent to a repairman for a tune-up before they returned, as good as new.

Nigel loved that car fiercely. He had driven it in college and held on to it out of sheer sentimentality, refusing to sell it even when Dana had pressed him to do so. Another indictment of his fatal mawkishness.

Nigel always drove at a respectable speed because he had no other choice when it came to the Civic, which was the only car he would touch. No matter how busted the Civic looked, he would not enter the new Subaru SUV that Dana had twisted his arm into getting to replace their other car—a 2007 Ford Taurus, cantankerous and unpredictable—because Emmie's arrival made a larger, safer car a necessity. The day that SUV entered the household was the day Nigel received the devastating news that, due to industry demand drying up, he was part of the team that would be let go (without so much as a paper parachute). The SUV was the harbinger of doom,

Nigel had decided. It wasn't fair—or even logical—to blame the car, of course. In fact, it was pure superstitious nonsense, but Nigel needed an outlet for his rage and despair. To this day, even seeing the Subaru in the driveway could make Nigel's vision swim. Maybe he needed therapy, but therapy wasn't a strict necessity, *not yet*, and they, a single-income household, had not a lot of wriggle room for *not yets*.

Nigel blinked and tried to refocus. The stress of his misjudged, frankly fantastical flirtation—*with his daughter's girlfriend's mom, no less!*—had amped up everything in him to a thousand. His nerves sang, their ends scorched by the fire of his humiliation. To make matters worse, both the GPS and his phone's reception were on the fritz, leaving him completely lost as he exited Federal Hill, where Selvi and Shobana had moved from Catonsville after Selvi's promotion earlier this year. Nigel was about as familiar with this part of the city as he was with Texas. On any given day, his sense of direction was barely functional.

He saw the time on the dashboard. If Dana'd really taken up a shift, she'd be right in the middle of its third hour by now. *If.* But he was darn sure she was not at work right then—she'd been lying about needing to go in for work for some time now, thinking Nigel wasn't paying her close enough attention to realize. Dana had a tell when she fibbed—she had an excellent poker face, no doubt, but she would ball her left hand into a fist. And suddenly he just wanted to get it all over and done with, excavate everything and dump the rotten carcasses out in the open, force them both to face the fact of their individual crimes—chief of all, the crime of possibly not loving each other anymore. It crushed him to think that.

He tried to call Dana to see where she was. He needed to see her, talk to her—*really* talk—now.

"Come on, Dana, pick up," he muttered. It took him five tries before he realized that it was futile; she was avoiding him.

He was all alone.

He drove up Hartford, took a left onto East Lafayette, and had just turned onto Hope Street when a white-clad figure—a girl—darted across the street to his right. A girl who turned and Nigel screamed. She *had no face*. The sight was so shocking that he swerved instinctively, eyes locked on the faceless girl even as he yanked the wheel. The car bounced off the curb, and the driver's side slammed into a lamppost. His foot reflexively crushed the brakes, but the impact had already thrown him forward and back, his seat belt snapping him in place as his neck whipped back with a sharp, sickening clack.

Then came the airbag—a loud, useless pop of inefficiency.

He could almost hear Dana's voice, prim, a shade of violet these days when it was once spring-summer blue, saying, *I told you so. We should have traded in your precious Civic years ago.*

Nigel's vision swam. He had bitten his tongue, and his mouth was awash with the tang of blood and mucus. He found it difficult to breathe; his rib cage hurt. *Shit. I think I hurt myself pretty bad.*

Maybe he was dying. The idea flooded him with a kind of stoic relief. And sadness, because at that moment he recognized how fucked-up his relief was. How long had he been feeling this way? Had the times when he was staring at his toothbrush, numb with the weight of the day, been more than just fatigue? The nights when he would turn over, his brain fizzing with wasted potential, the news, the rage and bile of a new podcast he'd just binge-listened to, images from the Korean reality show he just wanted to watch fifteen minutes of before coming to himself five hours later, realizing he'd gone through the entire season, and only because the alarm was going off for him to pick up Emmie from her three-day-a-week half-day stint at a local day care so she could *socialize* (they couldn't afford the five-day package, something he was prickly about). What were those episodes about if they weren't just symptoms of boredom?

If he was dying—

He saw Gill, his serious, frowny boy; Bex, mercurial, teenage, snarky; Emmie, precious, adorable, chubby perfection; and Dana. Oh, Dana.

"Excuse me, sir? Are you OK?"

Nigel's eyes focused blearily on the girl outside his windshield. He croaked, "H-help me, please. I'm hurt."

"I can see that!" the girl said. "Are you OK?" She was in her late teens, brunette, with deep eyes he couldn't tell the color of. They were fixed on him, untouched by her concern. Nigel felt a strange crawling sensation on his arms, a vague awareness that something was *wrong*, but he was also in a lot of pain and a confusing, suffocating amount of panic.

"Call 911," he pleaded hoarsely.

"Someone else beat me to it," she said. "I was knocking on your window for some time before you responded." The window had shattered, Nigel now noticed. She was framed by a halo of shards. "I was on my way to get to this client of mine, but then the accident happened and I thought, *Gigi, if you don't stop to help this man, what does that say about your family values?*"

"You had no face," Nigel mumbled, confused.

"Man, you must have hit your head pretty hard if that's what you think you saw," the girl said with a chuckle. "Don't worry. There was a huge pileup on I-83, but an ambulance is on the way."

Nigel's head lolled forward before he forced it up with an audible snap. *No. This is how McDreamy died.* He died after a crash, didn't he? Some kind of brain injury? *I need to stay awake.*

Nigel turned his head and winced at the pain that shot through his side. The girl was still standing outside, watching him with those old eyes. She was dressed in a white T-shirt and jeans under a white hooded sweatshirt, like a normal teenager, but there was something unsettling about her presence. Like she was perfectly at ease in a place where someone else was suffering.

And the smell of incense: She exuded it like musk.

"Why?" Nigel asked, not sure what his question related to. He blinked furiously, trying to stay awake. "Why are you still here?"

"I was on my way home from . . . work. At Brightstar."

Brightstar. Nigel's breath became irregular, as though the word were a trigger for him. She studied him for a moment before tilting her head. "Dana talks about you, you know."

Nigel's voice came out scratchy. "Dana?"

"Your wife? You remember her."

"I know who *Dana* is." He gasped out the words. He tried to fix his slippery gaze on her. "B-but how do you know her?"

She shrugged. She leaned closer, and Nigel realized she was not a teenager but someone in her early twenties—or older. It was not her skin, which was perfect, that gave it away. It was her eyes: The eyes were all wrong. "I work in the hospital. Candy striper."

"There . . ." Nigel coughed. "There aren't candy stripers anymore."

She chuckled, like she was privy to a private joke. "Figure of speech. I volunteer there. I help patients in palliative care *transition* comfortably. Then, in my spare time, I hang out in the cafeteria and . . . study. That's how I bumped into Dana. Hospitals are filled with tired, overworked people. People who need to vent. We got to talking, she showed me some photos of her family, and I recognized you." She raised an eyebrow at him. "She's got . . . strong opinions about you."

Nigel didn't believe this girl volunteered at Brightstar, but he didn't have the energy to dispute her story. "That so."

The girl tilted her head. "Yes. You're not exactly pleasing her right now."

Nigel let out a short, humorless laugh. His head hurt and his vision was filmed with blood, but everything that the girl said landed with startling precision. "Well," he rasped, "th-that makes two of us."

The girl studied him. Then her gaze flicked to his left hand, which was bare. "Must be exhausting."

"W-what . . . is?"

"Being someone you don't even like. Being *with* someone you're not sure you even like, maybe even know, anymore."

Goose bumps broke out over his arms. "Excuse me?" he said, wondering if he'd heard wrong. Wondering how this stranger had laid bare all his thoughts.

"I could read every thought passing across your face right now, Nigel," she said, tilting her head. "You don't exactly have a good poker face." She reached in through the glass and picked up Nigel's phone, which was wedged in his lap, and dangled it in front of him, tutting, like he was a naughty child caught with his zipper down. "You were trying to reach Dana just before the accident, weren't you? Don't bother, hon. I saw her in the parking lot before she drove off in a hurry."

He didn't answer; his throat was tight with bitterness. *Where* is *Dana?* She clearly wasn't on a shift.

She had lied to him. The knowledge was the final slap to his face. They once were the kind of couple who proudly proclaimed, to everyone within earshot, that they hid no secrets from each other—*we don't need to!*—that they could tell each other everything and anything.

Not, it seemed, anymore.

How smug they'd been. How wrong.

Nigel turned away from her. "Please l-leave me alone."

The girl laughed. She had teeth like tombstones, much too gray for someone her age. "I don't think you want me to leave, Nigel. I think you've not had an honest conversation like this for some time, and I've hit some nails on the head."

Nigel closed his eyes, defeated. If this was his end, he wanted peace. He didn't want her to be the last person he saw.

Dana, where are you?

He felt a gentle touch on his arm and a burst of pain relief. His brain fog dissipated or at least retreated into the shadows of his mind. "Come now, Nigel," the girl said. "Don't be petulant."

"What do you want?" Nigel said.

The stranger clapped, delighted that he was paying attention to her again. "Oh, I'm good, Nigel. The right question is, what is it that *you* want?"

"It feels like . . . it feels like you know."

She put her hands on her hips like an extra in a hip-hop dance video. She regarded him for so long he thought the matrix had glitched, and her image had frozen—she didn't blink much. "I think you want clarity," she said at last. "You look like a man who wants out but doesn't know where his destination is."

Something about the words hit Nigel so hard he involuntarily flexed his abs, and a strangled noise escaped him at the jolt of pain.

She leaned in, lowering her voice. "Tell me, Nigel, if you could step out of your life, explore an alternate one, just for a little while . . . would you?"

He scoffed. "W-what kind of question is that?"

"A real one. An honest one. One you should endeavor to answer with honesty too."

Nigel let out a slow, wheezing breath. He should ignore her. But her knowing gaze pinned him in place.

She shifted, resting her chin on her hand with one eyebrow arched. "Say you had a week. Just one. No job hunting, no responsibilities. No wife."

He flared his nostrils and she caught it immediately, her grin widening. She had hooked his attention in spite of himself.

"A week to live as though you never married," she said softly. "To see who you'd be, what you'd do, if life had gone another way."

Nigel swallowed. His mind went somewhere dangerous, somewhere he hadn't let it wander before, not fully. A week without the weight of his marriage, without the constant delicate tiptoeing around each other that had become his homelife. He thought about the faded, almost faceless version of himself that never said *I do*, the one whose idea of a compromise was which bar or club in Midtown he should hit with his friends after work. The one who still dreamed instead of merely existing: the Old Nigel.

"Th-that's not how life works," he said finally, but his raspy voice lacked conviction.

The girl shrugged. "Most people never get the chance to find out. But you?" Her fingers tapped against the side of the car. "I could give you that week."

Nigel let out a painful laugh. "What, you wave a magic wand and make my wife disappear?"

She smiled. "Something like that."

"That's . . . that's impossible."

"Is it?" she said, watching him closely. "Or is it exactly what you want?"

"How would you do that?" This conversation was certainly taking a strange turn. Maybe he'd hit his head harder than he thought. Maybe he was hallucinating this.

"You're not imagining this, Nigel. Here, I'll prove it."

She took his free hand. Her flesh was alarmingly hot but he couldn't pull away, frozen by some invisible force. And then before Nigel's startled eyes, the entire car—the entire world—went black, with just her and him illuminated. That's when he saw her—*really* saw who she was under that teenage facade: something formless made of smoke and two gold spots for its eyes. Then the real world blinked back on.

A noise that he'd never made before in his life escaped him, and the girl—the human one beside him—grinned.

"Don't worry," she said. "I won't harm you. Think of me as like a Ghost of Christmas Past–type being."

The rational part of his brain screamed at him to get up, to crawl away from this . . . this . . . being. From this conversation. But after his racing heart slowed down, another part—the exhausted, beaten-down part—wondered what it would be like. Just one week. No expectations. No guilt. No regret. "One week?" he repeated.

The girl must have sensed his hesitation, and she pounced. "One week," she concurred.

"What's the catch? What's in it for you?" Nigel asked.

"Interesting. This one's less trusting," the girl mused, like he wasn't right there. "To be honest, Nigel, we don't have any skin in the game. We are of an order that has always existed—caretakers, if you wish, of the balance between living and dead. And we have the power to move persons closer to where they need to be. Their final destiny, if you wish."

Nigel shivered. Should he trust her? She was probably what the headmaster back in his Catholic primary school in Peterborough termed a *demonic being*. But then Mrs. Calper had thought that dinosaurs were a myth made up by godless heathens, so there.

"I know what you're thinking, but believe me, our order does not interfere with your world—we are neutral; we seek only to guide you to your final destiny, one way or another, as I've said," the girl assured him.

"And if I do agree?" Not that he would, of course. "What happens to my family?"

"Nothing. The timeline and their world proceed as though there's been no deviation in your life path—that is, unless you seal the return."

"Seal the return?" Nigel repeated.

"You refuse to return," the girl said softly. "You've made that much clear through your actions—or inactions—in that regard."

Nigel exhaled, looking away. The air around them buzzed with unseen life—bugs, sounds of traffic, people. Life, moving as it always did. But for the first time in a long time, he felt like he was back in the driver's seat, taking charge of his destiny.

She extended a hand, her nails dark and glossy under the streetlight. "Do we have a deal?"

Nigel hesitated a moment longer. Then, before he could talk himself out of it, he reached out and shook her hand.

"One moment," the girl said. She took off one of her rings and, before Nigel could protest, swiftly dragged it over the lifeline of his left palm, cutting him with the sharp edge. A drop of blood bloomed, and she took her thumb and smeared it over his palm, whispering words under her breath as she did.

The moment she released his wrist, the street outside flickered—just for a second, like bad reception on an old TV.

Then everything snapped back into place.

The girl's smile was placid. "Enjoy your week, Nigel. The ambulance is almost here."

She got up and left him sitting there, dazed. The pain returned almost instantly, fierce and insistent.

Nigel squinted through the film of blood at the world outside his Honda. Everything looked the way it should, but the air felt different. Before he could put his finger on what was different about all of it, a wave of fatigue broke over him. *I'll just take a quick nap,* he thought, blinking slowly. *The girl did say they'd come get me, so they'll be able to wake me up once they are here, right?*

Is that advisable? a little voice inside him asked, a familiar voice he couldn't quite place. *Don't people tell you to stay awake no matter what?*

They did, but it was a lost cause. For the life of Nigel, he could not force himself to stay awake. He shut his eyes and let himself be borne away in the dreamless night.

Dana

Day One

Dana awoke to the sound of waves crashing and unseasonal warmth, her head throbbing and her stomach roiling with sour unease. *What happened?* She struggled to sit up. She was on a crowded beach somewhere, an unreal one with deep-gold sand and water a shade of lapis so intense that she'd only ever seen it in filtered Instagram posts. *Where am I? And what am I wearing?* She looked down through the most ostentatious pair of sunglasses she'd ever worn at a two-piece white bikini and a floral sarong tied around her waist. And what's more, she was in open-toed sandals and her toes were *manicured*, a summery yellow. *Holy shit, when did that happen?*

You're dreaming, she told herself, wincing as she sat up. But that didn't ring true, especially when she pinched her arm and pain radiated from the spot. Wherever she was, it wasn't a dream.

Did that woman in the parking lot really transport me here?

"Oh my God, here you are," a worried voice piped up. Dana looked up to see Pia Nasution running toward her. "I've been looking for you *everywhere*."

"Pia?" Dana croaked, unease spreading through her. The woman squatting down beside her had Pia's features—her long brown hair, light-brown eyes, and slender build—but the energy was that of a twenty-three-year-old cheerleader for an NFL team and what looked like designer knockoffs; Real Pia would never be caught dead in fast fashion. "Where are we?"

Pia laughed. "Did somebody have too many sangrias yesterday? I told you it wasn't a good idea to hit that beach club the night before your keynote! Right now you're about one mile away from our hotel in Canggu. Thank God I can track you on Find My Friends." Dana looked down at the small knitted crossbody bag partially hidden under her sarong that Pia was pointing at and took out her phone. She unlocked it with the same passcode as always: the date of her marriage.

Pia made an impatient noise and stuck out her hand. "Now come, you have an audience waiting for you to tell them about midcareer changes and human connection in a little over two and a half hours! We've got to get you dressed."

"Dressed?"

"You're not delivering a speech in front of a convention hall full of medical professionals in a two-piece and sarong, are you?"

"What—what?"

"Man, what do people put in these drinks," Pia muttered. "I hope your drinks weren't spiked, because you disappeared before I could check on you yesterday, and now I find you dazed and disoriented on a beach on the day of an important speech you've been paid five figures to deliver in front of a captive audience that flew here from everywhere to see you! And maybe party in Bali after! And come on, heave-ho, let's go. Your driver is here."

Dana let herself be chivvied along by this woodland creature to a small, paved street, where a green-jacketed man on a motorbike passed her a helmet and gestured for her to hop on.

"What? No, no, I can't—"

"There's no time!" Pia barked. "The traffic is insane, and everyone uses them in Bali, so stop whining and let's go."

The man gestured again for her to climb on, and Pia practically heaved her onto the bike.

"What about you?" Dana said desperately as the man revved his bike. She had no idea what was going on, where she was going: She needed Pia.

Pia gestured at a second bike making its way toward them, a smiling man at its sputtering helm. "I'll be right behind you on that bike. Now go!"

—∾—

They got to the hotel in under fifteen minutes, bypassing everyone in cars clogging up the streets of Bali to the Regent in Canggu. Pia tipped their motorbike taxi drivers with cash, and they thanked her in Bahasa.

Then Pia brought her to their two-bedroom suite. "I'll be in the other room," she said, pointing at one of the doors. "See you out here in the living room in exactly forty minutes. We'll need to do one last AV check."

Dana closed the heavy wooden door behind her and blinked against the soft golden light that spilled through sheer curtains, bathing the luxurious room's beautiful batik-and-cotton textiles and elegant rattan and hardwood furniture—including a beautiful canopy bed—with its warm glow. A small clock on her bedside table showed the time: 7:45 a.m. The suite smelled faintly of lemongrass and an expensive creamy floral, and the quiet—the *quiet*, dear God, the blessed peace—was a balm. No beeping monitors, no PA crackle, no someone screaming down the hallway needing her *now, someone, please.* Just the hum of central air-conditioning and the distant rhythm of crashing waves.

Mine, all mine. She couldn't believe her luck—she was going to get her special fortieth birthday trip after all. Would she have preferred that her family was with her? The kids, sure, but Nigel? She couldn't say.

She disrobed and headed to the bathroom, her breath catching as she stepped barefoot onto cool marble floors and saw a gorgeous teak bathtub and the rainfall shower next to it. She couldn't remember the last time she'd had a bath in peace—and she definitely had never stayed in a place this special.

A bottle of something sparkly chilled in a glass bucket by the freestanding tub, and beside it, a handwritten welcome note: *Dr. Dana Smiley—Thank you for honoring us with your presence. See you at the keynote.*

The title struck her: *Dr.* Not *nurse.* Not *hey you.* Not *miss, can you get me the doctor?*

She pulled out her phone and googled herself:

> Dr. Dana Smiley is a former ER nurse who put herself through graduate school while working double shifts, eventually earning a doctorate in medical humanities from UTMB. Her #1 *New York Times* bestselling book, *The Tethered Heart: Connection as Cure*, which has sold more than three million copies to date, draws from her frontline experiences and explores how fostering empathy and presence in health care professionals leads to better clinical outcomes. Deeply influenced by traditional care practices, healing touch, and culturally rooted forms of caregiving she encountered in diverse communities, Dana weaves these elements into a modern philosophy of compassionate medicine. Praised for blending clinical insight with philosophical depth, Dana's work has resonated with caregivers and patients alike. Today, she travels the world as a sought-after motivational speaker, addressing global audiences of health care professionals, policymakers, and everyday people on the power of relational medicine and the quiet revolutions that begin at the bedside.

She huffed a surprised laugh. *Shit, will you look at that? I'm a goddamn star.*

She remembered Pia's instructions to meet in forty minutes—now thirty!—and chose the rainfall shower. Still, it was the best shower she'd ever had in her life: The water pressure was strong and consistent, the temperature went from cool to deliciously painful in seconds, and the toiletries were expensive and nurturing. Even in their good, dual-income days, a Holiday Inn was the best she'd ever experienced. She tried not to cry as she dried off with the softest cotton towel after and donned the fluffy *clean* bathrobe that no one else had used as an emergency hand towel.

She padded over to the vanity, where someone—probably Pia—had placed a printed program, its front page in gold foil: Integrative Health & Wellness Summit, sponsored by multiple familiar Fortune 500 companies. She flipped it open, and there was her face on the second page, with the same bio.

She was the keynote speaker.

Dana's hands trembled as the significance of that fact jolted her back to reality. She looked at the clock and ran to her wardrobe, frantic. She had another twenty minutes to get ready before Pia hauled her out of there. She threw on a silk blouse and a neatly pressed gray light Italian wool pantsuit from her closet and hurriedly patted on makeup she found in a travel case by the vanity. There was about an hour until she was supposed to walk onstage, fully made up and polished, to inspire hundreds. She could still smell antiseptic, a ghostly reminder of her past life, on her skin.

I don't know what I'm supposed to say. That frantic inner voice of hers spoke up.

Don't worry, there must be a PowerPoint somewhere, right?

She must have created one, right? Dana blinked and experienced a kind of doubling as her old life and her current life shimmered in her memory. The recollections of her older life sat like a ghostly imprint over those from New Dana, each vying for dominance in her mind. The only way she was able to keep them straight was how Nigel and her family were noticeably absent in her present world. In the flashbacks that Dana saw of this life, she saw scenes of herself and Pia, as well as a revolving cast of new friends whose names and lives were both oddly familiar and yet not. It was unsettling, but Dana was determined to roll with it. After all, it was just a week, and it was just a universe that didn't matter—even if she made mistakes here. Nothing of consequence happened in this world.

That doesn't sound right, a nagging voice said. Dana shoved down her doubts. It was just her other, less-fun self speaking, trying to establish status quo.

Dr. Dana Smiley—keynote speaker—is in Bali, folks!

This wasn't exactly what she'd had in mind when she asked for a break, but still—she could get used to this.

—∞—

The stagehand dimmed the pink-and-white stage lights: Her speech was coming to the end, and judging from the audience's expressions, it was going well. And all she had to do was let herself go into autopilot mode and the speech came to her almost immediately; New Dana had certainly gone over her presentation many times. You almost wouldn't have guessed that she was an impostor piloting the body of New Dana, like those zombie caterpillars held hostage by the baculovirus.

Dana came offstage and passed Pia her mike. Without being directed, Pia stored the custom lapel mike in a special case and tucked it into a hardshell piece of luggage that had been retrofitted with special compartments to store the gear she needed for her work, like spare wireless lapel mikes, clickers, backup drives, smartphone gimbals and travel and multiport adapters, and most importantly, a stock of her favorite lozenges, Nin Jiom Pei Pa Koa, and granola bars. Without further instruction, Pia passed her a container of coconut water, makeup removal wipes, and an Evian mist. Dana accepted them gratefully and went about her business, almost as though she'd done this exact dance before. The more Dana went on autopilot, the more she "remembered" details from her current life. It was as though she had been superimposed over the current universe's Dana, and when she took a step back from trying to act like this Dana, the shadow Dana guided her actions.

"Babe, that was amazing," Pia said, her eyes shining. "This was our largest crowd yet, and I mean, they are already asking if you can speak at their European edition in three months! I'm so glad I reached out to the organizers to pitch you—they usually just bring in all these boring policy folks."

It wasn't strictly Dana's doing—it was Shadow Dana—but all the same, she felt a thrill of recognition. She'd always liked public speaking, and she'd flipped through *The Tethered Heart* in the twenty minutes she'd had to herself in the greenroom before she went onstage and agreed with the messaging in it. Health care in America was unsustainable in its current form and had lost its way, and health care providers were being crushed in the process. She hadn't really had time to reflect on her own role in the general scheme of things, but now that she had a break, maybe she should read the book to see if she could take some of the learnings from it and apply them to her team once she got back to her original timeline.

She focused her attention on Pia, who was bouncing on the balls of her feet, waiting for feedback. "Thanks, Pia. I appreciate this. You're getting a bonus for this, obviously."

Pia pumped the air. "Yes! I can finally justify getting those Chanel Coco Crush earrings I've been eyeing forever or maybe upgrade my gym membership when we're back in New York!"

New York, the city where New Dana was based. The words triggered another flow of memories, mostly of Dana and Pia working out in gyms and having power lunches and then going to parties, concerts, bars—basically living it up. Dana couldn't believe her luck. She'd always fantasized about living in New York. Now here she was, based in the Big Apple, with a job that paid her well and allowed her to travel in style, with *vacation time*.

"Why are you crying?" Pia asked, concerned. "Are you OK?"

Dana swiped the tears from her eyes. "Probably just my hormones—my period is coming." *Pull yourself together, Dana.* In her real life, she was known as the Diagnosis Massager (not ideal as a nickname, but close to the truth). Whenever bad news had to be delivered, the doctor spoke first, and then she was sent in to shoulder the tears, a steady beacon of stoicism. "When are we flying back?"

"The day after tomorrow," Pia said, already scrolling through her calendar app. "Late afternoon."

"What are we doing for dinner?" Dana wanted to know. Maybe Pia had something fun planned for them. Dana had done a quick search online and couldn't wait to explore the sights and try out all the luscious local food.

Pia squinted, too vain to wear glasses. "So far, nothing. I mean, we're invited to stay for the conference dinner—"

"No," Dana said immediately. She had only seven days to herself, she was not spending them hobnobbing with other medical professionals.

"Oh, OK," Pia said, looking slightly taken aback. "You usually want to stay to mingle, because *every conversation is a lead*, that's your mantra. You did that in our last keynotes in Croatia, Singapore, New Delhi . . ."

Man, even this Dana was hardcore. Dana wanted to kick her. *Hello, you're in Bali! A place that normally takes a whole freaking day of travel to get to! What are we even* doing *in a goddamn conference room?*

Or maybe this annoying version of herself had already been to Bali so many times, she didn't care? Dana didn't bother searching her new memories to find out. "I'm not hanging around this room, and you're off the clock," she said firmly to Pia.

"OK," Pia said. "I guess I . . . I guess I'll—take a break?"

"Absolutely!" Dana enthused. "Take the rest of the day off! Go sightsee! Eat! Make new friends."

Pia's face told Dana that days off weren't really par for the course for their dynamic. "Um, sure. I guess I can sightsee. After I follow up with some emails and clear a couple of other things off my plate. If you want to wait for me, of course."

"Nope, I'm off to do a bit of sightseeing myself."

"Oh!" Pia said, sounding surprised. "Um, do you . . . do you want"—Pia paused, clearly thrown by this version of Dana, who did not work hard on top of playing hard, before saying, in an overtly casual voice—"company?"

Dana shook her head. Wow, she was being so up front about her desires, it was almost as though she had no filter. "It's OK, Pia. I just need some time alone to, um, brainstorm on my next book." Besides, this version of Pia fatigued Dana; she was even more energetic and bubbly than her old Pia, without any of their shared history to anchor Dana emotionally to her. This Pia seemed like the type who would chatter nonstop while rappelling down a cliff, whereas Dana just wanted to relax, visit the Uluwatu Temple, and photograph sunsets like a goddamn tourist.

After two decades of working, she was going to do this break properly.

—∾—

Dana went shopping, first because this version of Dana had only heels and strappy sandals, and one did not explore unpaved terrain or hike in heels. She booked herself a private driver for the rest of the day, as recommended by travelers on various forums, and said she wanted to shop for clothes. The driver nodded and, almost an hour in torturous traffic later—during which Dana saw mostly the backs of cars and other motorists and plumes of exhaust and very little by way of scenery except the beautiful rice fields that still remained as they left Canggu—dropped her off at Seminyak Village mall.

Despite the crawling traffic, Dana was elated, enjoying every moment of her newfound freedom. For the first time in a long while, her life felt wide open, as though someone had flung open a window she hadn't realized was shut. Possibility shimmered at the edges of everything—her time, and money, was hers to command. She even had the luxury of doing absolutely nothing if she chose. Such bliss. *This must be what heaven feels like.* It wasn't freedom in the dramatic, cinematic sense but a subtler sense of returning to herself, of rediscovering her own desires and impulses, something she'd neglected to do in a long, long time, chugging along as she had been, fueled by the belief that if she stopped, the house of cards would collapse.

At the mall, she stopped by a kiosk selling to-go coffee with beans from Indonesia and grandly bought herself a flat white—she'd never had a flat white before—not that she knew how different it was from a latte or even a cappuccino. The first sip of her freshly brewed coffee, perfectly balanced and rich, unlike the slightly burned, sludgy coffee at work, almost made her tear up. And it was only coffee!

She heard her phone vibrate—texts from Pia, indubitably about work—and felt a little guilty about ignoring them, but it wasn't as if she were going to stay in this world, anyway. She just needed to do what the Gen Zs called *quiet quitting*—doing the minimum just so she wouldn't mess up New Dana's life once she left and put her own enjoyment first. She deserved this time off.

She finished her coffee and headed toward a sports boutique, fully intending to buy herself sneakers and local weather-friendly outdoor gear, practical things for the rigors of tropical exploration, but she got sidetracked by a window display and soon found herself the owner of a cute floaty white dress—white!—and her eyes prickled again with emotion. She couldn't remember the last time she had spent any money on herself. Her needs always came last in the hierarchy of household expenses. To be able to grab a cup of coffee, to look at things that weren't related to work—beautiful things, pleasing things—was stupefyingly moving.

I better get going before people think I'm on drugs, she thought.

She bought the things she came for—T-shirt, shorts, and sneakers—and changed into them in the mall's bathroom before rejoining her driver. Then they drove to Uluwatu Temple, one of the main temples of Bali, which was perched on the edge of a cliff. It was late afternoon by then. She put on the sarong and sash handed to her by the temple guard and made her way up the cut path. The air was thick with salt, incense, and the faint echo of chanting. She moved past mossy stone guardians and playful monkeys, one of which made a move as if to grab the sunglasses on her head before Dana remembered the warnings and hurriedly stuffed her glasses in her sling bag.

The temple itself wasn't grand—a cluster of dark thatched roofs nestled among flame trees and frangipani. No towering spires or gilded domes or ostentatious columns. Bali had grander temples in that sense—at least from what she could read online. But Uluwatu's claim to fame wasn't its astounding architecture—it was its rich sense of history, of atmosphere, palpable in the windswept, timeworn stone, the wizened trees cradling it, the worn rocks that met the rays of the sun so whitely. The temple made sense of and paid homage to the world around it. It would forever be the most breathtaking place Dana had ever been to. She was in Bali. She was *in* Bali, a place she had only dreamed of visiting. All she felt was gratitude and awe.

She walked its hallowed ground and admired the view as the sky turned from gold to crimson, took the selfies she had come for, then picked her way through the throngs of people who'd gathered to do the same and headed back to her driver, who was engrossed in a local telenovela on his phone. *Turns out you can get inured to beauty,* Dana thought wryly.

They were almost back at the hotel when Dana's phone vibrated with a message from Pia: Hey, wanna have dinner with me at Finns? Apparently it's the place to be i.e. gorgeous people, good food, vibes

Dana grinned. Sounds like a plan. See you in an hour?

Back in her hotel, after taking a long, hot bath—the sheer indulgence of it!—Dana put on her new dress and admired herself in the mirror. She threaded chunky good huggies in her ears and a cuff of gold and wood around her arm and piled her hair up so that her shoulders shone under the light. She looked ten years younger and felt it.

Pia met her in the lobby and gave her a loud wolf whistle. People turned and Dana flushed. "Stop," she muttered, embarrassed.

"Stop what, telling you you're a queen?" Pia said, playfully smacking Dana's butt with a leather clutch.

"You look great," she told Pia, not just to change the subject but because it was the truth. Pia pulled off a chic white long-sleeved off-shoulder flowy top that would have looked homely on Dana, and black jeans and gold sandals, topped with a denim Chanel Boy bag.

"I want to say 'this old thing,' but I bought my entire outfit today, aside from my evening bag," Pia said. "You know, when you told me to . . . sightsee."

"I'm glad you're stimulating the local economy," Dana said. She glanced down at her dress, worried about the deep V of the cleavage. "Do you think this is too much?"

"I think it's just right," Pia said sincerely. "In fact, I'd even say your boobs aren't nearly displayed as often as they deserve to be. You've got a *great* pair."

Dana reddened at the compliment, delivered within earshot of everyone in the lobby. "I don't remember the last time I wore white," she deflected.

Pia laughed. "Well, you're certainly living on the edge tonight."

The car arrived and dropped them off at the beach club, a sprawling institution on Berawa Beach, around 8 p.m. They entered and were swiftly seated by the poolside and handed two menus. A DJ was spinning before a noisy crowd, and the atmosphere was relaxed and fun. Pia excused herself to go to the restroom, leaving Dana to order the drinks and food. And order she did—the seafood platter, truffle fries, two rounds of passion fruit mojitos "to start," all without a second glance at her Amex Black Card.

I'm in Indonesia! Dana thought, with a small shiver of excitement. Somehow, the old woman—that caretaker lady—had *known*. Greece had become *Pia's* dream, not Dana's. Now that she was older, Greece didn't intrigue her the way it did Pia, who had always loved Greek mythology. No, Dana had always wanted to go to Asia, especially to Southeast Asia, since her dad had Vietnamese heritage. She'd never been farther than Europe—that was when she'd visited Nigel's hometown, Peterborough, and that was only because she had to see Nigel's family after they had impulsively tied the knot all those years ago, and then they'd had a brief, lovely little honeymoon in Italy, at Cinque Terre, while Dana was already five months pregnant with Bex. After that, they'd pretty much stayed put in the States, and now almost seventeen years had passed in the blink of an eye, and the farthest she'd traveled since then was Cincinnati for a medical conference.

Nigel had promised her they would visit Singapore one day, where his father, who was half Chinese, half British, was born. One Day. But they never did because they were just so busy being busy, and the children! The children kept having school plays and flus and playdates and soccer and more playdates and birthday parties and extra credit assignments and life, life kept happening. And now with Nigel being out of his advertising job, they probably never would, at least until one of them won the lottery—or he found a new job.

But she was here now.

Their drinks arrived, as did Pia, who came back bright-eyed and bushy-tailed. "I've just met a unicorn. A single, attractive, successful man who's in his thirties, built like Adonis, and not a walking red flag."

Dana raised an eyebrow and made a disbelieving noise. "Those exist?"

"Apparently they vacation here in Bali," Pia said. "He and his friend are in town for some corporate retreat for a global advertising firm. He told me to come to the VIP section and he'll let us in—it's open bar and seafood buffet, apparently."

Trust Pia to sniff out the fun like some kind of party truffle pig. "Won't his colleagues mind some random gate-crashers?"

"Not when they find out it's you, the famous Dana Smiley—who's looking to rebrand her image, wink wink," Pia said, also winking. "Why not, right?"

Why not, indeed.

Buoyed by lightness, Dana stood and made her way to the DJ booth, where beautiful bronze and tanned bodies swayed to the hypnotic beats. They were so lithe, so free, that even though Dana thought she looked good, she couldn't help feeling self-conscious that she was older than most of them.

As she moved, something crinkled in the pocket of her swishy knee-length dress (one of the reasons she got the dress—pockets;

you could take the nurse out of a hospital, but not the nurse out of a person)—something that had not been there before. She fished out a Polaroid and pushed her hair out of her eyes to get a better look and gasped when she realized what it was.

It was a photo of Nigel, the three children, their home, the Subaru, and Moped, the dog.

She vividly recalled when this photo—or the real version of it—was taken last spring. Emmie was a year old—to celebrate, Dana had wanted a good group photo they could use for that year's Christmas cards. Nigel was looking at the camera, unsmiling—he and Dana had just exchanged a few curt words; Emmie had been wailing, implacable; Dana's eyes were half shut from fatigue and anger, trying not to cry herself because her nipples hurt from breastfeeding and the back of her throat was stippled with spots that would later be diagnosed as Hand, Foot, and Mouth Disease, and Gill's gaze had been fixed on his phone. But here it was, perfectly posed—and she wasn't in it. Almost as though the universe was trying to tell her that they were better off without her—if it was, it was certainly helping with her homesickness.

She flipped the photo over. A handwritten message: *Use your time well, Dana.*

Dana squared her shoulders—it was already the end of Day One. If there was ever a time to YOLO, this would be it. To forget about what people she didn't know thought about her, forget about the worries of her other life, to forget all of it—she was someone else here and now, she had been given an opportunity to escape. So she closed her eyes, raised her hands, and danced like no one—and everyone—was watching.

Use your time well, Dana.

"Dana, oh my God! Is that you?"

Dana looked up and her mouth went dry, pretty much a first in her life. Standing in front of her in an immaculately white polo shirt, chino shorts, and a jaunty panama hat was none other than Yomi Owope, her high school crush.

Dana

Day One

"Dana, Dana, Dana!" Yomi said, throwing his arms around her for a quick hug that Dana reciprocated like it was nothing when internally she was panicking, before stepping back to give her an admiring once-over. "Wow, it really is you—Sweet Dee in the flesh! What are the odds?"

"Yomi, Yomi, Yomi," Dana said, her lips curving into a friendly smile. Old Dana would have frozen and flailed for words—ironic, since she had nerves of steel around open bodies but was so bad at small talk. Go figure. "What are you doing here? What's it been, like, almost two decades?"

"Two decades too long," Yomi said with a grin. He looked her over again with frank admiration. "Wow, you look better than ever."

Dana blushed. She was sure she did not, but all the same it was nice to hear a compliment, especially from the only guy she'd ever been head over heels in love with in high school. Yomi had been a very popular senior when she'd been a junior, and excelled in everything he did—music, sports, classes. He had always been unfailingly polite and kind in her original world, and it looked like he hadn't changed in this one. Here he was, smiling down at her with those melty-brown eyes of his, his hair now in braids. And he looked good, the little crinkles near his eyes adding depth and character to his face. They'd all aged, so she was glad that Yomi hadn't lied and said she hadn't aged a day. She didn't fear aging and what it meant in the hyperonline world they lived in now, didn't fear not looking like a twenty-year-old the way some of her peers did. It was a privilege to age—that is, if one had lived well.

But you haven't been living well, have you, Dana?

She hadn't, she'd be the first to acknowledge it now. She'd lost her light somewhere along the way.

"Oh my God, *Dana*, there you are! I've been looking everywhere!" Pia had somehow procured a tray of lime-green frosted shots. "Yomi Owope! What a pleasant surprise! How are you?"

After Yomi had given her the highlights—he was a hip-hop violinist now (six million followers strong on TikTok and half that on IG, Dana later found out) and touring in Bali with his band—Pia enthusiastically updated him on all her moves since high school. Yomi's eyes slid over to Dana a couple of times to try to draw her in—little glances, subtle cues trying to pull her into the conversation as Pia unleashed a relentless stream of updates about her life. Dana met his look once, then again, but didn't try to speak. She knew from experience that once Pia was in full flow, there was no stopping her. Words weren't invited; they were run over. So Dana just gave Yomi a faint shrug and a small, complicit smile—*you know how she is.*

Still, she noticed the effort he was making. It was a considerate, gentlemanly gesture, him trying to include her. She appreciated those little offerings of kindness. It had been a while since someone had noticed her and tried to fold her into a moment.

When Pia finally ran out of breath, Yomi pounced. "Sorry to dash, but I've got a late gig at midnight, and my band is waiting for me." He nodded at a group of five men and one woman milling about the entrance, their body language and expressions tinged with mild impatience.

"Oh," Dana said, her poker face falling. "That's too bad."

Yomi chuckled ruefully. "Honestly, I wish I could ditch, since you know, how often does one run into your schoolmates randomly across the world?" His eyes lingered on Dana. "But work is work and these guys are depending on me. I do want to catch up again. I'll be here in Bali till the day after tomorrow. You down for a catch-up, maybe tomorrow evening?"

"We're flying back in two days and we have work during the day, but we can try to meet up in the evening—at least, I think Dana can. I might have . . . a conference call," Pia said, lying breezily. Not that Yomi cared.

"Perfect," he said with a grin. "I'll see you, Dana?"

"Um, I'll have to check my schedule."

"It is absolutely free after noon tomorrow," Pia enunciated.

Dana dodged by responding, "Yes, but I might have a private . . . thing." She still wasn't sure how she felt about meeting up one-on-one with Yomi—not when every glance between them felt combustible.

"Don't worry about it," Yomi responded diplomatically. "We can always meet up in New York—that's where you're based, am I right?"

"Yes, you?"

"Same."

"This is fate," Pia said, eyes shining. Dana blushed—she wasn't subtle at all.

Yomi cleared his throat. "All right then, let's play it by ear, OK?"

They quickly exchanged numbers and IG handles in case they needed another way to contact each other.

"Well, goodbye," Yomi said softly. Then he reached over and gave both Dana and Pia hugs, lingering especially on Dana, before he turned and left with his band. Pia waved goodbye and started heading in the opposite direction, muttering something about their private car arriving.

"Pia, I—I don't know if I want to meet him in Bali tomorrow. It feels like I might be sending him the wrong signals," Dana said breathlessly as she tried to keep up with Pia's strides.

"Ah, I see." Pia nodded. "Look, if you're worried he'll think it's just a fling if you meet up in Bali, why don't you wait until you're both back in New York for a proper high school reunion?" she suggested slyly, sliding Dana one of those knowing winks of hers.

Dana muttered that high school reunions never turn out well. "Remember *Romy and Michele's High School Reunion*?" Pia said she had never heard of the movie, in spite of how Dana recalled that, in her parallel life, she and Pia had definitely watched it together a few years after it was released.

They had, right? Dana blinked and experienced a kind of doubling as her old life and her current life shimmered in her memory. The recollections of her older life sat like a ghostly imprint over those from New Dana, each vying for dominance in her mind. When she closed her eyes and focused, her old memories appeared in richer detail, felt *truer*, compared to New Dana's, but it took her effort to sift through confusing threads.

It was hard to think about her old life when this one was going at full throttle. Her phone was already vibrating: even with Pia's help, her inbox had thirty-plus new threads that needed her response. Hey Dana, thanks for everything you've done at the last AGM, your speech was powerful. And then there were her DMs, which normally Pia responded to, but with 380,000 IG followers, Dana received regular unsolicited DMs all the time. Hey Dana, I just read your book The Tethered Heart, and it was everything. Your words really impacted my life. Hey Dana, I loved that clip of yours on the podcast Medicine with Intention; it's so true that a kind touch can be incredibly healing.

Dana already knew she was going to reply to every single message of gratitude. She couldn't let any of them down.

Back at their table, Pia was trying to guilt-talk her into going up to the VIP section. "The cute guy I met earlier could really be the one! Plus the agency might be able to help you expand your reach beyond the US, so it'll be like killing two birds with one stone."

The last thing Dana felt like doing was socializing, but Pia's love life was supposedly on the line. "Are you sure he's a good guy?"

"Totally. He volunteers at an animal shelter during the weekends, Dana. And he's a hot Cambodian guy who grew up in rural America for most of his life and is now based in Tokyo, so he hasn't actually worked out how attractive he really is!"

Dana made a face. "All right, let's get you your man."

"It's going to be incredible, you'll see," Pia said, tugging Dana by the wrist. "They've set up a private firepit and live DJ set. You need *joy*, not spreadsheets."

Dana barely had time to protest before Pia ushered her past velvet ropes up to the slightly elevated VIP terrace with a prime view of the ocean, where a bunch of relaxed business-wear folks—at a beach club! Maybe they'd just come straight from a conference—were chatting with distinct Look at Me energy. The air smelled of frangipani and woodsmoke from the firepit nearby, and expensive cologne from the group of overconfident people dancing badly on the VIP deck.

"Look at that," Pia whispered. "There's buckets of champagne everywhere—decent nonvintage stuff too."

"Pia, *we* drink vintage champagne all the time. Like, after every successful keynote."

"Yes, but it's more fun when it's *other people's* champagne and doesn't eat into my very big end-of-the-year bonus."

Dana had to laugh—that was a classic Pia Nasution comeback in any timeline. She couldn't believe she'd not seen her friend in her real world in close to three years. It was a crime, and one she intended to rectify as soon as she got back.

And then she saw him, and the deck beneath her feet shifted.

Nigel. Laughing, drink in hand, long-sleeved white shirt unbuttoned at the collar, backlit by string lights and sunset. Tan, magnetic, surrounded by people who clearly thought he was a catch in every way.

Pre-Dana Nigel.

Pia leaned in and pointed excitedly in Nigel's direction, where her crush stood. "See that man, Tommy? My future husband? You *have* to meet him. And maybe that guy he's chatting with, ooh la la!"

A coldness settled over Dana's heart. "I already have," she said, the words catching in her throat. "In another life."

Nigel

Day One

Nigel woke up on the floor of his bedroom with a rude thump and the sound of very loud lovemaking coming from the room next to his.

"Goddamn it," he muttered, rubbing his forehead, where a bump the size of Texas was making itself felt, and trying to ignore the noises from his peer from the Hong Kong office, who was definitely married and *not* here in Bali with his wife. "How did I fall off my bed like a kid?"

He sighed and cast an eye at the time: 2:33 a.m. His body clock had been completely out of whack since he landed in Bali. "Thanks a lot, old age," he muttered. The top management from the four Asia-Pac offices were planning on convening for a full day of meetings at 9 a.m., hours away—and here he was, too alert to go back to sleep, but not sharp enough to work.

Still, he couldn't complain—he was in Bali for the Asia-Pac offices' corporate retreat, which was really just an excuse for teams across the region to meet in a beautiful location and drink on the company's dime—and why shouldn't they? They'd earned it. The group had had a bumper year, securing major deals across key markets under Nigel's leadership, especially with the AmorePacific group, which owned several of Korea's most influential skincare brands.

Plus, this would be Nigel's final quarter in the Singapore office—his term was up, and he was supposed to relocate back to New York in two months, although he planned to fly in earlier to sort out the handover of his apartment from a friend who'd been renting it from him before going on a much-needed break. His next role hadn't been made official yet, but there were whispers about a promotion. Everything hinged on what the board was deciding—he checked his watch—right about now, in New York. Nigel was trying not to spiral. He knew he was in the running for group CMO of the Black & Hansen Agency, but so was Angela Kasdin, his peer in Dubai, and she had more experience. Still, he had a feeling. And he'd learned to trust his gut over the years—it had served him well so far.

Good luck/break a leg, boss.

Clarissa, his soon-to-be-former PA in Singapore, had texted while he was asleep—likely just after the board convened in New York. She knew better than to jinx things. Nigel had always been a little superstitious about early congratulations; Clarissa had worked with him long enough to know that.

Anxiously refreshing my inbox and yours in hope!!

Her last login, based on their live chat app, had been twenty minutes ago. Night owl.

Go to sleep, Clarissa, he texted, just in case she was dozing at the table in front of work again.

He shouldn't obsess about the board meeting, but what else was there to do before it?

Out of habit, he went on his latest dating app and set it to within three miles of his apartment in New York. In mere minutes, five DMs hit his inbox; he had a very popular profile (shirtless, Singapore head of a global ad agency; hobbies: fine dining and gym). He scrolled through the profiles and chose the most interesting one: a woman six years his senior, tech executive, Pilates enthusiast, divorced with three kids. She even lived close to his bachelor pad, his one-bedder that he would be moving back to.

He contemplated texting her and asking her out for a coffee date in five days, a couple of days after his arrival back in New York, but something held him back. Jet lag, maybe, or nerves. Damned board meeting was taking forever.

If that's the case, then you've been having a very long stretch of nerves, my boy.

For the last two months, Nigel had not been on a single date. He wasn't sure what had brought this dry stretch on, but just the thought of going through the whole rigmarole of embarking on a first date with a stranger made him cringe.

He got himself a coffee from the Nespresso machine in his room—a nice-enough executive room in the Destin, a local five-star boutique hotel, of which all forty-five rooms had been booked out for this retreat. A hotel that he'd been planning to rate five stars on Google before experiencing how bad the sound insulation was. His Hong Kong colleague was at it again.

Guess I'm headed to the gym then.

He was about to leave when he saw the photo by the coffee machine.

It was a Polaroid. One of those cheesily posed photos in front of a cute house with a lawn, a dog—or something doglike, it was hard to tell under all that fur—and an ugly SUV. The kids were cute, though. And the woman's squinting face was half hidden by her mass of curls. Her hair could use a root retouch and a fresh cut, and she should, and he hated to say it, smile—it would completely transform her face, if looking attractive was her aim.

Nigel kept it aside, meaning to take it down to reception once the front desk was staffed; it looked like an important memento, the kind of thing someone might call the hotel about, frantic. People were such sentimental creatures—and that's why he made a mint at his job. He understood what made people tick.

He made his way to the gym, already planning his workout. If he did this right, he'd even have time to squeeze in a morning surf before the meeting, where he hoped to get the news that would validate his entire life.

—w—

He got in his surf session and was out of the water by eight. By now, he was ravenous.

As he approached the shaded lounge area near the pool, he spotted Marco (head, Sydney office), Farida (head, Jakarta office), and Xing Chen (head, Shanghai office)—basically, his peers from the region—sitting at a table having coffee and chatting while scrolling through their phones.

"You asshole," Marco said, mock-angrily as Nigel approached. Nigel and Marco had risen up the ranks together in New York, and had always had a friendly—and sometimes, less than friendly—rivalry.

Nigel laughed. "Say what?"

"Sit down," Farida said, patting the deck chair beside her. "The board has made its decision."

Nigel froze inside and tried to act nonchalant. "It's out?"

Xing Chen held up his phone. "Have a look, my friend."

Nigel tried to look blasé as he took the phone from Xing Chen, then read the subject line:

RE: Global Leadership Announcement

"Shit, it is out." He noted the time stamp. Poor Clarissa must have been trying to call him for the past hour.

He tapped it open.

Dear colleagues,

I am thrilled to announce the appointment of **Nigel Bradshaw-Cheng** as our new **Group Chief**

Marketing Officer of Black & Hansen Agency, effective immediately.
Since joining the group, Nigel has . . .

Nigel stopped reading and put the phone down with a loud plonk that elicited a protective cry from Xing Chen, who snatched it from the table. "Watch it, asshole, that's not my work phone!"

Nigel didn't hear Xing Chen. He was in shock. His mouth was dry and his blood was rushing in his ears, and he was *this close* to passing out.

"Is that a real email from our actual group CEO?" he asked when he could finally make his vocal cords work.

Marco grinned. "Yes, my friend, it is. The board must have timed the announcement to go out this morning Bali time. Maximize the pain in case some of us couldn't sleep."

"It's yours, Nigel. Soak it in," Farida said, clapping his back a little too heartily.

Xing Chen raised his mug of coffee. "To the man we all love to hate, who put all our numbers to shame and still showed up for sunrise surf. I hate you. You deserve it."

Nigel blinked down at the table. *You are not going to cry, you big gibbering loon.*

"Oh Lord, he's going to burst," Marco said. "Get the tissue box ready. *Garçon, les mouchoirs, s'il vous plaît!*" He motioned toward a mystified pool attendant, who ran to get his manager.

"Stop being so European and speak English," Farida said, elbowing Marco, who pretended to be mortally wounded.

"See, the available talent pool was absurdly shallow," Marco said, pointing at himself. "How can you be proud of being promoted when this is your competition?"

Nigel's lips actually trembled with emotion.

"If you cry, I will lance you with this pen," Xing Chen muttered, holding up his Montblanc. "Just let me hate you in peace, OK? Don't soften me up."

Nigel snort-laughed, the tension of trying to hold back his tears temporarily broken, "Thanks, pal. As if I'm going to lose it in front of you jackals."

Marco clapped him on the back. "That's the spirit."

"To me, your future boss," Nigel said with a wink, and drank Xing Chen's coffee down in one gulp.

—∾—

The rest of the day passed in a daze. There were strategy sessions, creative showcases, performance reviews with the regional teams, and endless video conferences—praising standout colleagues, laying the groundwork for next year's targets, even hinting at bonus pools. But Nigel barely absorbed any of it. All he could think, looping like a prayer in the back of his mind, was *I made it. I made it.*

By the time the last session wrapped, the sun was already sinking low over the water, painting the sky in streaks of gold and violet. Someone announced they had booked tables at Finns, a famous beach club and a local institution, and the entire group spilled out of the conference rooms in a rush of laughter and loosened ties.

He was still in the conference room on his phone, lost in thought, when someone tapped his shoulder. Farida. She was in her early forties and effortlessly chic the way only some women are no matter what they wear, and whip smart—a combination that was exactly his catnip. "Seriously, congrats again."

"Thanks," Nigel said, putting his phone down and looking up at her. "I didn't think I'd get it. I thought it'd be Xing Chen or Renee from Tokyo."

"False modesty doesn't suit you," Farida said archly. "Celebratory drinks at my place later? Just you—and me?"

Nigel raised an eyebrow. This was a first—a peer hitting on him. "I don't know if that's a good idea, Farida." Normally, he would have jumped at the opportunity. But lately—

Farida met his gaze squarely. "It can be whatever you want, Nigel, platonic or not. We're responsible adults here," she said. Then she turned and walked out of the room.

What do you want, Nigel? he asked himself.

He knew what he didn't want: to mess up workplace relations. Best to keep it simple.

But why, though? that new insistent voice said. *There aren't any reporting lines here. What would you be jeopardizing?*

Farida was age appropriate, witty, good-looking, a genuine catch. *Are you really keeping it simple, or are you just chicken? What are you really running from?*

He had a hunch, but he wasn't going to dive into that cesspool of doubt tonight. He went with his colleagues to Finns.

By the time they arrived at the VIP section, the sun was just beginning to set, and predictably, the place was packed. Gorgeous people dotted the wooden decks, dancing to the music that a bikini-clad DJ was spinning. And beyond the bodies, the Indian Ocean blazed crimson and gold, the rhythmic crashing of the waves on the shore underscoring the pulsing bass.

The day's congratulations were still pouring in. He tried to keep pace—firing off short emails, texts, messages consisting mostly of emojis and memes in group chats and DMs.

But beneath the flurry was something else: an unsettling stillness. After the initial wave of euphoria and excitement had vanished, all that remained was a dull thrum in his chest. He didn't have a name for what he was feeling, because it wasn't an easy emotion to name; it was how he felt when he observed Martha Hong, the Tokyo CFO, dancing with her wife; John Ferris whispering a private joke to his fiancée; and even the cheating husband from Hong Kong, Alvin Sim, who was now video-calling his wife to show her the stunning Balinese sunset.

"Hey, man, why the long face? Oh, wait, it's just your face!"

Nigel turned and greeted his oldest friend, Bart Middleton, a.k.a. Hong Kong Bart.

Hong Kong Bart was actually a New Yorker; they'd met nine years ago at one of the Advertising Club of New York's mixers specifically catered to folks in advertising, marketing, and PR, and Bart had been one of two Barts introduced to him that night. To distinguish between them, Nigel had christened him Hong Kong Bart, given that he'd been a director of Ogilvy in Hong Kong. They had bonded that night over a friendly competition to see who could gather the most business cards: a competition that Bart, ludicrously handsome and charming, won by a mile, although Nigel claimed it was because he'd been walking around with a piece of seaweed stuck in his front teeth.

Since then, they had become fast friends, sharing as they did many of the same interests, and both being from the same industry meant they always had something to talk about when the conversation had to stay light. Like Nigel, Bart was chronically single, but luckily for Nigel, their tastes and target demographics were quite different, since Bart was gay.

Black & Hansen had originally poached Bart to lead the Seoul office three years ago, but Bart had given it up this past January to move back to HQ for the simple reason that he'd found the love of his life in New York last year and wanted to be closer to him. The thought of being back in New York and able to hang with one of his oldest friends cheered Nigel up somewhat.

"I saw your Bart Signal," Bart said. "You looked like you needed my shoulder to cry on."

"Have you even congratulated me?"

"Decidedly not. But under duress—sure. Congrats, Mr. B-Cheng. So tell me, why the sour face?"

Nigel said, "I think . . . I think I'm wondering what it's all for."

"Ah," Bart said, raising an eyebrow. "The old coming-of-middle-age, single-man's dilemma. *What will be my legacy? Who's it all for?*"

Nigel groaned. "Am I a cliché?"

"Do you really want me to answer that?"

"OK, fine, I'm a stupid cliché."

Bart crossed his arms and grinned at Nigel. "We all are, in one way or another, clichés. After all, clichés exist because we as a species actually like being predictable—it helps us categorize the uncategorizable."

"What the—are you high? You sound like a dime-store therapist. Look, I need help."

"And I want to help you, but what seems to be the problem, my man? You're youngish and relatively successful and fuckable enough, I suppose."

"Gee, thanks for the compliment?" Nigel rolled his eyes good-humoredly, then sighed. "In all seriousness: I am at a dating crossroads."

Bart held up a finger and handed Nigel his mug. "Hold my beer and let me get the good stuff."

Bart left and came back with two old fashioneds. "OK, now I'm ready. Let's go somewhere a little more private."

They moved to a quiet standing table next to the railing that divided the VIP section from the general public.

Nigel stirred his old fashioned with the end of his cocktail toothpick, watching the ice cubes glisten under the soft bar lights.

"I think . . . I think in celebratory moments like this, I feel . . . well, I feel lonely. And tired of the scene."

"No shit, Mr. Serial Dater. You've not had a single stable relationship since your ass got dumped by Katie Purniss seven years ago. Anyone would get tired of your, um, dating lifestyle."

"I didn't ask for the lecture. Also, you're one to talk—you were way worse than me, pre–Love of Your Life. Zero vetting procedures so long as the man was hot."

Bart waved his hand away like Nigel was spouting pesky lies. "What happened? Isn't Singapore filled with eligible women?"

"Yes, it is, but none that have struck me here." Nigel patted his chest.

Bart slapped his forehead. "Oh my Lord, he *is* having a midlife crisis."

"I'm tired of dating," Nigel admitted. "It's a nightmare, and I might be sleepwalking through the process."

"Please tell me this is not a euphemism."

Nigel leaned forward, animated. "No, literally, I've not been paying attention during my dates, just half-assing them. I actually realized midway during a date seven weeks ago that I'd dated the girl before, and that the date didn't end well."

Bart let out a whistle. "That's got to be some kind of record. What happened after?"

"The crazy thing is, she knew who I was," Nigel said, taking a sip of his drink. "And she was just waiting for me to remember. And all the time she was stewing in her seat and I couldn't understand why she was so mad. I thought I'd gotten her drink order wrong or whatever."

Bart reached over and patted his hand. "Sweet child of mine. You have got to date with intention. Surely you don't want to be stuck in first-date hell forever? You're, what, forty-two?"

"Trust me, I think I'm officially done. Everything just kind of blends together after a while. The same opening lines, the same so-what-do-you-do conversations, the same trying-to-impress-you-without-seeming-like-I-am, studied banter over overpriced cocktails. It's a waste of energy. And money."

"And that's why I stopped doing that, my friend. Deleted all my casual-hookup apps and used an actual old-school matchmaking agency for millionaires."

"Humblebragger," Nigel said, punching his friend's arm.

"All facts, bro. All facts. Listen, that's how I met Mr. Homesteader. I'm done with the dating scene; it's too complicated now. I didn't even know about attachment styles when we were growing up. It was either 'Hey, are your parents around? Good,' versus the alternative. That's it."

"You're making me feel old," Nigel complained.

"Dude, we're early millennials, we *are* old."

Nigel groaned and socked his friend in the arm again.

Bart eyed him for a moment. "Let me ask you something. Are you actually looking for something real?"

"Yes, absolutely," Nigel said. "I need someone I can connect with on an intellectual and emotional level, aside from the physical."

"So let's start today. You say you want connection, so manifest that intention. Act accordingly."

Nigel sighed, running a hand through his hair. "But how do you meet someone organically anymore? I mean, sure, I could bump into someone I would vibe with at a bookstore or coffee shop, but that's statistically so unlikely in real life. And the reality is, my schedule is insane. I don't have time to linger around hoping for fate to throw someone in my path."

"You're approaching this all wrong, my friend. It's not about where or how you meet someone—it's about your mindset. How quickly do you dismiss a prospect? After ten minutes if she likes cilantro or tells you she has a pet iguana? Do you ever give people second chances with a follow-up date? And are you allowing yourself to be vulnerable? I don't believe in The One either, but I do think we can guide our interactions toward finding someone who both meets our requirements and makes our heart flutter, then nurture that connection into something real. Your problem isn't that you haven't found the right person; it's that you're not making space, in your head or your heart, for something real. Maybe deep down, you're afraid of what would happen if you actually found it."

Nigel opened his mouth, then shut it. He looked down at his drink, watching the way the amber liquid caught the light. "Ouch. You might be right, old man."

"Watch who you're calling old man," Bart protested. "You're two years older than me."

Nigel clinked his drink against Bart's. "It's a night for hard truths, isn't it?"

Bart left Nigel to call Giorgio, his homesteader flame. Around him, colleagues were popping champagne and drinking harder stuff. The night was rapidly descending into slightly debauched chaos that would only end badly.

Maybe I should find Farida, he mused. If there was ever a person to date with intention, it was her. He lifted his eyes and saw Farida by the uncordoned poolside bar with a couple of other colleagues, chatting with a well-dressed stranger dripping in arm candy. She was probably networking, as Nigel would be on any given day. Two peas in a pod. He should duck out and go over, get Farida somewhere away from their colleagues. Have a real conversation with her in some romantic beachside tavern.

And yet, he stayed rooted on the spot, sipping his Coke, the beginnings of a dehydration migraine hitting him.

I don't want to be alone—but I don't want to be with Farida either. He knew enough about her to know that she wasn't right for him.

He didn't know how long he stood by the railing facing the ocean, pondering his future, his body language deliberately closed, before he sensed a tingling and turned to glance at a woman standing by the railings—someone who wasn't from B&H, half lit by the flames, her profile sharply elegant against the darkening sea. A woman dressed in white, late thirties or early forties, a stunning woman.

There was something about her—something that snagged his attention and refused to let go. Compelled, Nigel walked over to introduce himself.

"Good evening," he said, his voice easy, confident.

She turned, and for the briefest second, something flickered across her face. Recognition maybe. Shock, even.

And then it was gone.

"I'm sorry," he said, a slight tilt of his head. "Have we met?"

Her mouth tightened. "No," she said coolly. "Now if you'll excuse me." She stepped away from the railing and left him.

The brush-off was so swift, so absolute, that Nigel almost laughed aloud. *When was the last time someone did that to me?*

And because he had never been very good at letting things go—certainly not women who fascinated him—he followed.

"Do I know you?" he said lightly, falling into step beside her.

This time, she didn't even respond. She simply kept walking, her head ducked, her strides hurried.

Nigel hesitated, watching her retreat across the boardwalk toward the road. Something about the moment—about *her*—felt heavier than it should have, because this felt like more than the simple rebuff of a stranger uninterested in flirtation.

It felt like unfinished business, and he wasn't the kind of person who left business unfinished.

He caught up with her just outside the beach club's gates, where the night air smelled of frangipani and salt. She had her phone out and was about to make a call.

"Wait," he said, not touching her, but standing close enough that she stopped.

Reluctantly, she turned, putting her phone hand down. "Can't you take a hint?" she said sharply.

Nigel flinched and held his hands up. "Look, I . . . I'm sorry I'm being so persistent. I'm not usually in the habit of chasing after women who clearly don't want to be followed," he said slowly. "But I'm getting the feeling that . . . I don't know, you know me? And not, I reckon, in a good way?"

Her expression thawed—not with warmth, but with sadness.

"I don't know you," she said quietly.

Nigel wasn't convinced; the heaviness in her voice was unmistakable. "Really? Because your dismissal feels personal. Like I hurt you in a past life or something."

Her lips flattened. It wasn't a good line, sure, but now he was thinking he was right and her reactions so far indicated something more substantial, something bigger than disinterest at play. Nigel could almost see the debate playing out behind her eyes. "It's complicated."

He exhaled, feeling vindicated by his hunch. "Tell me."

"I don't think that's a good idea," she said.

"OK, fine, don't tell me. But can I . . . Can I take you out for drinks? I just can't shake the feeling like I know you."

"Of course you know her," a voice behind him said. Nigel turned: It was the woman Farida had been chatting to at the counter, Arm Bangles Girl. "This is *New York Times* bestselling author Dr. Dana Smiley. You might have seen her on, like, I don't know, *Good Morning America*? Times Square? All the major airport bookstores across the globe?" She squinted at him.

"Pia," Dana said, her embarrassment evident even in the dim light. "It's not like I'm a household name."

Dana was right: The name had not struck any bells of recognition. But now he had a name. "Dr. Dana Smiley. Wow. That's so cool. An author."

"And *doctor*," Pia added pointedly.

"So cool," Nigel said, hurriedly.

"Let's go, Pia, the car's here," Dana said, businesslike. "I've got to attend the conference tomorrow."

"You do?" Pia said. At Dana's sharp glance, she hurriedly added, "Oh, right. I guess you do want to, um, speak to the organizers."

"Which conference?" Nigel asked, focusing all of his charm on Pia.

"The wellness one at the Regent," Pia chirped. At the corner of his eye, Dana was quietly wincing.

"Let's go," Dana said, almost dragging Pia to her car.

"One drink," he said, following them, not caring how desperate he looked. "Please. I'll come over to the Regent, or I'll take you out to dinner anywhere you want. No expectations."

Something about the way she hesitated by the open door, her arms folded across her body as if she were bracing for an impact she already knew was coming, unsettled him more than any outright rejection would have.

"Fine," she said at last, finally looking up at him. "One drink. At the Regent."

Pia leaned across the back seat and shouted, "Her IG is @DrDanaSmiley—DM her! And if she doesn't respond, DM me at @PiaThePA."

Nigel grinned. "Thank you. See you tomorrow. You won't regret it!"

But as her car pulled away and the elation ebbed, Nigel realized that her reticence when it came to him hadn't been about potential regret: It was the memory of something important in the past that Nigel hadn't quite grasped—and that she couldn't forget.

Dana

Day One

He didn't know her. Not even a glint of familiarity. Last she saw him, he'd been wearing an old, faded bathrobe and sporting a bad haircut. Now he was dressed like he owned the resort she was staying in, from the Royal Oak on his wrist to the sleek brogues on his feet. Like he'd never eaten moldy bread from the trash in his life.

Maybe this was only Alternate Universe Nigel, and there was no one else behind those eyes. Why should there be? She was in her vacation, her wish, and she hadn't included Nigel.

"Who *was* that?" Pia asked.

Dana could tell Pia was itching for answers, so she gave her the abridged truth. "Just someone I had a thing with in another life. He doesn't remember me."

"Impossible," Pia said loyally. "Anyone would remember you the moment they met you."

Dana laughed. Across the universes, her Pias would always be her number one cheerleaders.

"Are we really going to the conference tomorrow?" Pia asked uncertainly.

"Nope, I lied," Dana said. "I'm going to spend my day in a spa. So take tomorrow off too."

"Cool. I'll go meet up with a FateAble date then."

"Is that a new dating app?"

"It's the latest and the best. As a woman, you—"

Pia nattered on and on about the features of the app. At some point, Dana pleaded jet lag and said she was going to snooze in the back seat. It was almost midnight, and so much had happened that day she was surprised she hadn't crashed yet.

The biggest shock of all was seeing Nigel again, whatever version of him had been at the beach club. What did it all mean? Did it mean anything, or at least more than it had to mean? Didn't that older woman say she would be in a universe where she could potentially replicate the relationships she'd forged in this one, meaning it made sense that she'd have the same-ish characters to interact with?

She waited till she had said good night to Pia and was back in the room before she went into sleuth mode. She opened her IG app and there it was—a notification from a new follower with an anonymized account handle @BLieve865.

Hey, lovely meeting you today

Nigel. Dana's heart fluttered in spite of herself, then she scrolled down and saw the next message:

It's been twenty years too long. Let's not let another day pass
—Y.

The message was from Yomi, not Nigel.

Dana's reaction was complex. The previous excitement she'd felt about running into Yomi had faded in light of her running into Nigel and the mixed emotions that dredged up.

Of all the beach clubs in all the locations in the world, he had to walk into mine. Or she had walked into his VIP section. Right after she'd found Yomi too.

What is he doing here? Is this my version of him—or this universe's version? He certainly hadn't recognized her, so it was more likely to be the latter.

After casually checking if some version of her older children existed in this universe—she ran their names through the search engines on some wild hope, not expecting and indeed not finding any trace of them—she turned her attention to Nigel. She found him easily on IG, saw that he was a Singaporean marketing director of a reputed advertising firm. His public-facing socials were carefully curated to be personable, fun, with a dash of aspirational. Nigel went to the trendiest restaurants and nightspots, was constantly surrounded by attractive people, and occasionally posted Reels of himself giving out industry sound bites or life advice on various podcasts. Nigel was not disappearing in his midlife. He was leaning into it—and he was succeeding in every aspect.

Not for the first time since Dana had met him, she wondered about this Nigel's dating life. Based on the flirtatious comments on one of his recent IG posts, he was spoiled for choice: My favorite adman. Looking good Nigel, can't wait to hang later. And Nigel's winking and devil-face emoji response.

What about Yomi? Dana reminded herself, not wanting to spiral into obsession over the man she'd literally parallel-universe hopped to escape. If the connections unfolding here were possibilities in her real life, then she needed to pay special attention to Yomi Owope, because Yomi wasn't just any boy: In fact, Yomi had been *The* Boy. All through high school, Yomi had been the guy she'd obsessed over. Not solely for his looks, which weren't the flashy boy-band kind the other girls seemed to go gaga over, but because of him as a person. He had been into woodwork in Old Dana's universe—she was just going to refer to her real/former life as "Old Dana," to keep the versions straight in her head—and always had these adorable little carved wooden charms on him as key chains no one else except she and a couple of other girls noticed. He had elegant, dexterous hands that lent themselves to the multiple instruments he played: violin, trombone, guitar, piano. And he was a decent basketballer (on the school reserve team), a mathlete, and just a good person, unfailingly polite, articulate, and quietly confident the way many teenagers weren't, the way she wasn't. When he hit it big, she wasn't surprised. It was inevitable. He was destined for great things.

In New Dana's world, Yomi was not only more famous, but more . . . fantastic, if that was even possible. A jazz hip-hop artist with a worldwide following, multiple bestselling albums, sold-out appearances, a major collaboration announced with a famous rapper.

This man could give her some answers to the questions that plagued her waking hours—who should she be, who should she be with?

Dana's finger danced over the screen: Hey Yomi. So glad to see you too. We should catch up soon.

She sent it without hesitation, whereas Old Dana would have hemmed and hawed, twiddling her thumbs, and ultimately done nothing. Just tucked her wants into another box to be stored in some corner of her mind until it was too late to do anything about them when she finally retrieved it. Maybe it was because her time here was achingly finite: *I'm not going to wait around—this is my week to take action.*

Her watch beeped at the top of the hour, reminding her how late it was. Dana put down the phone, ready to undress and crawl into the beautiful canopy bed she'd been waiting to try all day, when a flash of heat shot through the fabric of her dress.

Dana yelped and pulled the fabric away from her skin. "What the heck?" Something was *burning* in the right pocket.

She fished the offending item out of her dress pocket with a wince and held it up. She gasped: It was the Polaroid, the one of the Cheng-Smileys she distinctly remembered putting on the vanity in her suite. That alone would have been creepy enough, if not for something way more concerning: The composition of the photo had altered, and it was now missing the Subaru SUV. Only the faint outline of its shape remained, a pale ghost where it should have been.

A strange unease trickled down her spine. She flipped the photo over:

Six more days, Dana. Use your time well.

Dana tossed the photo onto the perfect sheets of her canopy bed and pressed the heels of her hands against her eyes, willing the slow, creeping dread to dissolve.

It's probably nothing. Just a visual marker of a day spent in this world. There had to have been seven objects in the photo for a reason. Still, she couldn't shake the feeling that something important had shifted around her, something she couldn't yet see—and that this was just the beginning.

Nigel

Day Two

Nigel slept badly after he and the most hardcore of his colleagues left the beach club at 3:45 a.m. Considering how early he'd gotten up before and how he'd been stressed about the board meeting for the month leading up to the announcement, he was surprised he didn't crash as soon as he got to bed, but he stayed up till 5 a.m., then woke up, panicked, at 8:30 a.m., just in time to grab a coffee and a croissant before the second day of the corporate retreat began for everyone at 9 a.m.

The truth was he'd stayed up hoping to get a reply from Dana Smiley after he DMed her around midnight with an erudite Hey.

Then he panicked and unsent that message.

He finally settled on, Great meeting you. Let's hang, do drinks tomorrow like you promised.

Then he panicked and unsent that too. *Hang?* "Do" *drinks? What are you, twenty-two? And "like you promised"???? What is she, beholden to you, a crazed stalker?*

He groaned and palmed his face. Hi, it's Nigel. I really hope we can meet up, I really feel like we have an unusual connection that I'd like to explore.

He unsent that and threw the phone at Hong Kong Bart, hitting his talking friend almost squarely in the chest. The phone bounced and landed on the deck, whereupon it died. Either from secondhand embarrassment or a dead battery—he was too mortified to check. He picked up its carcass and stashed it in his back pocket, where it stayed for the rest of the night.

He'd like to believe she hadn't seen the messages, but the read notifications showed him she had—and what's more, she hadn't responded to any of them even though she stayed online till 2 a.m., posting a story about the conference around then. Then she dropped off, probably disgusted with his basic pickup lines.

This was partially the reason why he downed two espresso martinis and three tequila shots after. Partially.

He got back to his room somewhat hungover, plugged his phone in, and hoped for the best. His sleep was plagued with strange dreams, an especially memorable one in which he kicked a ball in a playground with a toddler who looked remarkably like the one in the photo on his vanity, while an older boy—the other kid in that photo—skulked about in the periphery, occasionally clapping when the toddler's foot made contact with the ball.

The power of suggestion, he thought, upon waking up in a cold sweat.

He spotted the notification just as he stepped out of the shower, still toweling his hair. A DM from *her*.

Drinks, 10 PM at my hotel. Regent, lobby

No greeting, no filler words, no doubt. Somehow, he'd known that was exactly how she would respond—she didn't strike him as a woman who wasted time.

If the tone hadn't been so dry and it hadn't been her, he might have hoped that this was a booty call, but instead he hoped that she had been too busy to meet earlier and this was the only slot in her busy schedule. He wanted to start right with her—she was special.

He stood there for a moment, dripping onto the cool marble tiles, his heart pounding with excitement edged with a rare edge of anxiety.

He typed, See you then, and threw his phone into a drawer before he could undo his text.

The rest of the corporate retreat passed in a blur. As he tried to reconcile the calm professionalism expected of him, his mind kept drifting back to Dana and her reaction when he first approached her: She had *recognized* him but pretended she hadn't. And it wasn't just the dismissal of a disgruntled woman he'd gone on a date with: She'd been guarded, disturbed—even angry at the sight of him. And while he was sure he'd never met her before—how could anyone forget that face? It was striking, even if it wasn't classically beautiful—she felt familiar to him. The whole encounter had left him shaken, intrigued, obsessed. More than anything, he wanted to understand why he couldn't stop thinking about her. Tonight he hoped to get the answers he needed regarding this . . . this undeniable connection between them, something familiar yet disquieting. Those answers flickered just at the edge of his memories.

Maybe this is how it feels to meet your soulmate, he thought half jokingly.

At six, as soon as the retreat was officially over, he eschewed hanging out with his colleagues and went back to his room to prepare for the date. By six forty, he was already standing in front of the mirror, adjusting the cuffs of his linen shirt for the third time. He told himself it was ridiculous—he was in his forties, for goodness' sake, he'd built brands from scratch, steered billion-dollar campaigns, built emotion out of nothing. And yet here he was, slightly sweaty around the shirt collar despite the air-conditioning, debating whether to button one more button or leave it casually undone. *Just like a teenager before prom.*

In the end he had to change out of the linen shirt anyway, since he'd sweated through it so much. He put on a casual pale-denim shirt—his last clean, smart-casual item he'd packed for this work trip; no way he was going to wear a corporate polo—and hoped for the best.

He had a quick dinner at a restaurant down the road away from his hotel, just in case he got pulled into any after-work hangs he couldn't talk his way out of.

The Regent was only a motorbike ride down the beach, but he called for a car anyway, not wanting to arrive looking windswept. The lobby, with its soaring cathedral ceiling of teak and coconut shells, was hushed and elegant, filled with the faint scent of creamy florals and old wood.

And there she was, sitting in the lobby, waiting for him. She stood up as he approached. In her casual outfit of soft jeans and a loose white top, golden sandals, no makeup, hair down in loose waves, she looked at ease, with an almost gamine charm.

"Hi, Nigel," she said.

Her voice sent a shiver of recognition down his spine. Like he'd heard it before in a thousand dreams.

"Hey, Dana," he said.

Then before he knew what he was doing, his hand reached out—for a handshake.

A *handshake.*

Nigel wanted to crawl into himself. A slightly bemused look flickered across her face as she took his hand—calm, firm, businesslike. Still, the warmth of her touch lingered, and for a moment, he didn't want to let go. She was magnetic. His other hand joined the first, enclosing hers in an odd, almost reverential clasp—like a religious leader greeting a disciple. Up, down, up, down, then an abrupt release.

And just like that, Nigel's humiliation was complete. Forget the friend zone; he was now a guru.

For a second, neither of them spoke. Nigel's blood was rushing in his head—and this was literally the first time he'd ever experienced it the way it was written. He could *hear* the blood whooshing through vessels he'd never known existed. He blinked, and his vision actually started spotting with flashes of light. He'd never been this nervous in front of an adult woman before. *Dear God, please don't let me pass out in front of her.*

Then she said, "Come with me."

"Wh-where?"

"To my suite," she said. "So we can have some privacy to discuss . . . some, um, sensitive matters."

Nigel followed her with his heart pounding a stricken beat. On the one hand, it was the best outcome he could ever have hoped for—privacy with this intriguing, sexy woman—but on the other hand . . .

He was not going to sugarcoat it: He was afraid for his life, though how literally that threat assessment level skewed, he wasn't sure.

But he kept walking anyway, curiosity powering his steps.

When he reached her suite, she turned to him and said, "Yes, you can leave your shoes by the side of the door," taking the question right out of his mouth. She did the same. Nigel experienced an almost overwhelming sense of familiarity in witnessing this act of her sliding her pale feet out of her gold sandals. Like he'd done this before with her. He shook his head and tried to clear his confusion. *The brain isn't foolproof—sometimes there's a glitch in the matrix,* he reminded himself. Nostalgia, déjà vu, could be triggered through a complex alchemy of stimuli, and sometimes the brain's recognition and recall systems misfired organically. He was probably just severely sleep-deprived, jet-lagged. *Keep your wits with you—you need to impress this impressive woman.*

Because Dr. Dana Smiley was clearly going places. The suite was simple but beautiful, full of character, unlike his sterile business hotel with its IKEA-looking "sleek" furnishings—beautiful locally sourced hardwood, linen curtains billowing in the sea breeze. He noted the elegance of the cut and fabric of her clothing, the expensive lowlights in her hair, her discreet but expensive jewelry. And then there were her achievements—the way she'd juggled shifts and night school to get a master's at NYU, then enrolled in her doctorate at the University of Texas (it was fascinating the trivia that had turned up when he'd done a quick sweep of her online before their meeting). She was obviously someone who didn't shy away from hard work in order to achieve her goals, and she certainly spoke like someone with empathy and heart for others.

But even if she hadn't had a fancy doctorate, even if she wasn't a *New York Times* bestselling author with all those intimidating accolades, Nigel thought he would have found her fascinating anyway. Some people just compel you with a glance, a gesture. Seep into your thoughts like ink in water.

Snap out of it, Nigel. Poetry has never been your forte.

A bottle of wine—Chablis, expensive—and a bottle of sparkling water—San Pellegrino—sat in a cold bucket on the dining table of the suite. *It's like she knows what I like.* Nigel noted these details absently, trying to keep his nerves in check.

"Thanks for coming," she said, her voice steady, almost formal.

"Thanks for inviting me over." Wow, the quips kept coming.

They hovered in the center of the room, neither making a move toward the sofas or the dining table, the air charged with tension. *How do I know you?* Nigel wondered. *Who are you, really? What am I missing here?*

Finally, she gestured for him to sit at the dining table. She remained standing, arms crossed over her chest like she needed the extra barrier.

"How was your day?" Nigel said, before internally smacking himself for saying something so inane. How was it this stranger had the ability to make him second-guess even his gift of gab? He was the king of small talk, the guy the other partners carted out to soften up mulish clients before they discussed contract terms.

He shook his head.

"What?" she said, confused.

"I give up," he said, throwing up his hands. "I don't know what it is about you, Dana, but you get under my skin and make me doubt myself. No one has ever made me feel the way you do."

She crossed her arms over her chest. "I'm sorry I seem to have this destabilizing effect on you. The way you phrased it . . . I somehow don't think you meant it in a positive way."

Nigel let out a rueful laugh. "It's complicated. Like, on the one hand, you've been playing on my mind 24-7 since we met, and on the other, I'm terrified I'll say the wrong thing and you'll brand me." He'd thought he could be casual about this date—if it were a date—but it was impossible. Nothing about their interactions was reading casual.

"Sounds like our real life," Dana muttered, turning away and pacing the room.

Nigel cocked his head. "I'm sorry? What do you mean by that?"

She stopped pacing midway and turned to face him. Nigel's face burned under her piercing gaze.

"You really don't remember me, do you?" she said.

"No," Nigel admitted. "Although there is something about you . . . that is . . . very familiar. I can't place my finger on it. Like maybe I know you from a past life or something."

He meant it as a joke, a figure of speech, but Dana's face drained of color.

She nodded to herself, as though an internal argument had been resolved. "That settles it." She sat down and seemed to be bracing herself to deliver bad news. "I thought I could go through this evening acting as though we're strangers, but I can't. I don't have a poker face strong enough for this kind of charade."

"Wh-what? What d'you mean?" Nigel said, completely caught off guard by the evening's change of tone. She was visibly upset and he'd only *just* got there.

"The reason why I'm familiar to you is because I'm your wife, Nigel."

Nigel let out a surprised laugh until he saw that she was serious. "I'm sorry, *what*?"

She got up and fished out a photo from the lit counter where the coffee machine was and shoved it under his nose. "Look at this photo. Does it jog your memory?"

Nigel dropped his eyes reluctantly and gasped. It was a Polaroid, eerily similar to the one in his room, only instead of the woman being in it, it was Nigel instead, standing with the same three children, the house, and the rodent-dog.

It was the exact same photo he had—only *he* was in it.

And suddenly Nigel realized that the woman in his version of the Polaroid—that ungroomed, unsmiling woman—was *her*: Dr. Dana Smiley. This polished creature in front of him.

Nigel dropped the photo onto his lap, almost recoiling from it, stunned into rare silence. His thoughts were galloping wildly in myriad directions. He licked his lips and managed to whisper, "I don't . . . I don't understand." He glanced up at her. "What the hell is this? Who are you? How did you get this . . . this photo of me? Who are these people?"

"Take a good look," Dana urged. "Are you sure none of this is familiar?"

"No, none of it is," Nigel exclaimed. "Why would I lie?"

"Damn it," she muttered, disappointment etched in the lines of her face. "I thought that since you're such a visual person, a photo of us might jog your memory."

Nigel was flailing. "What do you . . . how would you know whether I'm a visual person? Isn't everyone?"

"Not the way you are," Dana said softly. "Although you're good with words too. You were known as the jack-of-all-trades at your Baltimore agency, great with copywriting and graphics, with vision and strategy. I'm glad it's the same here—and I'm not surprised they promoted you to group CMO. You were wasted in that small agency in Baltimore."

Her face clouded, lost in some private thought. "I'd actually forgotten about that. That was a huge sacrifice that you made for me right from the start, by moving to Baltimore just because my career didn't have the same flexibility. One I'd somehow forgotten . . . or minimized, maybe to assuage my own guilt." A weary look crossed her face. She sighed and pushed her hair out of her face. "God, I've stopped seeing so many things, haven't I?"

A strange dissonance settled over him—again, the familiarity of her actions, her tics, the truth of her words, and this odd kinship he felt with her, despite knowing she was a stranger that he'd met only yesterday. He blinked, trying to clear his head. "Look, is this some kind of prank? Did Bart or Clement put you up to this?" His friends were notorious pranksters, never hesitating to go all out on an elaborate scheme. This had Bart's sticky fingerprints all over it.

She shook her head somberly. "I wish it were a joke, believe me. But this is a photo of us, your family, Nigel, in the other universe that I—*we* came from."

"Did you just mention you're from another universe?"

"Yes," Dana said simply. "A parallel one. I know it may be hard to believe."

And now another universe was involved.

If she's acting, she's good. I'll play along. But just in case it wasn't a prank and she was a legitimate unhinged person—*I need to keep an eye out for a weapon I can use.* The bottle of wine. *I can use the bottle.* "OK, Dana, if you're from another universe, how did you find me?"

"I didn't—we ran into each other at the beach club, remember? In fact, someone from your firm invited my PA and me to the VIP section because they were hitting on her or something. Believe me, I certainly wasn't hoping to run into you in this world." She sounded miffed, not like a stalker at all, but Nigel had watched too many true crime documentaries to let his guard down.

"So explain. How about starting with who exactly you are and how you—we ended up here?"

With great conviction, Dana said, "My name is Dana Smiley, and I've been married to you, Nigel Theodore Bradshaw-Cheng, for the past sixteen years. We got spirited here to this parallel universe when I made a wish to explore an alternate life for a week—and somehow, I believe my version of you ended up here too."

Nigel broke out in the first cold sweat of his life. *Wow, she really believes this.* "Shit, how come I don't remember anything from our long history together?" he said jokily, forcing himself to stay bolted in his seat.

"Look, this is going to take a while, so . . . would you like to have that drink I lured you here with?" She was already opening the wine bottle in front of him, stabbing the cork with a simple twist-and-pull corkscrew with the precision of a brain surgeon. Wryly, she added, "So you know I didn't poison it. And please go ahead and choose the wineglass you'd prefer. I'll drink mine first so you don't panic."

She knew how paranoid Nigel was. "Um, sure. Yes, please. A nice big glass of unpoisoned white wine, please."

"Right away."

He let her pour him a glass and chose the one farther from him and took a long sip after she did. He didn't know why he hadn't already left the room but instead found himself drinking wine with her. It was her authoritative, no-nonsense air, he decided. *You'd have to believe anything she said.*

To be fair, he could easily overpower her. He was fit: A regular half-marathoner, he weightlifted and he boxed. Whereas she—he gave her body an assessing once-over—looked soft, curvy, and—he swallowed, flushing at the direction his thoughts were headed, and pulled his eyes up to rest on her face—not threatening.

In fact, she was just sitting there, wearing a sheer shirt that you couldn't hide weapons under, looking up at him if not trustingly, then without fear. Unless she possessed some deadly martial arts skills, he reckoned he was safe from bodily harm. Still, he shouldn't let his guard down. She might be unarmed, but she definitely had a screw or two loose. "OK, Dana. So we're married."

"Yes."

"How did that happen?" Nigel asked, actually curious. He'd never seen himself as the marrying kind.

She ducked her head and spoke in a matter-of-fact manner that did not quite mask the hitch in her voice. "You and I met while you were visiting Baltimore for a bachelor party seventeen years ago, and . . . and then"—she bit her lip, met his eyes almost defiantly, almost as though she was challenging him to disagree—"we fell in love and got married."

An image, blurry and unfocused, of Nigel and a woman who could've been Dana darted through his mind but vanished before he could grasp it. "Tell me more about our relationship. How did we fall in love? How did I propose?"

She told him with the precision and heart of a seasoned and skillful storyteller. How they'd met in the hospital when he came into her ER, the many attempts he made to get her attention, how they ended up dating—reluctantly from her side, Dana emphasized, at least in the beginning—how he ended up winning her heart, and the quirky proposal that involved a ring hidden in a bowl of sauerkraut that her favorite deli in Baltimore had prepared for their to-go order.

The stories were lovely, shot through with eye-catching, nostalgia-inducing detail, but Nigel felt nothing. Not even a flash of recollection, no matter how hard he focused. He couldn't help the disappointment that landed in his gut—maybe deep down he had hoped for an epiphany that would confirm that this woman was not mad, that she was someone he should run to, not away from.

"And our family, what's it like?"

"We have three lovely children, the kids in that photo: Bex, sixteen; Gill, eleven; and Emmie, two."

"Wow," Nigel said. "Three kids. And that's quite the age gap."

"Emmie was a surprise—a happy one that came in the middle of a rough, *rough* time; she's our little pandemic gift," Dana said softly. "Although . . . although there are some days, if I'm being honest, when I've been rather bad at showing her just how much she's wanted. In fact, I think I've been absent for most of her young life because of work—" Her voice faltered and she ducked her head to surreptitiously dab at her eyes. She clearly wasn't comfortable breaking down in front of him, even if they were supposedly married. *This other guy must be a real winner,* Nigel caught himself thinking before he mentally shook himself. Damn, she was so convincing, her anguish so real, he couldn't help getting swept up in all of it.

Nigel awkwardly handed her a linen napkin from the table. She accepted and started sniffling into it. He hesitated for a moment, debating whether to offer some kind of physical comfort, a gentle pat on the shoulder or a hug, but he held back, feeling somehow *guilty* for causing her grief, like this Other Him existed. "It sounds like you have a lot on your plate," he said instead, still wanting to comfort her. "Do you want to talk about it? Was it work stress or . . . ?"

"My work, your lack of work, money stresses . . . all of it compounded together." She blew her nose, hard. "That's the reason why I made that wish. I just needed a little break, you know? I've been putting out fires nonstop since the pandemic and I-I'm so tired."

"You don't sound happy when you talk about our life. Were you . . . were you happy?"

Dana shook her head. "It doesn't matter how I feel. What's more important is the health and happiness of my kids."

That's a terrible way of looking at things, Nigel thought.

"These are all valid reasons for wanting a vacation from your life," Nigel said quietly. The low light from a lamp bathed the room in a warm, amber glow, casting gentle shadows across the curve of Dana's cheek and threading her hair with sumptuous gold lowlights—with her curls and her figure, she looked like something out of a Rubens painting. The faint scent of vanillic musk from a nearby oil diffuser hung in the air. If this had been a real date, the setting would have been perfect for romance. "I'm sorry Other Me didn't seem to be pulling as much weight as he should be. You seem like a good woman."

Dana flinched as though his words were barbed. "Thanks," she whispered. The wineglass shook in her hand as she visibly swallowed. "That's . . . that's nice to hear from you."

They locked eyes and Nigel felt that strange tug again—not something as superficial as attraction, although it was there, of course, but that same sense of complicity, of kinship. It was disorienting, as if he were looking at a photograph of someone he could not remember meeting but felt certain he knew.

A beat passed. Outside, wind brushed gently against the hotel room's windowpanes, making the glass creak ever so slightly.

"Have you always wanted to go into medicine?" he asked, his voice lower now, as if afraid to break whatever delicate thing had just settled between them.

"No, that's the thing. I never grew up wanting to be in medicine," she admitted. "But it was always a career I thought I should embark on, given my dad's past. My dad would have become a doctor if he could—he left Vietnam in the early seventies and never got to finish his studies. He worked in administration for a hospital." She swiped her nose with the back of her palm, and Nigel was overwhelmed with the familiarity, the intimacy of that gesture. "Being a nurse was a safe, stable bet. Once my dad suggested I try it, I never really thought of doing anything else." She chuckled, looking awkward. "I was always trying to please him. He was so unhappy. I think he never really got over the trauma of leaving his motherland."

This was the first nugget of her personal history, aside from the "alternate universe" married-life insanity she'd spouted, and Nigel was enraptured. "Were you close to your dad? Your mom? If it's OK I ask."

"Of course you can," Dana said. "I was never very close to either parent, even though I love them both, the way we can't help loving our parents. My parents split messily sometime during my junior year, and my mom remarried her high school sweetheart and moved back to Houston while I stayed with my dad here—I mean, back in Baltimore. When she was alive I would see her, like, once every year over Thanksgiving—she had stepchildren and my stepdad, and it always felt like I was, I don't know, a reminder of a chapter of her life she'd rather forget, even if she loved me. And then my dad got sick a couple of years before Bex was born. Alzheimer's. He's in a home. I . . . I visit him every week."

"I'm sorry," Nigel said, genuinely affected.

She waved his apology away, immediately businesslike, *like someone used to putting on a stoic face*—a crucial aspect of her job, he guessed. "Don't be. I've had time to grieve that aspect of my life. What still affects me, what makes me sad sometimes, is knowing that our kids won't grow up with grandparents around them, because even your parents live too far away and are too old to travel much."

Nigel tried to suppress the impulse to agree with her—that would mean agreeing with her version of the situation. He fought to steer the conversation back to less emotionally charged grounds. "Did you dream of doing something else when you were much younger, or was there anything you particularly liked doing, growing up?" he asked. "That can be quite illuminating."

Dana smiled at some private memory. "I loved sculpting and making things. I was good at it—got my pieces displayed at a showcase hosted by MICA—that's the Maryland Institute College of Art—I gave it up as soon as I graduated from high school, but I've always wondered—and in this universe, apparently, I have biweekly pottery classes and a shelf at home full of twisted animal figurines."

He raised an eyebrow. "Twisted?"

She tugged at the neckline of her shirt, exposing more skin. "They're more *Nightmare on Elm Street* than Disney woodland, is what I mean."

Look up, you're staring at her neck. "Interesting."

Dana cleared her throat, and Nigel came to his senses with a start, because in spite of his inner voice, his gaze had *not* lifted from her winglike clavicles. "Sorry," he said, blushing. "I was thinking about work."

"At least that hasn't changed," Dana said. "You were always a consummate professional. That's one of the main differences between your other life and this one—besides the family, I mean."

"And how did you, um, parallel-universe jump?" he asked, if only to remind himself that she was not completely right in her mind. "Forgive me, but you don't seem to be particularly magical or in possession of some futuristic technology that would allow you to do such a thing."

"There's someone else involved. Psychopomps."

That sounded ominous. "What the heck is a psychopomp?"

"Guardians of the balance between life and death, like Anubis or Saint Peter; they shepherd souls through states of transition, and I—I suppose they have the power to alter your destiny."

"Ah," Nigel said. *Of course it gets worse.*

Dana sighed and rubbed her eyes. "Let me prove it to you. There's a reason I invited you over this late." She looked at the clock. Four minutes to midnight. "Wait, where's my photo?"

"What photo?"

"The photo of our family. The one I just handed you."

Nigel picked it up from the floor and wordlessly gave it to her, noting the possessive pronoun *our*.

She plunked the wineglass down on the teak dining table, missing the coaster. Nigel winced. "Let me show you."

She sat back down on his side of the table with her photo and bent her head close to him. Nigel caught a whiff of her. Underneath the salty tang of sea air was a nutty, buttery scent to her that he found extremely comforting—and alluring. He had to stop himself from drinking in her scent.

Goddamn, maybe *he* was the one who was unhinged.

She held the photo up. "Watch very closely at what happens next."

"What am I looking for, exactly?" Nigel wanted to know.

"You'll see. I think the dog will disappear."

"Uh-huh," Nigel said. Whatever happened between them, this was going down in history as his most eventful date—ever.

The clock struck midnight in delicate mechanical beeps.

Nigel stared at the photo of three kids, him, and the rodent-dog standing in front of the house. He stared very hard at them, wanting, like Fox Mulder of *The X-Files*, to believe.

Nothing happened.

"Umm?" he said, clearing his throat so she too would stop staring at the photo.

"Wait, why didn't it work?" Dana shook the photo hard, as though doing so would erase the fact that the photo had not changed a bit.

Nigel sighed, feeling drained by his conflicting emotions at the picture having not changed—there was a part of him that had been holding his breath, hoping for some supernatural sign. "Look, Dana, this has been oddly compelling, but I really need to get some shut-eye if I'm going to get any work done tomorrow." Plus his flight left early in the day and he didn't want to miss it.

"What? Already?" Dana said, "It's barely midnight."

"Alas, I belong to the 5 a.m. club and I'm already two hours behind my usual sleep schedule." *Also, you are definitely unhinged.* "Plus I have early-morning calls tomorrow before I get to work at 8:30, so, you know, chop chop." He got up to go, regretful that the evening had turned out that way.

"Look, Nigel, I'll bring you proof, I promise."

"Uh-huh."

She stopped by the door so abruptly he crashed into her with a yelp of pain. She didn't seem to feel the impact, though. Instead she turned to face him with a wounded expression. "Nigel, how could you forget me so easily?"

She looked up at him with her hazel eyes. Nigel's breath hitched—something about the moment made him freeze. A strange, disorienting sensation gripped him, something more acute and disorienting than déjà vu. And then, suddenly, he wasn't in her hotel room anymore.

He was in a memory seventeen years ago, standing in the dim blue glow of the National Aquarium in Baltimore. The air smelled of salt and damp metal, the low murmur of families and hidden machinery that kept the show running. He was on a date with Dana, and it had been going well enough that Nigel was working up the courage to ask her for a kiss. He'd never waited before—never had to wait, to be honest, never felt the need to hold back on making a move, but he'd wanted to wait for the right moment. And the aquarium had a certain romanticism to it, despite the press of crowds. You couldn't help but be infected with excitement in a place like that, surrounded by the wonders of the deep sea—you couldn't help but feel privileged to be given a seat in this show.

And that's how he saw Dana—he was lucky to be in her presence. Few people had ever captured his attention the way she had. She could be reading a placard out loud and Nigel would be enraptured by the cadence of her voice; he'd catch himself staring at the perfect line of her neck, the cut of her jaw—not as narrow as she would like, she'd confessed, but wonderful in Nigel's book—the tiny dent in her bottom lip. More than anything, he thought her kind and gentle, traits he'd always sought in others because he'd found them lacking in his own home; he found her bitingly funny; he believed her to be the smartest woman in any room.

There he was, standing before the massive Atlantic Coral Reef exhibit, the swirling fish casting rippling shadows on the floor, waiting for the right moment even though he knew there would never be a perfect moment—life wasn't one of his show reels, one of his ad campaigns. So he finally went for it. He tapped her on the shoulder, she turned, and he gently leaned forward, someone jumping off a cliff with no safety net. She could reject him. She could punch him. But then their lips met, and everything changed for Nigel. He knew he never wanted to kiss anyone else for as long as he lived.

The memory was vivid, real—but impossible. His breath caught as he snapped back to the present, staring at her. He was deeply shaken by that flashback, but his common sense wouldn't allow him to admit to it. He had his own pragmaticism—it was what had allowed him to climb the ranks in his industry, and to outlast his competition.

"I'm so sorry, Dana, but I really don't remember any of it," Nigel heard himself say. "Now, good night."

He turned to leave, but not before he glimpsed the crushed look on her face as she shut the door.

—∾—

He walked to his waiting car, his thoughts and emotions in disarray. He hadn't meant to lie to her, but the truth was too frightening for him to comprehend, much less accept. Apart from the utter freakishness of seeing her with the exact photo, only with his mug in it, there was that aquarium flashback, as real as any core memory of his. And the feelings brought up by that flashback—those were even scarier.

He shook his head, hard, as though he could rid himself of the aftershocks. There had to be a logical explanation for this—*had* to be. Whatever had prompted that larger-than-life flashback had been a glitch in the matrix, nothing more. His overactive imagination, his creative mind filling in the blanks from her anecdotes.

Wait, how did you even know where that was—that it was even an aquarium in Baltimore? There was no signage in your flashback. He'd never stepped foot in Baltimore—how was he supposed to have gone to that aquarium? Plus she had never told him about that date—if it had happened, that was.

The photo in his room—he had to see it, now.

He ran all the way to his room on the second floor once the car dropped him off. Ran to the F&B counter where he'd stashed the photo. His heart pounded, caught between hope and fear—desperate for answers, terrified of what he might find.

His shaking fingers fished the photo from behind the pod machine and he had to steel himself before he could look at it. Maybe it would be the same as it had been when he first laid eyes on it two days ago. Maybe . . . maybe . . .

The evidence was irrefutable—this time, there was only Dana, and the kids and the house . . . *the SUV and the dog had disappeared.*

The noise that left his throat was that of a child. *No. It* can't *be.*

He flipped the photo around and sucked in his breath: There was new writing on it.

You have five days left, Nigel.

And just like that, Nigel saw a vision of the young woman watching him through a broken car window, framed by shards of glass. *The accident, and the woman—no, the being who brought you here,* his mind whispered.

The Polaroid fluttered to the floor. Unless someone was tampering with or replacing the damned Polaroids, and unless someone was implanting memories in his head, it seemed that Dana Smiley had not been lying to him. Far from it.

Dana

Day Three

What happened? Why didn't it work?

Dana had been so sure the photo would alter at the stroke of midnight. She poured herself a glass of white wine and downed it with a wince. The memory of Nigel's face as he excused himself and practically hightailed it out of there told her everything—it wasn't him. Maybe that's why the photo hadn't changed in front of him.

Or maybe the magic hadn't worked when she tried to show it to Nigel because the photo was a countdown timer for her eyes only.

Or maybe she was going insane and this was all in her head.

She reached for the Polaroid again, second-guessing herself, but lo and behold, Moped was indeed gone.

I knew it! she thought, vindicated, although she now understood that only she could discern the supernatural touches in her world.

She flipped the photograph over.

Five more days, Dana.

Dana put the photo down and sighed.

She was sorry not to have a photo with Moped in it—she loved that dog. She had rescued the Russian Toy terrier and German Spitz mix from a local animal shelter after his owner, an elderly man, died. He was the sweetest little dog that none of the other family members cared for much—they were more cat people on the whole, to Dana's deep regret—but Dana and Moped were pair-bonded for life. He had helped her through the worst of her postpartum depression and anxiety, as she did what she'd always done whenever the going got tough, which was to paper over her issue of the day with the wrong solution, in this case a rescue dog who ended up now being more in Nigel's care than hers.

Emmie will be the next to disappear, Dana thought. Even if it was just a photo, she hated the idea of her kids being erased, even for the little while she would inhabit this universe. (She always had a photo of the kids in her pocket.) This photo was a precious memento.

She tried to take a photo of the Polaroid using her mobile phone, then her laptop and iPad, but nothing worked. She even went to reception to get someone to scan the photo for her, but no luck. There was some kind of magical cast on the damned Polaroid that prevented the photo from being transcribed on a new medium, and the receptionist was perplexed by why their scanner seemed to have malfunctioned. Dana left with the Polaroid, muttering excuses, and went back to her room, where she finished the rest of her Chablis. Then she opened and finished the champagne too.

Spending the night alone in her suite binge-drinking—she'd not expected that. *What outcome did you expect, Dana?* Anything involving Nigel in this universe had to be a mistake. Hadn't she wanted to leave because of him—mostly—in the first place?

She should never have met up with Nigel tonight—in fact, she should never have connected with him on social media, checked her DMs, and clicked on his message. His nervousness and second-guessing, reflected in his repeated undoing of his DMs, had been amusing, even endearing, especially coming from such a confident man. Like her old Nigel had been. She was transported to when they first started dating, and a horrible nostalgia rushed over her, frying her neurons and clouding her good judgment. She was curious to know what a Nigel who had never met her was like. It had seemed like a harmless idea, a situation she would be in control of.

She *should* meet him after running into him like that—it had to be fate, right? Also, why was she projecting her anger and baggage on this person who might just be an innocent doppelgänger? He deserved an apology—in person.

That's how she'd found herself responding to his DM and inviting him over. Then she turned off her phone, floored with adrenaline, then the alcohol crash came, and she fell into a dreamless but fitful sleep at her desk. She woke up, sore everywhere and remorseful, determined to spend her free day sightseeing and not thinking about Nigel and her old life. She would be alone with her Thoughts. Maybe she'd even get a massage! But then he'd DMed to say he'd love to have drinks, and after that, Bali had been a wash. She'd walked around in Canggu, browsed the shops she'd heard about in forums, then asked her driver to take her to a couple of other famous landmarks, rice fields, and stunning temples after that, but barely saw or enjoyed anything. Her thoughts were, once again, on Nigel and their situation.

Because a small part of Dana couldn't help but wonder if her gut had been onto something—that her Nigel was in there, under all the polish and bluster. If that was the case, their meeting tonight would've taken on a deeper meaning. It wouldn't have been about flirtation, it wouldn't have been about nostalgia—it would've been about better understanding his Dana-less life to see if she could get the answers to the existential questions that had been plaguing her since she saw him: Was he better off without her? Was *she* better off without him? Had they made the right choice when they chose each other?

And so the evening hadn't unfolded with the casual ease she'd hoped for when she first invited him to come over. In retrospect, she'd been foolish to think it could: The informational asymmetry alone would have made it hard to stay surface-level with Nigel, not when the weight of their shared history was so heavily palpable on her end. And there was the pulse of attraction she could clearly pick up from him—and, let's face it, her. She still wanted Nigel after all—that much was clear. There was something about stepping outside your everyday life, away from its noise and obligations, that forces you to face the truth of your own desires. However inconvenient they might be.

But what really disrupted her plans to stay cool was her realization that he could indeed be *her* Nigel, even though he didn't seem to be aware of their past. There were many clues: his careful avoidance of saying anything that might "trigger" her, his inexplicable fascination with her, a middle-aged woman of average looks, and his quiet insistence that there was something about her he couldn't shake . . . It was all too telling. The signs were unmistakable. He didn't know he was an interloper in this universe like she was, but she knew, and that was enough.

And once that certainty settled, everything she'd worked so hard to suppress—the resentment, the grief, the white-hot sour anger—rose up in toxic, unstoppable waves. A year's worth of buried emotion spilled out, messy and uncontained. It didn't matter that he couldn't remember her. That should have softened something, she supposed. But it didn't. She couldn't help how it made her feel. So she'd gone straight for the jugular and revealed who she was. And then everything kind of fell apart.

At least your doubts are cleared up now, Dana thought acidly. *You really are that forgettable—even to the man who's shared your bed for seventeen years.*

He claimed she felt familiar. Familiar. And yet he couldn't hold on to a single core memory—not of their life, their love, not even of their children. While she lay awake worrying about them, wondering how they were coping, if they missed her. Even though the guardian had assured her time wasn't passing the same way back there, it didn't matter. The ache still found her.

Dana let out a shaky sigh. God, Day Three of her fabulous escapist vacation, and all she had was more questions that needed answers. Her neck and shoulders were all knotted up and tense—she'd never even gotten to have the spa day she'd promised herself.

I love this for me, she thought wryly.

She was glad she had told Pia to fly back the night before and to take the rest of the week off in New York. Whatever happened after Dana left, she hoped that Pia took away some life lessons from Dana's time as New Dana—knowing when to relax and take a break was a crucial survival skill, an act of self-love. A skill she was definitely going to work on once she got back to her original timeline. At least she understood that now—she wasn't a robot, she wasn't even a superhuman, and she should stop acting like she was either.

—w—

Ngurah Rai International Airport was heaving. Dana took a deep inhale and moved through the throng of stone-faced people at the check-in counter, determined to make the best of her third day. Pia had booked her a business-class ticket, which was the standard way New Dana traveled. Apparently. Well, Old Dana would definitely appreciate this rare luxury for her. Once they departed from Bali, she planned to order champagne, put on a sheet mask from one of her favorite Korean brands, and watch the latest Hollywood blockbuster—Old Dana hadn't been to the movies in almost a year!—until they arrived in Singapore for the stopover. *Bliss.*

That's when she spotted him.

At first, she thought it was just her eyes playing tricks on her—the man who had ruined her vacation even in this world, the man she least wanted to see—but no. It was Nigel, as sure as bottled water was bad for the environment.

He stood a few counters ahead of her, laughing politely at something the agent had said, running a hand through his messy hair—kept somewhat longish in this world. Same annoying, easy charisma that seemed to hum off him even when he wasn't trying.

Dana ducked her head and busied herself with her passport, praying he wouldn't turn around.

She wasn't ready. Not for casual small talk. Not for forced smiles. No.

It's OK, he's headed to Singapore and you're bound for New York. He's Singapore's problem now.

She cleared security, hung back as much as she could before making her way to the gate, and there he was again, ahead of her in the throng of last-minute boarders. Dana clenched her fists. On the same flight to Singapore, of all things. Out of all the carriers, all the connections on this popular route—it had to be hers. *Of course.*

They both peeled away from the general queue and took the Business Class lane, Dana trailing a few steps behind. *Of course* it had to be Business. And *of course* the agent would look at her boarding pass and smile, pointing her to the cabin next to his.

Someone was having a grand old laugh on her behalf. Escape her old life for a week? Good luck!

It's OK, Dana, it's only a short flight to Singapore. Then she'd never have to see him again—at least, until they got back to their real lives.

She took a deep breath, walked down the aisle, purposefully glancing at her phone and hoping he wouldn't look up, since he was already seated. All she needed to do was get in her cocoon-like seat and the divider between them would swallow her from view—he'd never have to know she was next to him. *Almost there—*

"Dana?" His voice was low, tentative, his gaze on her as she slid into her seat.

"Oh, it's you," Dana said, acting surprised to see him next to her. She gave him a neutral smile. "Didn't see you there."

"I didn't think you'd be on this flight," he said, voice light but edged with something—nervousness?

"Neither did I," she said. She smoothed the blanket over her lap, pretending to fuss with her seat controls. "Small world."

She pointedly turned away and pulled out the novel she'd purchased at the airport bookstore. *Please don't let there be a delay. Please let the plane depart on schedule.*

The plane shuddered as it pushed back from the gate. They both fell silent, the hum of takeoff filling the space between them.

Dana stared out the window as the plane climbed, her heart in her throat. Turned out she was still a nervous flyer in business. She focused on the drone of the engine, the sterile comfort of business class, trying to enjoy her champagne and her reclining seat (it took all her self-control not to recline it fully even for that short leg of the flight). But the minutes stretched awkwardly—she could sense him glancing over, could *feel* that he was assessing for the right moment to speak to her.

He finally did, about twenty minutes after takeoff, tapping the divider until she looked up from her book reluctantly. "Look, about last night—"

"Forget it," she said. She retreated back into her seat and pointedly held the book up as if she were reading. It wasn't like he remembered her, and she wasn't about to rehash the past now. Besides, someone in *Dead Hot Girl Summer* was going to get murdered in a bad way in a remote cabin on an ill-fated girls' trip, and the only person who could solve it before the killer struck next was a kindhearted but snarky cold case enthusiast. Dana would much rather have put a face mask on and rewatched *Pride and Prejudice* and objectified Matthew Macfadyen, but that would no longer be possible now. Why was the universe being so unkind to her? Why did it have to center her number one antagonist? She just wanted some me time, goddamn it. She didn't want to face her feelings.

You never want to face your feelings, that annoying judgy voice reminded her. *You literally universe-hopped to get away from confronting your feelings.*

"Shut up," Dana said.

"I'm sorry?" Nigel said from the cocoon next to her. He sat up and glanced over. "Are you addressing me?"

"No," Dana retorted. "It's not always about you, Nigel."

"Gotcha," Nigel said.

Good God. She was a terror. She put the book down and turned to face him. "I'm sorry, that wasn't fair," she said. "It's just—I hate flying and I didn't get much sleep after you left."

He held her gaze and something in Dana's gut twisted.

"I . . . I'm sorry I ran out of there," he said. "It was . . . it was a lot. You can admit that, surely. Put yourself in my shoes."

Didn't she know. A traveler from another universe? Pure sci-fi fantasy. If Nigel had told her that and she'd lost all memory of him, she probably would have turned and run, too. "It's not—look, let's just . . . let's just forget we ever had that conversation and mind our own businesses."

Nigel's jaw worked as though he was holding back from saying something, but then he smiled politely. "Sure. I'll leave you to read"—he glanced over—"*Dead Hot Girl Summer*."

"It's very intellectual," Dana said defensively.

"Clearly."

They lapsed into a polite silence. Dana tried to focus on the jumble of words on the page, but that too was ruined. She slid the book back in her tote and palmed her eyes. This was, without a doubt, the worst flight of her life.

Especially when the captain announced they would be hitting a bout of turbulence next, thanks to a tropical storm.

Of course. Why not. She wouldn't be surprised if those monsters from *The Langoliers* appeared midflight. After all, she knew that supernatural caretakers existed—now what was stopping the Langoliers from appearing, Avengers universe–style?

She might have squealed when the plane shook alarmingly. That prompted Nigel to look over.

"You OK?"

"I'm *fine!*" she barked.

"Want to watch a movie?" Nigel checked his watch. "We have about an hour and fifty minutes left. Take your mind off the turbulence. Anything you want to watch in tandem?"

Dana doubted she could watch anything under these conditions, but she lobbed her choice at him like a grenade, hoping to get a reaction. "How about *The Notebook*? Have you seen it?"

They had, once upon another lifetime. It was the first movie they'd watched a couple of days after they'd moved into their new home together. It was one of Dana's favorite movies that Nigel had never watched before, and she'd been surprised when he agreed. As expected, she had ugly-cried when it was done. Nigel had pulled her to him, offering her solace, and then proceeded to dry her tears very creatively and assiduously after.

If he remembered, it would have struck something in him. But nothing flickered in those brown eyes.

"Sure," Nigel said. He flipped through the selection on his screen. "It's a pretty long movie, though, so we won't be able to finish it."

The plane shuddered and Dana went pale.

"Where you headed next, after Singapore?" Nigel said in his maddeningly calm voice.

Dana gripped the handrests, white-knuckled, as another bout of turbulence rolled through the plane. "New York. Meetings with new clients for speaking engagements and such."

Nigel broke into a smile. "Me too. Laying over at Changi, then nonstop to JFK."

"With Singapore Airlines?" Dana exclaimed before she could stop herself.

"Yup."

"On flight . . ." She blurted out her flight number, and he confirmed it.

Dana let out a frustrated grunt. "Just my luck." She would be hostage to him for the *next twenty-four hours*.

"Thanks, you're clearly thrilled, I can tell," Nigel said dryly.

"You have no idea," Dana said. Another roll of turbulence rocked the body of the plane and Dana shut her eyes and gritted her teeth. Between the storm and Nigel, the Langoliers could not come fast enough.

Nigel

Day Three

They landed in Changi on time. As the plane taxied down the runway and Dana started tapping away on her phone, pointedly ignoring him despite having grabbed his hand several times during the last hour at particularly hair-raising parts of the flight. Nigel debated if he should invite Dana to come have drinks with him. She looked like she could use a couple of stiff drinks, given how tightly she'd been wound during that last hour of nonstop turbulence—heck, *he* could use a couple of drinks, especially when she looked up at him like he'd personally skinned their—*that* dog in the photo, which, in the light of day after an uneasy sleep, had not seemed so plausible after all.

Speaking of which, are you going to tell her about the disappearing dog?

Nigel shook his head. *Nope,* he told himself. Maybe he had imagined the dog—after all, he'd only glanced at that photo briefly before slotting it next to his coffee machine.

But it's her! And the same kids.

Was it, though? That Polaroid had been blurry—and now that he had taken it out surreptitiously to check it, had it gotten fuzzier than it had been the first time he laid eyes on it? The squinting woman standing in front of a two-story colonial behind her—was she really the same woman as this boho-chic, quiet, luxury-wearing woman in front of him, whose clothes, jewelry, and casually capacious designer tote bag screamed C-suite executive? *Well, maybe, yes.* And if the kids in the photo were supposed to be his, then they were a miscast: They were so golden, their smiles too perfect, even the littlest one's—his had been preposterous growing up, Invisaligned into submission only a few years ago. And the rat-dog, as far as he could remember—he would never have let that creature into his home. Never. Nor bought an SUV that screamed *suburban dad.*

He put the photo back into his jeans pocket and came to a decision of sorts. The smart thing to do would be to wait and see what happened at midnight, if his photo really did lose another member of its cast. Dana had been so adamant that the dog would disappear, but nothing had happened to hers, and if Nigel could not be sure that there had even been a dog in his original photo, why should he say anything unless he was sure? What if he'd been wrong? What if these Polaroids were of different families?

Maybe he'd misremembered the photo. Maybe he'd misremembered everything.

Nigel shook his head again. He wasn't sure what exactly had happened with Dana, with his Polaroid, but there might still be a logical explanation that didn't involve any supernatural angle. Maybe she was just an honest-to-God scam artist, or an honest-to-God prankster connected to that rascal Bart. There needn't be—what was that again, psychopumps? psychopomps?—involved in the equation; it could just be a wonderful, elaborate, human-orchestrated, old-fashioned hoax.

Either way, human or supernatural scams were involved, and that alone should have made Nigel run for the woods, but here he was, being problematic, hanging around this woman like some kind of a persistent diaper rash, apparently having lost all good sense related to mate selection.

And of course, something in him couldn't shake the feeling that Dana was right. That aquarium flashback and the emotions involved—the anticipation, the euphoria of that first contact—had sent chills down his spine, had shaken him to his core in its wake. It didn't feel like he had concocted it in his overactive imagination.

He needed to find out more about this inexplicable connection of theirs, needed to get her to talk about their life together, but how could he engage with her after what had been a less-than-ideal end to the night before?

But then the captain announced that those taking the connecting leg to New York would be delayed. Instead of the original one-and-a-half-hour layover, which would have been too short for them to spend quality time together, it was now almost a four-hour layover. Dana looked up from her boarding pass with an exhale so heavy it made the woman across the aisle from her turn and stare. "Is anything ever going to go my way this freaking trip?"

Nigel decided he would wait for a better moment.

They started walking down the gangway into the terminal with their bags. With both hands occupied with bags, she could no longer use her phone as a shield. Nigel struck. "Drinks?" he said, his voice casual but every fiber of him hoping she'd say yes.

She threw him a glance, half exasperated, half amused. "Are you sure you want to hang with the crazy woman from another dimension who might just be your ex-wife?"

"Angry ex-wife," Nigel filled in automatically, and her eyes narrowed. "Just a joke!" he said hurriedly. "Look, all the drinks are on me, OK? It's the least I can do if you're visiting from another world. Might just have to start believing in karma."

She sighed again, but he caught the slight quirk of her lips before it vanished. "All right."

They headed to the nearest bar they could find in the transit zone—a sushi bar, hardly Nigel's idea of the best place to partake of fresh seafood, but he had a niggling feeling it would be a good choice instead of the boring pub a few steps away. Nigel ordered champagne and a dozen oysters, despite Dana's protest that she wasn't a fan. But he suspected she didn't really mean it. Maybe it was pride, or discomfort with letting him pay. Or maybe—if her story about universe-hopping was to be believed—she just hadn't settled into this version of herself yet—the Dana who belonged to the good life, who could sit in an airport bar drinking champagne without needing to explain it to anyone, not even herself.

Whoa, what's this about there being two versions of Dana? Remember, this is literal crazy talk!

He tried not to watch her mouth as she ate her oysters.

"My goodness, but these are *fresh* airport oysters. Who could have guessed?" she murmured.

"You know, normally I'd stay away from consuming oysters that aren't served in an actual seafood restaurant," he commented, which led to a chuckle. "But it is Singapore, after all."

"How did you know I'd want oysters, in spite of my protests?" she wanted to know—she'd taken four by then to his two. As she bent down to dine on the fifth, Nigel discreetly ordered another dozen before she noticed.

"I don't know, I just had a hunch."

Her eyes darted to his, startled. "I love oysters," she said. "In real life. But I don't remember the last time we had any. They are quite pricey, and we were going through a belt-tightening exercise."

"Then . . . then I'm glad." What he actually wanted to say, quite cheesily, was that even if he had to starve, he would have gotten her oysters as a monthly treat, if that was what it took for her face to do what it was doing now—which was smile like she'd won the lottery.

He suddenly wondered how the other Nigel—if he existed—could have let it get this bad. What had the situation been like?

"Was I a good husband?" he asked suddenly. Dana had mentioned that both versions of him were very much extensions of each other, that they were similar where it mattered inside, although he was probably much fitter in this universe—he'd clocked how often she darted admiring glances at his biceps.

Dana tilted her head and regarded him for too long a beat before saying, somewhat stiffly, "I guess."

"Elaborate."

She laughed, flushing, visibly uncomfortable. "I don't want to ruin our non-date rehashing the past."

"Maybe rehashing the past and processing what went wrong might be the key to understanding what got you—us—here."

She shook her head.

"Tell me, what was I like as a parent?"

"Very good," she said emphatically. "You're basically Gill's best friend. And I know Bex confides her crushes to you. And there's this thing you do with Emmie—"

Miracle Beanie Baby.

A memory flashed before his eyes, one of a young child with curls the color of burned sugar—the toddler, Emmie—running away from him as she squealed and giggled into a room with a handwritten sign—BEX'S LAIR. ENTER AT YOUR OWN PERIL. He heard his voice saying, "Emmie, no! Bex is in her Angry Alone Era!" But his voice was giggly too. They were in on this together.

The hair on Nigel's arms rose.

Nah, this wasn't anything real. It was just his brain supplying him images. He was an adman, and this was what he did daily: construct videos and images in his head. Dana had just opened the floodgates of that creative part of his head by supplying facts and a photo to him. She was manipulating him, no doubt. This must be a new method of catfishing. If it was, it was very efficient.

Another image surfaced, vivid as a daydream: that of him and Dana dancing on a moonlit patio perched by the cliffs of a seaside town, so idyllic it could have been plucked from a dream. The music playing over the speakers sounded Italian, punctuated by the crash of the waves below. Beyond the patio, the rugged cliffs fell sharply into the inky sea, where the moon's reflection shimmered in fragmented trails on the rippling water. The air was tinged with salt and the scent of almond oil that Dana had slathered over her skin. She was pregnant. A server came up to them and spoke in Italian.

Nigel put the oyster down. He was suddenly scared. For all his bluster, he wasn't actually prepared for what to think if everything this woman told him was the truth.

"Are you seeing someone?" Dana asked, realizing that he'd stopped listening. She blushed. "Sorry for the absence of a segue, but I don't want to monopolize the conversation with my past-life talk either. Tell me about you. Your life. Your job."

Nigel didn't answer right away. He swirled his drink, watching the bubbles rush toward him. "Define *seeing*."

Dana gave him a look. "Seriously?"

"I go on dates. Humble, FateAble . . . the usual suspects. You know how big cities are—Singapore is . . . frenetic."

Dana didn't smile. She just watched him. Nigel guessed that she'd cased his IG and seen the women. "Anyone serious?"

He opened his mouth, then shut it. The bravado slipped, just for a second. "No," he said quietly. "Not really. My work takes precedence now." He finished his champagne. "The dating scene gets tougher the longer you're in it, I suppose. I just dismiss people so quickly because I know what I want and I don't have the patience for bullshit."

"Spoken like every single person above the age of forty," Dana said wryly. "*I know what I want,* but I wonder, do we also become less patient when the exact inverse is what's needed as we get older?"

"Maybe. Was I like that in the other life too? Impatient? Intractable?" Nigel wanted to know. He caught himself saying it like he believed in the other universe now. And maybe a delusional piece of him did. He swirled the dregs of his champagne around its glass, torn between dread and curiosity.

"I wouldn't . . . I wouldn't call you that, more like you were always so sure of yourself and what you wanted." She gave an awkward laugh. "Remember I told you that the first time we met, you hit on me through a fog of painkillers."

"That—I must have been cute," he said.

She chuckled at the memory. "It wasn't, and you weren't, not really. You were, in fact, quite hard to understand. But there was an underlying . . . charm to the moment."

That smile, genuine and dazzling. Nigel thought, *Other Nigel's a lucky bastard.*

"So Other Nigel's charming like me? Is Other Nigel a total workaholic too?"

Her smile slipped. "Not exactly. He always found time for his family, even though he was ambitious."

"But you said you're the sole breadwinner now—and he's the main parent?"

He could sense that this was a sore point for her. "Yes."

"What's that like for you?"

"Stressful. The hospital is always threatening to cut our budget, so I'm always giving 200 percent, ready to pull double shifts whenever I'm needed. I'm Super Nurse at work, and when I'm home I'm Shit Mom. Shit Wife."

"You don't mean that," Nigel said softly.

She let out a humorless bark of laughter. "I do, actually. I don't kid myself. I barely see my family, and when I do, I'm about as fun as a basket of dead fish."

"Have you . . . have you told your Nigel how you feel? Or let him explain himself?"

Dana shook her head. "At first I wanted to give him space to process his grief—he loved his job, and the agency just folded. AI came for it and brought many creative industries to its knees." She saw the questions on his face and added, "Generative artificial intelligence in our old world has become quotidian. People use it for everything, and they aren't burdened about the ethical and financial repercussions of these companies gorging on stolen source material these models are trained on; they just care about the end product."

"Soulless consumption at the expense of people's livelihoods."

"Exactly." They said nothing for a while, just watched the bubbles in their champagne fizz. Nigel couldn't remember the last time he'd had a conversation like this. A conversation about real things, real life. He genuinely enjoyed talking to her.

He wished he didn't have to ask difficult questions, but he felt compelled to dig further, really get to the root of everything. "What happened after he was fired?"

"He was devastated, although he tried not to show it. He'd been with them since . . . since we got married. He'd built a client portfolio he was genuinely proud of during his time as creative director—solid relationships with local and regional businesses. Advertising in Baltimore isn't like it is in New York or other global cities; it's smaller, more limited. But he carved something out for himself. Then the layoffs happened. Three months went by, and still nothing. No job leads, no interviews. Just him, still in his pajamas, drifting around the house, bingeing reality shows, pretending he wasn't down. I started to get a little worried—but I didn't feel it was the right time to say anything. So I didn't."

She put her glass down hard enough that the bartender winced. "Then another three months passed and he's not just watching reality TV, he's gaming with our son. But also doing all the school runs, PTA meetings, the works. I'm pissed. I'm exhausted. I'm concerned. But still, I say nothing, because it's gotten harder to broach the subject by now when he's basically become Super Dad to the kids even as he's stopped trying to find a job—and stopped communicating in any real way with me. I fester quietly. I get even more upset, because I don't know how to tell him what I feel. What I want and need from him." She said all this in a rush, as though she'd been holding it back for a long, long time.

"Whoa," Nigel said, wincing.

She sighed. "We've obviously not been communicating openly with each other for some time now. All that comes out now are platitudes and half-truths, and family admin. Not the real stuff. The hard stuff that needs to be said. On both sides. We're basically two ships passing in the night at this rate."

Nigel bit his lip and considered Dana. With everything she'd told him, it was no wonder their relationship was fraying, and they now found themselves in this supposed alternate universe on a coincidental whim.

Other Nigel deserved a good shake and talking-to, as well as a hug and some therapy, so it seemed; as for Dana, burned out and unappreciated, likely starved of affection, of touch—

"Look," Nigel said on impulse. "I'm sorry I don't remember this other life of mine, but if I can be of any service to you, then please—use me."

"I'm sorry?"

"Use me as Other Nigel's placeholder," Nigel said, his eyes fixed firmly on hers, so she couldn't misread his intentions. "Pretend I'm him and get rid of whatever demons you have with me using whatever methods you'd like and then go back to him. I'll be glad to help. In any way you need."

Dana's gaze dipped toward his mouth. It was quick, but he caught it, and she saw him catch her in the act. The air between them thickened with a different kind of tension.

"And what *exactly* would you have me do with you in place of my real husband?" Dana said slowly.

Yes, what exactly do you mean by that, Nigel?

Nigel shrugged with faux nonchalance. "Anything. Anything you want."

He had a few very conventional ideas, but he tried not to let his face betray those thoughts.

And judging by the way her face was flushing, he wasn't doing too good a job at being discreet.

"Are you suggesting what I think you're suggesting?" she scoffed. "Is that how you get laid? Offer sex as a solution to real problems?"

It wasn't too far from how Nigel operated, but he didn't want to admit that.

"I never said anything about sex," he said in a low voice. "Unless that's what *you* want."

Her breath hitched and she picked up her phone, pretending to be distracted by work. But her hands trembled.

Aha! Got you.

A hollow victory, though, because he didn't kid himself that he was probably more invested than she was in her saying yes to any naked shenanigans happening between them.

She downed the rest of her champagne in a shot and looked back at him. "OK, stranger, then let's get out of this place."

His pulse spiked and he struggled to keep his cool facade intact. "Wh-where do you want to go?"

Her lips curved into a slow, amused smile, as though she'd seen through the act. "Let's go see that damned famous airport waterfall everyone's raving about."

Keeping it professional, I see. Nigel glanced at his watch and made the calculations. In any other airport it might have been difficult, but he knew Changi and its layout well, and he was confident in its efficiency. "Let's go."

—

Of course Nigel had seen the Jewel Rain Vortex, that overhyped indoor waterfall—in fact, he'd seen it many, many times; every time some out-of-towner visited him in Singapore, they always had it in their itinerary. If this was a nightmare, then this tracked. But hey, he'd never seen it with a woman he was into before, so that was at least the bright side of this layover.

She wasn't just any woman he was into either—no, she was more than that. Ever since that conversation at the oyster bar, Nigel had felt closer to Dana than he'd felt to anyone in a very long time—perhaps closer than he ever had to anyone, full stop. It wasn't just that she had shared so much with him in such an unguarded, vulnerable way, but something about her had reached into a quiet place inside him and stirred it awake. She felt like a missing piece he'd been searching for all his life. And while he didn't believe in partners completing you, he did think that some people amplified the good, admirable parts of you, and of life, so that you remember what life is truly about: connection, intimacy, love.

It struck him then how rare those kinds of conversations had become in his life. Real ones. Not about campaigns or clients or what fancy wine to pair with dinner—but the kind where you lay yourself bare without shame or performance. He realized with a twinge of discomfort that the last person he'd come close to opening up with was Bart—and even then, their chats mostly revolved around half-serious jokes and dating. This was different. Dana had given him something rare—a glimpse into another life, of what he could be if he didn't have his career to drive him, to make him happy; she'd shed light on truths that he hadn't been aware of.

That he might want and need more than this—this exciting but ultimately other-serving life.

And now he was diving into dense crowds to see an overhyped monument—he'd seen the Vortex *nine* times since the year started—just so he could almost imagine them on a summer vacation together, maybe to Crete or Lisbon, braving the mad tourist crowds while being utterly wrapped up in each other.

They skipped past immigration without issue, since both he and Dana—in this universe at least—were enrolled in a frequent traveler program and were holders of American passports.

After they cleared immigration, they followed the signs to Jewel, the newest shopping complex of Changi Airport, heading aboveground into the humid late-afternoon outdoors briefly, before entering the shopping complex adjacent to the airport, where the infamous Rain Vortex was located. The air was thick with heat, noise, and unspoken things. They followed the signs, Dana two steps ahead of him, her silhouette cutting through the crowd with unthinking grace. People streamed around them—families, couples, squinting travelers dragging luggage with weary determination—but he could see only her. His hand twitched as if it wanted to reach for hers, to close the distance, but he didn't. Not yet. If he messed this shot up, it could be a point of no return, and he didn't want to run that risk—already she mattered too much to him to lose her now.

They heard it before they saw it—lush trees under a glass sky, the endless curve of storefronts, and above it all, the incredible man-made waterfall plunged in a roaring, jaw-dropping purple cascade, a spectacle so perfect it might as well have been conjured by a computing program itself. A marvel of technology and imagination. Here was Man playacting as God.

"Incredible," Dana said, her eyes on the water.

Nigel gazed at her instead. "It's all right," he said. He knew what he was here for.

Without another word, he reached for her hand.

Dana

Day Three

She kept a safe half step ahead as they wandered through the Shiseido Forest Valley. It was quiet except for the sound of cascading water from the Rain Vortex and the occasional awed murmur of tourists as they wandered through the sprawling indoor garden.

Quiet except for the confused pounding of her heart, the roar of blood rushing in her ears.

Earlier he'd brushed her hand as they stood by the waterfall, and she'd jumped back as though she'd been electrocuted. "What are you doing?" she said, harsher than she'd intended. It'd been a while since any touch between them hadn't been a result of purposeful scheduling, and the spark from the unexpected contact had spiked her heart rate—just like he used to in the early days of their dating life.

"Nothing," he'd said. He held up his hands, apologetic, eyes wide with innocence in a gesture that Dana recognized her kids had copied. "Someone bumped into me."

Dana made a show of pursing her lips in displeasure, saying nothing but privately, oh, privately, she hadn't minded the contact—far from it. That touch had lingered far longer than it should have, reverberating across the plains of her soul. And maybe that was the problem—she'd wanted more from him, in every aspect: his voice, his glances, his touch.

But this man, she reminded herself, was not her husband. She should not confuse his attraction for real connection. It was becoming increasingly clear that he was only a pale echo of the real man, a cipher, a Nigel-shaped canvas and nothing more. Maybe everything she'd sensed that first night—the way he seemed to recognize her, the magnetic pull she mistook for proof that he too had crossed universes but lost his memories—had been nothing but wishful thinking. A projection of her deepest, secret hope: that it was not too late to fix things with the real Nigel.

The relationships you forge here can be replicated back in your real life. That was the comforting part of this unusual situation she found herself in. This parallel universe was a sandbox, a space to rehearse desire and consequence beneath the soft illusion of safety, of impermanence—that was what the woman promised her.

But now she was confronted with a new and more unsettling question: She'd been looking at their relationship as one to be saved, as though it was the best outcome for them both. But what if she was looking at the situation from the wrong angle? If these were just versions of them—refracted by the choices they'd made differently from the original Dana and Nigel—then who was to say Nigel hadn't made the wrong choice from the get-go?

What if he was never meant to marry her at all?

A brutal, chilling thought. Because here, in this universe, he looked so at ease. So happy. As if this life—this skin—fit him better than the one they'd shared.

This was how Nigel used to be when she first met him. The vibrant, assured man she'd fallen in love with. This version of Nigel had faded somewhat in the last two years of their marriage—was *she* responsible for his diminishment?

This realization hit her with the force of a vortex.

They had another two hours and fifteen minutes until boarding, but suddenly Dana couldn't wait to get away from him, put physical distance between them. Buffer herself from further disappointment or rejection.

"Excuse me, but I need to go."

"Go?" Nigel said, looking crushed. "But . . . but I thought we were—"

Dana brought up the only excuse she knew would work. "Yes, well, I have a work call I need to take in private."

"I can walk you to the Kris Lounge—"

She shook her head, already backing away from him. "No need." Without another word she turned on her heel and melted into the throng of visitors, heading purposefully toward immigration again. Already the emotional shields she would employ in her old life were coming back on. She didn't want to give him more of her—that would be a mistake.

She needed space from her husband's ghost, here made flesh.

—∾—

She spent the next two hours shopping and burying herself in work, answering Pia's emails and texts, giving her the go-ahead to scheduling requests and other demands on New Dana's time, and even taking a quick call with a potential client, because once she left, the original Dana in this timeline would have to pick up the pieces.

By the time they lined up to board the flight to JFK, the air between her and Nigel was neutral again, if not safe. Still, Dana hoped they would not end up next to each other on this leg. The longer she spent time with him, the more confused she'd feel about Old Nigel in their real timeline and New Nigel in this timeline, and she couldn't risk that. She needed all her wits about her so she could figure out her next steps, here and back home.

They didn't end up next to each other—thank God for small mercies. His lone seat was across the aisle from hers, and there was a woman between them.

Feeling his eyes on her, Dana angled her body away from him, put a sheet mask on, and slept.

—∾—

There were a few times—six, in total; she was counting—during that flight when she woke up due to body-clock chaos, jet lag, or noise, and glanced over, almost involuntarily, to where he was seated, and each time he'd either sense her gaze and turn to meet her, or she'd find that he was already watching her. His screen was usually black in those instances, but toward the tail end of the flight she saw that he'd been watching *The Notebook* with his headset on. He was crying noiselessly. It was the only time he didn't react to her watching him.

Almost irrationally, she began to hope again. Something loosened in her—the tight knot of certainty that he was better off without her and that he knew it began to fray. If he was her Nigel, then maybe, beneath the wreckage of their past, something green could still push through the muck. The thought that he might still remember her, that he might still care, unsettled her more than she expected. It made her feel seen in a way she hadn't dared to hope for in days. That there was something there worth fighting for.

Or maybe she was just kidding herself? After all, she'd tried everything, and he was still drawing blanks when he looked at her. Could she realistically expect a movie to draw him out, if he was really in there?

She gave herself a hard mental shake: No, she was deluding herself.

—ᴧᴧ—

They landed and Dana shot out of her seat as fast as she could, wanting some space to process what was happening here. She just wanted to go home—well, this timeline's Dana's home.

The wind slapped her awake. JFK's chaotic arrival hall pulsed with fluorescent fatigue. She blazed through the entire process and retrieved her checked baggage, before heading to the curb outside to flag a taxi.

Nigel walked up beside her, slightly breathless from dragging his much larger suitcase. "You're really leaving without saying goodbye?"

"Goodbye," Dana said, attempting levity, not looking at him. "Normally I'd say, 'See you around,' but that would be a lie." She never wanted to see him again, not in this timeline.

He put his hand on her arm and Dana froze in her tracks, causing a mother-and-daughter duo to nearly crash into her with a volley of curses. She jerked out of his grasp, angry now.

"Dana, come on," Nigel said quietly. "Is this how we're leaving this?"

"How else would you have it?" she shot back, angry now. "I give in to your badgering, head to your place, and we have sex? Would you leave me alone then?"

He flinched and took an involuntary step back. The words she had thrown in his face hung between them, sharp as icicles. She didn't know why she'd said that—or rather she did. Hurt people hurt others. She put a hand on her face and massaged her brow. "I'm sorry, that was uncalled for. There's no excuse."

"I don't want you to come home with me," he said roughly. "I just can't bear for us to part on these acrimonious grounds."

She had to laugh. "We're not parting, because we were never together. So don't beat yourself up."

They stood on the sidewalk, suspended in a strange stillness. Not lovers, not quite strangers—just two people taking each other's measure. Like gunslingers at an impasse, only now too worn down to shoot. "I should go," Dana said at last. "Grab a cab."

"OK," he said quietly; he had his hurt-mouth look.

"What about you?" Dana asked. "As in—do you know how—"

"Yeah," he said, looking down at his phone. "I got a Lyft. In about ten minutes."

"OK," Dana said. "Goodbye."

She expected him to leave but he stayed. They stood together, bodies facing out toward the night. Silence bloomed between them, thick and unfinished.

He tried again. "Do you want me to drop you off? I'm not, you know, in a rush—I can just drop you off. I live in Chelsea, but I'm happy to go anywhere with you."

"I . . . I don't think it's a good idea." She couldn't be alone with him now—she might do or say something she couldn't take back—well, more than she had already done.

He cleared his throat and spoke up, his words a rush of throbbing emotion. "What's happening between us—I don't know what it is," he said, his voice thick with feeling. "I don't understand it. But I can't seem to let you go."

"Don't," she said, backing a half step away. "Don't say things like that."

"Why not?"

"Because it isn't real." She turned away from him so he wouldn't see her falter. "This version of you, of us . . . it's a fantasy. This isn't real."

"If this isn't real—" Nigel started to say. He reached for her gently, drawing her into his orbit, tipping her chin until their eyes met. "Then tell me to stop."

She didn't—she couldn't. She kissed him. Gently at first, the feel of him both familiar and new, comforting and dangerous. He made a noise when she sucked on his lip, drew him into her mouth. Felt him shiver when she wound her hands around his waist, guided by instinct and memory, the devastating drug of how good he could make her feel when they had been right with each other.

If it's a fantasy, why can't I live in it? What's the harm.

It would have been so easy to let herself be swept away—to let her use him, as he'd so callously put it—but it would be a cheap comfort and a false victory. In the end, she would have fallen for a straw man, and then how would that help her quest for clarity and peace? For a reset?

He was leaning in again for another kiss, and there was a secret piece of her that was eager to surrender to the passion, to forget and just feel. "No," she whispered, pulling away and shaking her head. "I can't.

I shouldn't have . . . I shouldn't have kissed you. Not when you're not the person I want you to be, and vice versa. It's not fair."

"What if—what if I'm the person you need me to be, right here, right now?" he said roughly, drawing close to her again.

"No," she said firmly, stepping back and folding her arms. "Please. Stop."

"Dana—"

"Stop. You know I'm right." She turned away from him, the naked look of want on his face—she had to remind herself why they shouldn't continue. "We can't. We're not a real thing, here. Exploring this any further would be a mistake."

"You think *everything's* a mistake if it feels good," he ground out bitterly.

Startled, Dana whipped around to face him. "What did you just say?"

And there it was—the flash of recognition Dana had been waiting for. Sometime in the last eighteen hours, the switch had flipped on. This was *her* Nigel—or a hybrid version, one that remembered her.

"What did you just say?" she repeated in a low, terse voice.

He met her gaze. "I . . . I got some of my memories back," he admitted. "It's all jumbled up, but I remember."

"Tell me one of them," she challenged him.

"Our shower." His cheeks flushed. "Kissing. We'd just moved in a week ago. The shower had olive-green tiles back then. A portable Bluetooth speaker was playing 'Wild Horses' by The Rolling Stones."

Dana sucked in a breath. She remembered exactly what happened next. The scene had the undeniable clarity of a core memory for her. *Our home,* came the thought. *We'd just remodeled the living room and were celebrating his raise; Bex had to have been three months old—*

This man recognized her. The knowledge was like a punch to her gut (and Dana had been punched in the gut before—twice, each time by a patient). It should have been a wonderful miracle, allowing them to explore this renewed connection properly—but now, she wasn't sure. "When did this happen?"

"Sometime during the flight, when I was watching *The Notebook*," he said. He smiled wryly. "Rachel McAdams got soaked in the rain and I remembered . . . us."

"Good God," Dana said. She felt betrayed. She'd been struggling not to feel attracted to a fantasy version of him, struggling with the guilt of it, when the entire time it was him, truly him.

"Did you—do you remember how you got here then? You know I made a wish to get here."

He shook his head. "It's . . . I—I don't . . . I'm not sure . . ." He hesitated before taking something out of his wallet. "I also found this, although I'm not sure how it fits with my new memories. But given that you have one as well—"

He passed her a Polaroid face up. It was just like the one she had, except it had the kids—and her. It was fuzzy, but unmistakably her, and like hers, it was missing the SUV and their dog, Moped. She was so shocked her breath seized in her lungs.

"When did you find it?"

"I found it the first day I arrived, thought someone had left it in my room by mistake, and didn't look at it again for two days until I came back from your hotel room. Even though it looked like yours and fit what you told me, I wasn't sure I should say anything—you can see it's quite faded and I thought it could still be a prank, nothing supernatural, you know."

She could tell he was embarrassed, that deep down he knew he was wrong—that was why he was speaking so matter-of-factly, almost tonelessly.

"You had a version of my Polaroid *all this time* and you *hid* it from me?" she said, sharp with anger.

"I didn't *hide* this from you, Dana. I was just . . . I wanted to find the right time before telling you. I didn't want to do it at the airport. I wanted to invite you back to my place as soon as we landed so we could figure this . . . this totally bonkers situation out together."

He sounded sincere but Dana's guard was up. "Do you remember when this photo was taken?"

"No," he admitted. "And to be honest, I've had flashbacks before, ever since that night in your Bali hotel, but they felt like scenes from a picture book or a movie—unreal. It was only after watching *The Notebook* that something clicked and the memories I saw felt lived in. Like I was truly remembering."

"You should have told me as soon as you got off that plane," Dana countered. "You should have let me know so I didn't spend another minute thinking I'm a fool for imagining you were my—you were the same Nigel I'd always known."

"I'm sorry," Nigel said. "You're right, I should have. I guess I just wanted to be sure what's what. I-I'm still trying to figure out what's up. Everything is jumbled in my head, and I don't even know where I end and this timeline's Nigel begins. I didn't want to ruin a chance with you in this world, before I was sure."

Dana blinked, stunned. "Even with everything you'd seen, you still dragged your feet? Would you even have said anything if I hadn't confronted you? Just so you could, what, kiss me?"

She was being cruel, she could feel it. Maybe there was an undeniable piece of her that wanted to hurt him in the name of self-defense. Nigel flushed. "I was going to tell you, Dana, of course I was! I just wanted to find the right moment, and it felt like a terrible time to do it right after we had a breakthrough." Bitterness crept into his voice. "But also, maybe I wasn't rushing to tell you that I remembered being unemployed, being useless, being the guy who couldn't even be a partner to you when you needed one. Maybe I wanted just a moment with you where you didn't look at me like I'm less than perfect."

How could he have gotten her so wrong? It made Dana wonder how far back they'd been growing apart, because these words could have been uttered by a stranger. "God, Nigel. You think I needed you to be perfect? Whatever for? We're *married*. We're past that."

Nigel laughed, a low, hard sound. "I don't know, Dana. You certainly were happy to kiss this different version of me—the successful, confident version I used to be. That didn't feel like pretense at all."

If she ever had a moment during this trip when she thought she might physically explode, this was it. She thought she might atomize—scatter into pieces too small to gather back.

He realized he'd gone too far. "I'm sorry," he said curtly. "That was too much."

Dana crossed her arms, retreating into herself. She said nothing.

"You're right, maybe *perfect* is the wrong word, the wrong . . . standard. I think you've been looking at me like a disappointment for so long, I didn't want to go back to that." His voice cracked. "I wanted to remember when I was enough for you."

A long, hurt silence stretched between them. His reasons were valid, of course, but they did not justify leaving her in the dark, not when she had been second-guessing herself and her motives, torturing herself for being attracted to this version of her husband. For leaning in to this fantasy version of him without the pesky overhang of their past.

"I just needed you to be present," she told him quietly. "That was all I ever wanted."

He took a tentative step toward her. "Could we please just talk at my place? Maybe we can spend the rest of this week we have here enjoying each other's company."

A Band-Aid. He wanted to throw a Band-Aid at the problem. Dana couldn't believe it. *Or maybe he is willing to take any scrap of love you throw his way?* a little voice inside her suggested. Dana ignored it. "No," she said. "I think it's a mistake to spend my time here pretending that things between us are all right."

They were past the point of no return, she realized.

Nigel's phone lit up with a notification as his car arrived, the headlights bathing the curb in yellow. Dana didn't move. Her phone buzzed. She glanced down.

Yomi: Back in NY last night, super jet-lagged but can't wait any longer to catch up. Lunch or dinner tomorrow? No pressure

She stared at the text. Impeccable timing, Universe.

"Yomi, from your high school?" Nigel said, an edge in his voice.

She lifted her eyes. *Don't squirm.* "Yeah. I ran into him in Bali."

He flinched; then his expression smoothed out, like a stranger's. "Then maybe you should see where that goes."

Dana's eyes flashed. "What?"

"Dating so soon in your new world." His lips twisted in a cruel smile. "Well, I don't blame you. You deserve to see if there's someone better out there for you. You deserve the second chance you came here to find."

Nigel the Poor, Lonely House Dad. Nigel the Unloved. Nigel, the Victim in All of This. Her anger flared but quickly burned out. She was too tired. Too heartsore.

"Don't make this out to be a noble move on your part," she said. "You're not setting me free. You're just giving up. Like you've been doing for some time."

Knives out. The air rang with their words, drowning out the airport traffic.

The cab pulled up behind them, engine idling.

Dana opened the door, then looked back.

"You were never beneath me, Nigel," she said quietly. "And by the way, I kissed you because even before you knew I wasn't delusional, this version of you gladly and willingly chose to spend time with me, which is more than I can say for the real you."

The car pulled away, just before her world was veiled in tears.

Dana

Day Four

New Dana's two-bedroom apartment on Rivington in New York—generally regarded as a promising neighborhood these days, for real estate investment—was the kind of space that looked like it was lifted out of an aspirational interior design Instagram account, the kind that Old Dana used to follow obsessively—natural travertine stone wall lights, warm oak floors, and linen curtains swayed gently in the breeze from half-open windows overlooking a quiet, tree-lined street. The living room was anchored by a greige couch in textured fabric strewn with soft throws in muted earthy tones, and books were stacked artfully on every surface, some opened midread. A small gallery wall displayed Chinese ink paintings and pencil sketches, and one glass cabinet held Dana's wire, pottery, and stone sculptures from her weekend sculpting classes—adding a pulse of intimacy to the otherwise minimalist wabi-sabi aesthetic. In the kitchen, brass hardware gleamed against matte cream cabinetry, and the faint scent of eucalyptus hung in the air. A monument to good taste—a monument to achievement.

It was the kind of home that Old Dana once vision-boarded for her fantasy life in New York, but now that she was actually supposed to be living here, Dana couldn't appreciate it. She'd entered with her bags, glanced around, and then thrown herself on the couch, fuming.

How dare he! How dare he accuse her of only wanting him when he was successful? How could he mischaracterize—twist everything around? Like he'd not had any part to play in this?

What happened to them? *How did we get here, to this stage? What happened—to me?*

It was funny that it was only after they'd arrived in this universe that she actually asked herself these questions.

In the past year, Dana had woken up more mornings than she cared to count with the following feelings: the unbearable itch to claw her own eyes out, as if doing so might somehow erase the relentless ache that had settled behind them; the ability to focus only when she was on specific tasks; the experience of feeling overwhelmed on some days and needing to shut the world out and lie flat on the bed, utterly exhausted—was this bone-deep fatigue a result of her unending shifts? But also needing the shifts to find any reason to get out of bed.

The other things she did:

Pretending to be asleep when Bex or Gill knocked on her door, wanting to chat.

Sleeping in the car or the living room after a shift.

Snapping when she was spoken to.

Doomscrolling in her room.

Feeling like she would never speak again sometimes after a long shift where a particularly terrible accident had happened, especially if it was a result of domestic violence or abuse.

Wanting sex.

Not wanting sex.

Feeling like clawing her eyes out.

Hating. Hating her husband, who loved her. Loving her husband but . . .

Hating herself.

Clawing her eyes out.

Going to work. Feeling like she could survive if she was surrounded by structure. If she was needed.

Clawing her eyes out.

Hating work. Needing to work.

Needing to escape this feeling. Feeling like she was drowning. Dying.

Clawing her eyes out.

I was drowning, Dana thought bitterly. And he hadn't even noticed. In fact, what had he said just now? The gist of it had been: *And what about me?*

Maybe we both are at fault here for what's happening. At least they weren't pretending that all was well anymore. In some ways that was a relief. Like waking a sleeping limb—it hurt, but at least you knew it was still connected to you.

She had three days left in this world, and after that, what was next? What needed to change between them? Was change even possible anymore, or had they crossed too many fault lines to imagine anything but collapse? What did she want from the two of them? What did she want for herself?

And Nigel—what did he want? What had brought him here? Had it been some cosmic accident, or had he made the same desperate wish she had? In the wake of his stunning admission, they hadn't circled back. But it felt crucial now, especially since she had been reminded by the guardian of one crucial fact—that she had options to explore in this world and back home.

Too bad it seemed like they were back to not talking to each other. Even in this world, it felt like they were at an impasse.

Why try to fix something that is so broken? Why not just start fresh? Maybe that was the wiser choice. Relationships had expiration dates too—just because you'd poured time and effort and grief into something didn't mean it was salvageable. That was the trap, wasn't it? The sunk-cost fallacy, applied to marriage. Sometimes you needed to walk away and let the ruins remain ruins.

Maybe she and Nigel were at that stage, and she just needed to wake up and smell the expiration date on their marriage. Or maybe . . .

Hey, Yomi texted. If this isn't Dr. Dana S, I'm sorry! I got this number from Pia, her PA.

She exhaled sharply and rubbed the heel of her palm tiredly against her face. She had more questions than ever, even without the added complication of Yomi.

Meeting Nigel on the same night as Yomi meant Yomi never got the fair shake at spending time with her that circumstances would normally have called for, and now she wondered if she had acted too hastily. She'd always liked Yomi—obsessed over him, in truth—and now the universe had handed her a blank slate. That had to mean something, right? And Nigel had practically encouraged her to explore it, throwing out the idea like it was a favor, as if she needed *his* permission to chase her own desires.

The memory made her breath catch. Dana's anger surged in her chest and made her vision pulse as she paced her living room. *How dare he.* How dare he dismiss her, even in this world? Why didn't he ever fight for her? She dashed an angry tear from her eye, struggling to tamp down the disappointment. *Keep it together, Dana.* But it was impossible to keep a cool head in this situation—or maybe she no longer could. It felt like she'd been walking on eggshells around him, around how she felt about him, for too long. And without the scaffolding of duty, the noise of daily distraction—the ER, the kids, the admin of life—the truth had nowhere to hide.

She had nowhere to hide.

Back in the real world, she hadn't had so much time—and energy—on her hands to address her needs, to process her thoughts and feelings; most days, she got home, kissed the kids, and was out like a light before she had to get up and go again. But here and now, she had time to herself—Pia had made sure of that—so she had to face her truth. Peel it back like layers of scar tissue, exposing the rawness beneath.

So maybe it was time to take stock of what was working in her life—and what wasn't.

She could see now that her anger wasn't just about Nigel's apathy. It was about the years she'd spent contorting herself to make things work for him, for the kids. Always putting her needs last on Maslow's hierarchy. The compromises that had turned into sacrifices. The way she'd stopped asking for more because it always felt like too much.

She'd gotten quite good at muting her feelings, out of necessity, out of survival. Being an ER nurse meant high stakes every day, with almost every case that came through those doors. Sometimes the wounds were hidden; sometimes they were self-inflicted; sometimes they were collateral damage that had no rhyme or reason. You learned to tune down certain sympathetic responses, learned to manage the stimuli. Learned to tell yourself, *Don't think about it. Just do. Just get through this shift.*

Maybe some of that muting instinct spilled over to everyday life. When things in her personal life got too big for her to handle, she turned to her best self-preservation skill—closing in on herself.

Turned out her relationships with her children and her husband were probably the collateral damage of her shutting down emotionally.

But could she pivot and do something else completely new with her life?

Dana glanced around her apartment. She could see clearly the seductions of this life: the glamour of flying to a new destination every week in business, addressing big crowds that wanted to be inspired by her words. She'd enjoyed the two days she'd spent in Bali, talking about a topic she could easily relate to. There was no clinical pressure here—no life-or-death decisions, no blood, no grief. Just the comfort of drawing on her polished anecdotes, a reliable rotation of personal triumphs and carefully packaged wisdom. Her social media following doubled as a built-in consumer base, always ready to applaud, to buy, to believe. It was all so much easier, so much cleaner than facing death straight on, day after day, daring it to do its worst—no, watching it do its worst and thinking anything she did mattered.

Could she fix everything by studying, leaving her job, and pivoting to *this*?

The answer came to her almost immediately: *No.*

She had gotten into this job for a reason. A lot of it had sprung from pragmatism—her father's cultural deference to the medical community as a mixed-race immigrant from Vietnam, a product of his own deferred ambitions; her mother's undiagnosed mental health issues, which meant she had a hard time keeping a job and running a household, made getting a stable, secure job as soon as Dana was out of college a necessity. Since she was their only child and thus their only safety net, nursing had been that pathway. She'd always wanted to help people, after all, and she didn't mind the context. So she took that path. The sensible path.

But she'd been lucky—the sensible path had turned out to be the right one. Over time, she'd grown to love the work. The long hours hadn't bothered her. She rose quickly through the ranks, eventually becoming a nurse manager, and pursued additional training with the aim of one day becoming a nurse practitioner.

She hadn't thought she'd ever be overwhelmed by the very thing she loved—but she was coming to the realization that she could. That her chosen career, at least at the rate she was pursuing it given her family's financial situation, was killing her slowly.

But that didn't mean she didn't love what she did, still—she just needed to find a new way to do what she loved. It might mean re-examining working in the ER. It might mean taking fewer hours. She wasn't quite sure how she wanted to go about it yet, but change was necessary.

A mechanical beeping interrupted her thoughts: midnight. Dana was prepared. She took the Polaroid out and stared at it. Given that her photo hadn't been altered when her phone, still set on Balinese time, struck midnight, she expected her timeline would reset to New York time—and she was right.

At the end of the twelve beeps, Dana watched as her youngest daughter's smiling face vanished before her eyes.

Dana leaned her forehead against the fridge and let out a breath that rattled. She'd convinced herself that she needed a vacation from her life, but maybe the solution was not escape but a re-examination of how she was living in the real world.

And maybe part of that re-examination exercise was to consider pruning the relationships that were no longer working, like hers and Nigel's, and giving herself space to develop new ones.

Starting with Yomi.

A quick lookup of the fusion dim sum restaurant in Midtown showed that it was small and terribly chic, which immediately made Dana, who'd grown up eating in authentic Chinese restaurants, wary of the place, even though it was supposedly on several critics' lists. She hated when nonethnic folks tried to *elevate* ethnic cuisine, and if food was a window to a person's worldview, then she hoped Yomi wasn't on board with that kind of cultural appropriation. *He must have chosen Mandarin Garden because it's a nice date place and it's got a great wine list,* Dana thought reasonably.

For their first date, Nigel had brought her to the park on a spring morning like this one and they'd had sandwiches from a famous local deli. They'd planned for the date to last an hour, but it ended up becoming a lunch and dinner date. It had totally changed the trajectory of her life. Maybe this sort-of date would change the trajectory of her life now.

Dana arrived ten minutes early, not because she wanted to impress anyone, but because she'd become used to arriving in places with chaos trailing behind or before her, so she always gave herself a generous margin of time to make an appointment on time. Here, however, everything was lovely, muted, intentionally bustle-free. And of course, Yomi was already seated, chatting with the waiter about items from the seasonal menu.

He stood as she approached. "You look incredible," he said, leaning in to kiss her cheek.

"You too," she said, pleased. He was wearing a sage blazer and a linen shirt paired with deep-brown pants, and scholarly gold-rimmed glasses. A handsome, well-dressed man. Dana waited for her heart to flutter like it used to whenever she ran into him in high school, but its reaction was unusually muted. *Well, you're not a teenager,* she chastised herself. *You can't expect to be swooning at your crush like one.*

They exchanged pleasantries, joked about jet lag being a thing at their age. "I'm still a little amazed you said yes," he said. "I half expected you to brush me off with excuses or ghost me."

"Flattering impression of me," Dana said.

Yomi chuckled. "Touché. But really—thanks for coming out."

She shrugged, adjusting the napkin across her lap, her gaze drifting over the curated elegance around them. "You caught me at the right time."

"Just my luck, then."

They lapsed into an awkward silence. Dana tried not to fidget. She really was out of practice when it came to dating and "fine" dining (i.e., anything fancier than their local diner)—what was she supposed to do with her hands? What was she supposed to look at? And say? Or not say? She tried to channel the ghost of New Dana, but it was getting harder and harder to access that version of her; the longer she stayed here, the more "Old" Dana seeped through and consolidated.

Yomi leaned forward and adopted a conspiratorial tone. "Look, I know Chinese tea is de rigueur for dim sum, but how about some cheeky white wine to celebrate our running into each other after two decades? I'm a big believer in fate and all that jazz."

Dana grinned. "Sure."

Yomi ordered wine for the table. It arrived swiftly, and he dispensed it with the relaxed confidence of someone used to closing deals and tasting flights.

"So," he said, leaning back in his chair. "Tell me, what is Dana Smiley up to these days?"

Dana wondered which truth she should present. She settled for a hybrid. "Lots of traveling for my speaking engagements. Overwhelming, in a good way. I haven't had this much quiet in years. You?"

"Now that I'm a touring musician, I travel way too much for my own good. I make it a point not to play any gigs whenever I'm back in New York. I just rest."

She nodded, watching the sunlight glint off the rim of his glasses. "It's good to rest," she agreed. It was such a basic response she flinched. She tried to think of a witty rejoinder. Instead: crickets. The only thing that came to mind was the morbid *You should never wait till you're dead to rest,* but somehow she didn't think that was any better, in terms of banter.

Yomi picked up the elegant gold-printed menu. "We should order."

The menu was shockingly simple and eye-wateringly expensive for a dim sum restaurant—it also had truffle. Dana was just about to raise this as a criticism when Yomi said this was one of his favorite dim sum places.

"I love dim sum but can never find one that's quiet enough to have a date in. So this feels like an acceptable compromise, even if it isn't authentic." He flipped the menu around, then grinned. "Oh, hey, they have a truffle oil siew mai! I love when they reinvent classics, play around with flavors."

It is *a fusion restaurant,* Dana reminded herself. *Don't get it twisted.*

Yomi refilled her glass.

"You seem different," he said after a pause.

"It's been almost two decades since we last saw each other," Dana pointed out.

"Right. I mean . . . I just didn't think you'd be a motivational speaker. I always thought you'd be working closely with people."

"I meet people all the time," Dana protested.

"Yes, but, like, I thought . . . I thought you'd be a teacher or a social worker, somehow. You always cared so much about people. You weren't even doing the volunteering so you could burnish your CV. You genuinely liked helping folks. I mean—you weren't transactional and tactical about it like I was, anyway."

She looked up, startled and surprised by his admission. "What do you mean?" She thought about the many hours she and Yomi had spent with the school counselor, helping the counselor organize her sessions, triaging and giving basic mental health support to peers who were too afraid of speaking to an adult yet. She'd always thought he was the sweetest, most empathetic person, contrasting to Nigel's perceived "lack" in that regard.

Yomi laughed. "I don't know if you remember, but back then Peer Counseling was one of the easiest programs to get a spot on—nobody wanted to work with the quote-unquote crazy ones, eh?—and that's why I knew it'd look great on my CV. And you know as much as I do that when you're angling for a spot at the best schools, you've got to stand out. I wanted to be seen as an all-rounder—and it worked."

"But . . . but you were so *involved*," Dana said, confused. "You even got promoted to student coordinator."

Yomi chuckled. "Exactly—which meant I didn't *need* to actually get my hands dirty"—he made air quotes around the word *dirty*—"and listen, I just managed the pool of peer counselors and the training thereof. Management stuff."

The casual cynicism behind why he did it surprised her, but then she supposed she hadn't known him before, not really. Not the way she knew her husband, who she'd seen through the good and the bad, naked of artifice. Except somewhere along the line, she had stopped seeing the good and started focusing on the bad.

The truism went *people changed*, but Dana didn't really believe that—it was more likely the case that our understanding of them changed. Or their understanding of themselves. Because at their core, people were who they had always been—just wearing new layers, shaped by time, circumstance, and regret.

Which meant that Yomi Owope must have always been more performative and superficial than she had given him credit for—she just hadn't seen it until now.

The food came and they continued to make small talk. Yomi was attentive and, for the most part, asked all the right questions, gave her the right responses. Dana tried to reset, to give the date her all. *This is Yomi Owope,* she reminded herself. Her mythical One That Got Away. She would fantasize about Yomi when things between her and Nigel weren't going well. *Yomi would never say this. Yomi would never do that.* She often wondered what would have happened if she'd said yes when he asked her to senior prom, instead of freaking out and rejecting him point-blank, thinking it was just a prank, because why would one of the most desirable boys in her school be interested in her?

Dana was beginning to discern a pattern here—of avoidance.

The lunch was winding down. Dessert came—fancy little salted egg yolk lava buns brushed with edible gold foil. He was gazing intently into her eyes. "I can't tell you how much I've thought about you over the years," he confessed. "Especially when you started appearing all over my socials with your book. Imagine—beauty and brains."

It should have made her glow, hearing him speak so highly of her, especially when she had always thought so highly of him. And maybe once upon a time, in another life, it would have. She had no doubt that a compliment from him in her youth would've had her floating for days. But now she just felt a gentle melancholy. Like rereading a poem written by an old flame to a version of you that they never knew.

He reached across the table, brushing a nonexistent crumb from her arm. The gesture was intimate, familiar, but instead of the thrill she should have felt at the slow drift of his finger against her bare skin, Dana felt nothing. Only a humming awareness that the intimacy of this gesture came from the wrong man.

"You ever wonder?" he asked, his voice dipping low. "What might've happened if we'd actually gone for it?"

She picked up her wine, cradling the glass between her palms. "I used to wonder," she said finally. "A lot."

"And now?"

Now. She thought of Nigel. Somewhere out there in this same warped, temporary world. Probably charming someone, cracking a joke that shouldn't have been that funny if it had come from anyone else but him, who she thought she'd stopped loving because he'd become a stranger to her.

He hadn't become a stranger to her—it wasn't as one-sided as that. She was at fault as much as he was. Somewhere, somehow, they'd stopped listening and communicating well with each other, and now the words had piled up between them like snowdrifts until they could no longer see each other in the storm.

Yomi was waiting for an answer. His "in." Dana decided to spare him her indecision. "I think you're great, but—I just got out of a relationship and . . . and I think I'm still not over it."

There was a sharp silence—Yomi clearly hadn't expected that answer. "Right," he said. "That's understandable. You need more time."

No, I don't need more time, Dana realized. *I needed some home truths pointed out to me.*

The coffee arrived—an impeccable flat white with foam art. Great, but totally wrong for a dim sum place.

An irrational urge to giggle bubbled up. She clamped her hand over her mouth to hide her mirth: *Yomi brought me to a fake dim sum place to have Western food.*

"Is everything OK?" Yomi asked a little stiffly.

"Not really, but I think it's going to be," Dana said, finally getting hold of herself. They weren't at the stage where she could share her truth with him, and it didn't look like they would ever be.

Dana picked at her dessert, feeling suddenly full. This Yomi had it all: He was stable, successful, attentive. He was Nigel before they met, before an unlived life together with Dana. Of course she was attracted to him—he was physical manifestation of her need to escape. Wasn't this the whole point of her wish?

But she was beginning to understand that a hard reset wasn't the answer to her problems either.

She thought about Nigel and the snowdrifts of unsaid words between them. *I guess I'm going to have to shovel my way through them and start finding out what I want from us.*

—~—

After she and Yomi parted, she made a decision: She'd somehow summon the psychopomp and go home to her family. The break had been an interesting experiment while it lasted, but she needed to go home. She booked herself a spa day at the fanciest place she could get an appointment at the last minute. A facial, a body scrub, and a two-hour body massage. Bliss.

At least she'd managed to have her spa day, Dana thought. This week had not, for the most part, felt like a vacation at all. She missed her kids. And she missed her life. Maybe what she needed wasn't less of her real life—what she needed was *more* of it: more of the parts that mattered and, certainly, more of herself in it.

Now the question was: Was she sure she wanted more of *Nigel* in her brand-new life?

Nigel

Day Four

Nigel wished he could say he'd spent his fourth day in this strange, parallel version of his life doing something meaningful—sorting through his thoughts, taking stock, building clarity in the wake of the merging of these two worlds, especially since he still wasn't sure how he got here in this strange timeline. Instead, he'd drifted through it, jet-lagged and hollow. After parting ways with Dana, he had collapsed into bed and slept far too long, waking up near noon with a gnawing hunger and an even deeper sense of dislocation.

He decided to fall back on his perennial anchor—work.

He wasn't even supposed to be in the office. This week was meant to be downtime: catch up with old friends, binge a show or two, enjoy being back in New York in the apartment he'd leased out to a friend for the past three years while he was seconded to Singapore. Instead, here he was, striding into the Black & Hansen HQ like a damn champ—or maybe just a chump.

"Aren't you supposed to be off this week, post the Asia-Pac retreat?" Li Fern asked, raising an eyebrow.

"Rest is for the weak," he quipped automatically. "I'm an addict, what can I say."

Almost as though his current life could sense that it was losing primacy as old memories resurfaced, as tangible as the concrete under his footsteps, New Nigel's thoughts made themselves known:

You have freedom here. You were ambitious once, but you shelved those plans when Dana got pregnant. Here—

His phone buzzed, interrupting his thoughts. More missed calls and emails from his partner, Stuart Morton; emails from his clients, from regional and national powerhouses to up-and-coming businesses who were used to liaising with Nigel directly instead of his subordinate directors—each person sounding panicked because they couldn't reach Nigel on his cell. *Where's Nigel? When will he be back? Have we locked in the brand narrative we want to push for the fall campaign for Avery's Hardware? Do Stuart and Nigel think we should spend X amount on traditional media buys, as opposed to digital marketing? Are we aligned with the client's direction for visuals on the subway posters or should we propose alternatives from our internal team?* Even when his PA Clarissa had been firm—*Nigel's on a corporate retreat and personal leave!*—and he'd turned on that cheerful out-of-office message, they still clamored for him. And in this world, AI hadn't been mainstreamed the way it had been in Old Nigel's world, thus it hadn't brought the industry to its knees—yet. His expertise, his skills were still relevant here, were still needed here.

Here, Nigel shaped worlds.

He holed up in the coworking suite, powering through the backlog of emails he'd neglected. The motions were familiar, but the purpose felt weightless, untethered.

You're thinking about her, huh? his Inner Bart chimed in.

Nigel gave a dry, hollow laugh. *It's that obvious?*

Buddy, it's written all over you. Just go talk to her.

I can't.

You can't, or you won't?

Nigel tried to shut Inner Bart up, but even with work, he felt unmoored. In this world, he had so much of what he'd missed in his other life, but none of it seemed to matter right now.

He felt completely lost and he missed Dana.

He went to the gym to lose himself in motion, to outrun the ache he couldn't name. Hard, fast, reckless. New Nigel ran an annual half-marathon and competed in Spartan races; the body knew what to do, even if the mind was spinning.

How did I get here? What did I wish for?

The question clanged in his head like a bell. *Tell me,* he begged the unseen forces he felt around him. *Help me understand.*

As his feet pounded the belt, rhythm steady, breath ragged, something shifted. A flicker in his peripheral vision—then, just as suddenly, a clarity. In his mind's eye, he saw the girl—the psychopomp, Nigel corrected himself—again. Not just her face, but the moment: the stillness outside time, the broken shards of glass from his side mirror, her ancient eyes, her voice like a chime in fog.

Would you like a week to live as if you'd never married your wife? she had asked.

And he—numb, bitter, maybe even curious—had said *yes.*

And what's more, she'd said, *you may remain in this world if you choose to.*

Unlike Dana, he could stay if he wanted to.

Now that the memories had returned—like fog lifting suddenly to reveal an entirely different landscape—new questions circled, low and persistent:

Why did he make that wish? Did he really think they were over?

He kept running.

No, he decided. *I didn't think we were over.* He was just done with being unseen by her. He was her husband, true, but she'd stopped seeing him as her partner somewhere along the way.

He ducked his head and ran ever harder, pounding the treadmill as though he could outrun his thoughts.

How easy it would be to blame her, to make this whole mess her fault. He'd always been a good husband to her—barring the one slipup with Selvi—hadn't he? Supported her through thick and thin. Yet, after he'd lost his job, she'd not returned the favor. She'd not been there for him. But sitting with the truth, he could feel how incomplete that answer was.

It wasn't just about her. She hadn't been the only one who stopped seeing him: He had stopped seeing himself. His career had been such an important component of his identity, his joy. Nigel, the Adman. Nigel, the man who shaped corporate identities, who made you dream. Yet he'd stopped dreaming when he stopped working. He'd closed down upon himself after losing his job. Made himself appear as small as he felt inside.

He'd made the wish because he missed the version of himself who had purpose, conviction, a sense of direction. Even clarity. And beneath all the anger, beneath the dull ache of disconnection, he still wanted to matter—not just to her, but to himself. He wanted to dream again.

And he wanted a partner who dreamed with him. Like Dana used to, back when they were each other's partner in life.

He slowed down on the treadmill. He wasn't sure if it was just sweat running down his face.

I want us to be like we were again, Nigel thought. *I want to get back to that.* And maybe the first step was communicating with her openly and vulnerably.

He texted her then. Hey Dana. I finally remember everything now—how I got here, what I wished for—and everything that happened between us in the other world. I'm sorry for my part in this, truly.

It took every ounce of courage he had to send that text, to put himself out there. To prevent himself from spiraling, he started on the treadmill again, a slower, more sustainable jog. For the next hour, he kept checking his phone every time it pinged, hoping it was his wife—but it was never her.

He was nearing the tail end of his hour jogging on that treadmill when a text landed. Dana, finally.

> Thanks for your text. I've also been doing some thinking about how we got here and I know some of it is my fault too. It takes two hands to clap and all that

A knot inside him loosened. It felt good to hear her acknowledge her part in this.

I'm going back, she said. I don't know if I can cut short my time here, but I thought I should let you know. Do you want to come back with me?

Did he?

He tried to imagine himself living in the perfect world the guardian clearly thought it had plunked him in, where he would be in the right place, with the right job, with the right toys, and friends and women.

And even then, she was winning. Dana and his perfectly imperfect, floppy-haired children.

Yes, he thought. *Yes, I do.*

—~—

She gave him the location of the Solomon's Porch Medical Center, a large public hospital in the Bronx, and told him to meet her there. SPMC was New Dana's former place of work before she took a sabbatical to be a motivational speaker—Dana theorized that since the beings had mentioned that they were there to help people transition, there was no better place to lure them out than a public hospital.

Dana walked in first, Nigel following a few steps behind. They entered through a side entrance, slipping past the main lobby, and made their way to an empty procedure room that Dana remembered from her New Dana memories.

Inside, the lights flickered faintly. The room smelled of antiseptic and something older, almost sweet and metallic. Old sweat, maybe, or the end of hope.

They sat side by side on a cot, their bodies almost touching, and waited. Nigel could hear the susurrus of low whispers threading through the hum of the central air-conditioning around them.

"Did . . . did you hear something?"

Dana leaned closer and whispered, "This room is famous for being haunted. That's why it's unused."

Nigel yelped and Dana chuckled. "I'm kidding."

Nigel drew his knees close to his chest. "I'm enjoying this thaw in our relations. What do we do now?"

Dana closed her eyes. "We made the wish to try a new life with intention. Maybe we need to unmake it the same way."

She exhaled deeply, then whispered, "Nigel and I . . . we want to go back. We've seen enough. Please. We want our real lives back."

Nothing happened.

"I want to go back, please!" Nigel echoed.

"Wait," Dana said. She went to the supply cabinet and picked out two packaged single-use blades.

She held them out to Nigel. "I remember that she said she needed blood to seal the pact and open the portal. So let's try to lure them out with blood."

"O . . . K," Nigel said, his stomach knotting at the idea of being cut. He was always the squeamish one in the relationship. "I, uh, I don't think—"

"It's OK, I've got you," Dana assured him, and this alone calmed Nigel. "I'll do it for the both of us."

"I need to sit down." He sat back down on the cot, as did Dana.

He turned away and let Dana nick his palm, wincing when the blade cut through skin. Then she took another blade and did the same to her own. "Please," she intoned. "Please send us back."

For a couple of beats, nothing happened. Nigel deflated. Maybe the guardians needed a more elaborate ceremony, maybe—

The lights snapped off with an audible *tak*! A hush fell, so thick it muffled even their breathing. Then, a flicker at the edge of the room—lightless but pulsing. The air dropped ten degrees.

She was back—the old woman that wasn't a woman. The guardian. This time, the guardian was dressed in all-white, floor-length robes, its lidless eyes two shining gold pits. "Hello, Dana and Nigel."

"Thank God," Dana breathed.

It lifted an eyebrow and its lips curled. "God? That's generous."

When the being spoke, it did not speak aloud. Its voice arrived directly inside him, and Dana seemed to hear it as well.

"I know we have three days left, but we want to go back, please," Dana said.

The guardian cocked its head. "What do you mean, go back? You sealed the portal back to your world yesterday."

Dana let out a surprised huff of laughter and said, "Wh-what do you mean? I asked for a week's break, not a permanent transfer to another world. We were supposed to be able to return at the end of the week."

"Yeah, that's what you—your colleague promised me as well," Nigel said.

"We never guaranteed you a return." The guardian's eyes were coolly assessing. "Your actions can affect the world you're in, Dana, I told you that."

Dana jumped to her feet, fists clenched. "But we never said we wanted to stay in this world!" she cried.

The guardian shook its head. "Consent, my child, can be implicit in your actions. By kissing Nigel, you closed that portal. You accepted the new world you're in."

"Wait, what? How is that even a logical conclusion just from a kiss?" Nigel demanded, also jumping to his feet. "It was just one kiss."

"I beg to differ, Nigel," the guardian continued, its voice flat and emotionless. Nigel's skin crawled, wondering if it could search his memories and see his almost-kiss with Selvi. It was right: A kiss wasn't just a kiss. "Everything the both of you have done since you got here is to seek each other out, even though you had ample opportunity to explore lives without each other. Your wish, Nigel, was to experience life as though you'd never met Dana—yet you chose to pursue Dana once you regained your memories—and by doing so, you altered the parameters of the wish world. Dana, you wanted a marriage vacation, but you still chose to remind Nigel of your old life together and even rejected a past suitor that was eminently suited to you. You weren't acting to uncover the truths that brought you here."

Dana made an anguished noise. "But that doesn't mean we want to *stay* here. You should have told us that was the worst possible outcome if we kissed."

"And let it influence your decisions and actions?" the guardian said, shaking its head. "Then what would be the point of this exercise?"

Nigel sat down heavily on the cot. He was still reeling from the gut-punch of this reveal.

"You both wanted an escape, now here it is. This is it. The portal is closed. You can have each other, here, for the rest of the week."

"Rest of the week?" Dana echoed. "Wh-what happens at the end of the week?"

"The parameters of Dana's wish were that there'd be no lasting consequences in her world. In order to keep within the parameters of both your wishes, with the altered circumstances of you both remaining in this timeline, then at the end of the seventh day, your old timeline will fold into this one. Your children, your memories, the world you left behind, all will become dust. And you, Dana, will cease to exist, while you, Nigel, will continue as though you've never met her."

"No," Nigel whispered. "That's . . . that's absurd. That's cruel!"

"It is the cost of your wish," the guardian responded.

"But we didn't know. We thought—you said . . . you said that my actions in this world would have zero lasting consequences . . ." Dana's voice dropped to an agonized whisper.

"That is a matter of *our* interpretation," the guardian said.

"But how can that be? If my world disappears . . . isn't that . . . isn't that a lasting consequence?"

"But if your world ceases to exist, and you're gone, you wouldn't be around to experience it, would you?" the guardian pointed out calmly.

Nigel and Dana exchanged horrified glances.

"Please, *please*, is there any way out of this . . . this shit show? What can we do to return to our worlds?" Dana begged, her body visibly trembling with desperation.

The guardian considered her. "If you wish to return, it must be earned. And as always, there's a cost."

"How?" Nigel asked, standing up excitably. "We'll do anything."

"Through choice. Through relinquishment. Through knowing what matters and what must be left behind. Your way home cannot happen without a cost. To open a portal, to create a passage back to your timeline, there must be sacrifice."

"Please, no more riddles. What kind of sacrifice is needed?" Dana demanded.

The guardian was impassive. "There is a way to return to the original timeline, but it means fulfilling your original wishes as is."

Nigel's stomach twisted as the importance of what the guardian was inferring hit home. "Meaning?"

"Meaning, your wishes taken together led to this specific parallel universe, so if you want to return, we need to close out those wishes."

"Close out—how?" Dana asked.

"Let me explain." The guardian pointed at Nigel. "Nigel, you wanted to know a world as though you'd never met your wife." The guardian turned to Dana. "And your wish, Dana, was that the time spent in this timeline would have no lasting consequences to your life. That means, taken together, Nigel has to remain here while the original Nigel—or rather his body—dies in the car crash."

"What crash?" Dana whispered, her lips pale.

"Nigel crashed his car on the way back from Selvi's. And that's when the wish happened."

Nigel sat down on the cot heavily, too stunned to speak further.

"I warned you—there will always be consequences to a wish of such magnitude. And Nigel, you will have to stay away from her from now on, so that you can live in this world. Respecting the parameters of your original wish."

"You tricked us!" Dana shouted.

The guardian turned to her with a cool, unblinking stare. "As I said before, we are guardians of the balance. We are neutral beings whose sole purpose is to help humans transition from one plane to another. My colleague was younger and more capricious in trying to put you both in the same timeline, but we do not meddle, and we have no agenda. This situation is entirely of your doing, Dana and Nigel. My colleagues and I will see you on the seventh day, at the stroke of midnight, to collect you to where you need to go."

And with that, she faded away.

Nigel put his head in his hands. He couldn't bring himself to look at Dana. "You made a wish to erase me?" he choked out. How could she be so cruel as to wipe him out of the life they'd built? To take him away from his kids.

"I didn't . . . It wasn't . . . Those beings twisted everything."

"Or maybe they gave you exactly what you secretly wanted," Nigel said bitterly. He dropped his hands and gazed at her. "You wanted me gone, after all."

"What about you?" Dana cried, whirling around to face him. "You're the one who wanted to know a world where I'd never met you. You wanted to be unburdened. You wanted freedom. Well, guess what—you got it. You'll have everything you want in this world. All the fucking career and women you want, Nigel, and none of the burden of family life—how about that? Whereas I . . . I'll have to deal with all the fallout—the consequences in the real world. Whereas you'll have it easy—you won't remember us."

"What? I would want to remember you, you and the kids!" Nigel shot back. He stood up, adrenaline coursing through his veins. "Christ, Dana, what kind of heartless bastard do you think I am? Did you think I'm in a better position just because I'll forget my family—you, the love of my life—existed? What kind of monster are you?"

They stood inches apart, fury electrifying the space between them. The horrible words they had thrown at each other reverberated in Nigel's mind. He felt physically sick. This was the worst it had ever been between them, and Nigel couldn't see how they could come back from this.

It was Dana who spoke first.

"Shit, I'm sorry, how could I say something like that?" Dana put her face in her hands and rocked back and forth on her legs. "Why the hell did I make that goddamn wish?"

They were quiet for a while before Nigel finally spoke up. "Because we needed help. And neither of us were giving it to each other. We'd checked out, Dana. That's the truth."

She wiped the tears from her swollen eyes. "Why didn't you tell me you were drowning?" she mumbled.

"Why didn't you notice?" he shot back. "Wasn't it obvious? Oh wait." His voice laced with irony. "Was it because in spite of all I did to run the household while debasing myself to look for piecemeal work on gig platforms—yes, Dana, I did do stupid copywriting work, if you'd actually asked me, did you think all the gas money and the kids' extracurricular activities were paid out of our joint account?—you came home radiating *fuck off, leave me alone* vibes. How could I be honest with you?"

Dana's voice was equally sarcastic. "Oh, poor you. I'm *sorry* I wasn't emotionally available, Nigel. Maybe because I was handling all our shit. Maybe because I had to keep us afloat, Nigel. I had to be the responsible one."

"Oh, spare me the martyrdom. You think I like feeling like deadweight you had to carry?"

Dana's voice trembled. "I think you gave up before I did."

Nigel stood up abruptly—he couldn't be in the same room as her anymore. Dana stood up as well, holding both hands up in supplication. "Nigel—please. I'm sorry."

"Don't worry, Dana," Nigel said. "You're going to get your wish. I'm leaving."

Dana

Day Five

Deep breaths, Dana. Deep breaths.

Long after her son vanished from the Polaroid at the stroke of midnight and Nigel had left her to make her solitary way home to her apartment, her heart was still racing out of her chest, adrenaline making her fingers twitch as she paced the living room, turning over the events in the hospital. Trying to find some piece of information she could use to get them out of the mess they had created, whether or not Nigel was ever speaking to her again.

Nigel. At the thought of her husband, a vise tightened around her chest, squeezing the breath from her lungs. The idea of losing him made her head spin. She kept replaying their last moments together, wishing she'd managed to explain the truth behind her wish. That she never meant to undo him, to undo them.

Focus. It took all her medical training and experience to stop herself from spiraling. The only way to stop her entire world from crashing down was to literally set her mind on finding a solution. Everything else could wait.

I need a game plan.

But her body had other plans. Fatigue pulsed behind her eyes, thick and insistent. She hadn't slept properly in days—jet lag still lingered, but worse than that, the existential weight of realizing that this alternate reality wasn't a detour. It might be permanent. A trap disguised as a second chance. And that her return to her real life meant Old Nigel—the Real Nigel—would die.

I'll get some shut-eye, she told herself. *Clarity will come with rest. Then I can strategize.*

She set her phone alarm for 6:45 a.m.—early enough to not lose the day—and collapsed into bed without changing out of her clothes or brushing her teeth. She fell quickly into dreamless sleep, then into dreams that twisted back on themselves: staircases that ended in the sky, trains running backward, a man with Nigel's voice but not his face calling to her through fog.

When the alarm rang, it pierced her skull like a spike. She sat up slowly, heart hammering, mouth dry, her thoughts immediately racing again. She dressed on autopilot, her limbs stiff.

There has to be a way back. For both of us. Or a way to break the wish. To beat the ones who did this to us.

But what did that even mean? Beat them how? The guardians had been cryptic, but not cruel. They'd said they weren't in control of what happened—and that they had no agenda. They were, it seemed, chaotic neutral beings. *So what are you trying to fight, Dana?*

She didn't know. But she needed something to work with. Some scrap of explanation. Some key to a door she didn't understand how to open.

She made a double shot of espresso, grabbed a breakfast bar from the pantry, and powered up her laptop at the small desk in the corner of her living room. The screen glowed too brightly in the early-morning dimness. She opened twelve tabs in under a minute. Searched everything from Reddit to obscure academic blogs, Google Translate, and AI trawlers, using the clues they had given her and Nigel. *Guardians of the balance,* they'd called themselves. No names. No origin. No clear cosmology. She kept skimming through resource after resource. Both Western and Eastern systems had examples of psychopomps and other vague analogs—tutelary spirits, devas, shadow judges—but nothing felt *right.* And some of the blogs clearly stank of conspiracy theories that sounded even more far-fetched—talking about government experiments, aliens, and the like. Her desktop search yielded nothing useful, just tons of unverified, unreviewed "experts" that made her yearn for trustworthy sources. Actual books. Peer-reviewed journals. Microfiche—well, not that she'd ever used a reader, but she could start now.

So she went to the New York Public Library and installed herself in the main reading room. She was only half present as her brain jumped from thought to thought. She pulled books off the shelves—witchcraft, ancient religions, spiritual mechanics—and scanned pages, searching for books related to psychopomps, until the words lost meaning.

Her notes became a tangled mess of keywords, barely legible diagrams, and dead ends.

By 5 p.m., she was spent. Her temples throbbed and her stomach was sour with hunger and thirst. And she had exactly nothing to show for it. There was nothing in her frantic research that gave her any clue about these beings—presumably because people only saw them when they were on the cusp of death or other equally transitional phases. So she went back to her apartment and did the only thing that made sense.

She called Pia.

Pia answered after two rings, her voice as comforting as a warm cup of cocoa. "Dana! Finally. I was starting to think you were ghosting *me*. All my emails and messages and not even a single emoji in response."

Dana leaned her forehead against the cool glass of her bedroom window. "I'm sorry," she murmured, her voice cracking. "I'm going through something."

There was a brief pause. "Where are you?"

"At home." She hesitated, then added, "Falling apart."

"You sound like you're about to crawl into the earth."

"Feels about right."

"You want me to come over?"

Dana hesitated. There was a part of her—always—that defaulted to no. To solitude. But that old coping mechanism had frayed lately, and right now it felt like holding her breath underwater.

"Yeah," she whispered. "Please."

By seven, Pia was at her door. She swept in like she belonged there, looked around at the clutter of notes from all of Dana's frantic scribbling at the library, and energy drinks, and crumpled clothes, and made a sound in her throat.

"What is this? Apocalyptic mood board?"

Dana didn't laugh. She didn't have the energy.

"OK," Pia said. "Don't explain. Let me guess—a guy?"

Dana let out a noise between a cry and a sob.

"Oh boy," Pia said. "And why didn't you call me sooner?"

Dana pressed her lips before the truth tumbled out. *How about I don't feel comfortable because you're not the real Pia—or at least not* my *Pia?*

Pia put her hands on her hips, closed her eyes as though overwhelmed by her thoughts on the subject, and then clapped twice. "I know what will cheer you up. Thai food, a shower, and then we get our girl back."

Dana opened her mouth. Closed it again. Pia had always known how to bypass her defenses—never pushing too hard, just showing up with presence and action. It was more grounding than any magic ritual.

They ordered Thai food. While they waited, Pia dragged Dana into the bathroom and pointed at the shower. "Get in."

The hot water seared her skin and loosened something clenched behind her rib cage. She stood under the stream, eyes closed, wondering how she'd ended up here—not just in this world, but in this state. Unmoored. Uncertain. And deeply, deeply lonely and hungry for real connection.

They ate cross-legged on the bed, the smell of lemongrass and fish sauce thick and comforting in the room. Dana's stomach rumbled for the first time in two days. Pia passed her a plate of pad see ew, and Dana scarfed the noodles down without hesitation.

"So," Pia said through a mouthful of noodles, "want to tell me why you look like you've been living in a bunker?"

Dana put down the plate. "It's this guy I'm sort of seeing."

"Ah. The guy from Bali?"

Dana nodded.

"What happened?"

"We fought. It got ugly."

Pia nodded, not surprised. "And now?"

"I don't know. He's gone. Again. And I'm here trying to . . . I don't know. Fix something that might not be fixable."

Pia raised an eyebrow. "You always do this."

Dana sighed. "What?"

"Run. The moment things get uncomfortable, you go full avoidance mode. You dig into projects, drown yourself with work. Retreat. You shut people out before they can leave you."

Dana flinched. There was nothing to say, not really, because every word, every sentence hung with the quiet weight of truth. Turned out New Dana wasn't much different from Old Dana, after all.

"That's not fair," she whispered, even though she believed otherwise.

"Isn't it?" Pia didn't sound accusing—just matter-of-fact. "Am I off by much?"

Dana said nothing.

"Look, I'm sure this guy probably comes with his own baggage—who doesn't, at this age? But if you still care—if you still want anything to do with him—you're going to have to stop retreating every time it hurts."

Dana stared at her, throat tight. Pia didn't know the half of it. Didn't know about the wish. The displacement. The literal dimensional rupture.

But maybe she didn't need to.

They finished eating in silence. Later, Pia threw on a rerun of a Japanese reality show, *Terrace House*, which she swore was the best cure for nerves. "Nothing and everything happens in a glance," she said.

"And the people on the show don't rush about trying to find resolution. They just sit in uncomfortable situations and let them unfold. Then they react, when they need to." She slid a glance at Dana. "I thought the lessons in them might be applicable."

Dana half watched, half sat in silence, thinking. Thinking about everything that was unfinished between Nigel and her. How maybe escape wasn't the point. Maybe sitting in the situation was. Sitting and learning.

Dana started to cry. Pia reached over, pulled her close, and gave her forehead a kiss. "You'll find your way out, Dana. Just promise me something?"

Dana nodded.

"Don't walk away from this—not until you know you truly have to. Don't shut him out by reflex."

"I won't," Dana whispered. "I promise."

—∾—

That night, she lay awake, fighting the old toss-and-turn, alternately staring at the ceiling of her room, her thoughts ricocheting without hope of resolution.

She and Nigel had two full days left in this horrible nightmare of a world. *How do you want this to work out?*

She pulled out her notebook, the one she'd brought to the New York Public Library, filled with random factoids and musings gleaned from her frantic research. In the margins of one page, she'd scribbled something in near-illegible handwriting: *Balance isn't about peace. It's about tension.*

She stared at the sentence for a long time. She didn't remember writing it, even though it was clearly in her handwriting. Either way, it held weight, resonating within her in a way few words had in a long time.

Maybe she and Nigel were part of the balance—not in opposition, but in flux. A dynamic system. Not something to fix or erase.

She pulled out her phone, stared at Nigel's name, and called.

No luck—she hit his voice mail. *You've reached Nigel,* the message began and continued for another minute.

No, I haven't.

She left a voice note on his messaging app, hoping the sincerity in her voice would convince him to call her back.

"Nigel, I don't know what I'm doing anymore. Our situation . . . I've been trying to fix this like it's a puzzle, to find a way to unjinx ourselves, to avoid one of our erasures. But maybe it's not . . . maybe I've been looking at this wrong. Maybe what we're living is a story. One we can still write together . . . that is, if you still want to."

She hung up. The silence that followed rang with brutal finality.

And then—

A message.

Nigel

Day Five

Nigel sat in the darkness of his apartment, nursing his glass of thirty-year-old single-malt whiskey that he'd been saving for a special occasion—there was no point to that now!—wondering how things had gotten to this stage.

The vicious things he'd said to Dana, that she'd said to him, lingered in his mind, replaying like a broken record.

He took a sip of the whiskey and felt the warmth as it went down. To most people, he must live an enviable life: enough disposable income where he could drink thirty-year-old whiskey in an apartment like his. This was proper *Architectural Digest* stuff, this midcentury two-bedroom apartment in West Chelsea with its exposed ceiling beams, reclaimed hardwood oak floors, Carrera marble countertops, and custom black steel and pebbled glass room separators. Nothing to sniff at. And he was in the position to scale greater heights: In little more than a month, he'd officially start as CMO of Black & Hansen. The emails in his inbox from his New York PA were already blowing up, lining up New Nigel's schedule for the next two weeks.

This is all yours now.

His hands trembled as he reached for the bottle of whiskey on the table. In two days, he'd forget his family, but he would have everything he'd ever wanted, career-wise.

It felt like death.

He could have stayed there on his couch. It would have been cathartic to wallow in the self-pity for a bit. But then sometime after the third shot, he put the whiskey glass down with a resolute thud on the coffee table and stood up.

No, if this is the end of the road for my other life, then I can't just give up and wait for the end.

I need to be with my wife and celebrate our life together, not feel sorry for myself.

He was a fighter—that's what drew Dana to him in the first place.

He replayed the months over which he and Dana fell in love, beginning with the fall that had nearly ended his life. He'd been hiking through the Patapsco Valley State Park with his college buddy, Clem, and some of Clem's friends, feeling like he was invincible—he'd just been promoted at his New York ad agency to account manager and he was in Baltimore celebrating Clem's engagement—and he remembered slipping from the cool overhang he'd been foolishly scaling without safety gear to impress his buddies ("I've rock climbed before, twice, I know what I'm doing!" when Clem cautioned him), the sharp, gut-wrenching sensation of free fall, and the sickening crunch as he slammed onto the rocky ground below.

The pain was unlike anything he'd ever felt. When the ambulance rushed him to the ER, he could barely stay conscious. Dana was the first nurse assigned to him, her calm, steady voice cutting through his haze of panic as she worked alongside the ER doctor to stabilize him. He'd begged her to hold his hand and she'd done that, as the doctor assessed his injuries—multiple rib fractures and a suspected abdominal bleed—and prepared him for the CT scan that would confirm the internal damage.

"I'm right here, Nigel," she'd said as they wheeled him toward imaging, her hand firm on his shoulder. Even through the fog of pain, he'd been comforted by her touch and drawn by her voice.

After surgery, Nigel spent nine days in recovery. Dana wasn't his assigned resident nurse—she was on rotation in trauma—but she came around to check on him anyway. She'd appear in his room during her rounds, wearing her no-nonsense demeanor like armor, but the fact that she was there when she didn't need to be, the fact that she stayed and chatted and was interested in his care, made Nigel think he stood a chance.

The rest was history. A lot of it happened long distance. They went from flirty banter over late-night pizza to realizing they fit together in all the ways that mattered. A few months later, Dana was pregnant. And just like that, Nigel left his life in New York behind and moved to Baltimore, because that's what you do when someone like her walks into your hospital room and changes your life.

I'm a fighter.

Then fight for her, a little voice responded.

Had he truly fought for her—for them—lately? Had he even fought for *himself*?

It was always easier to assign blame elsewhere, to point at circumstances or choices that weren't his. *She started it, she withdrew first.* A convenient out. The truth was harder to swallow: There had been a lack. His lack. He'd been drifting for a while now, a passive participant in his own life. Becoming a willing addict to life's easy distractions—reality shows, social media, computer games. Yes, he'd managed the logistics—kept the household running, handled the schedules, played the part of a doting father—but he'd avoided the real work. Of confronting his own depression. Of not checking in with himself, and with his wife. Of neglecting to tend to the uncomfortable work of growth, of vulnerability, of mending a relationship before it cracked. Of showing up, fully, when and where it mattered most.

Boo-hoo—life's hard—and here he was, choosing to believe in the inevitability of his failure.

He should be fighting for every single goddamn second with her, now. Eke out whatever goodness was left of their allotted time together.

He'd read this factoid somewhere, that for an average millennial to exist today, they were the product of approximately forty generations, which equates to millions of ancestors, and the very fact of their existence hinged on billions of decisions, coincidences, and improbable events, compounded over time. That the odds of their existence were virtually zero—yet here they were.

Decisions and luck, essentially. You couldn't influence luck, fate, or whatchamacallit, but you certainly had control over your decisions in life. So why shouldn't you?

Why aren't you doing all you can to be with her, Nigel Bradshaw-Cheng?

Because what a life they'd had—what a life they'd *made*—together.

He relived their memories as though he walked in them, real life—they were high contrast and lived in, instead of muted, faded, back when he first got them. His daughter Emmie, her tiny, grease-smeared hand slipping into his as she toddled beside him at the park, a duck-hunting, Moped-chasing duo. The way she chuckled when he made faces at her; the way she made him feel when she giggled. Gill, his brave, wonderful boy, turning to him after a recent game of *Fyodor's Quest: Annihilation of the Damned* and proclaiming him "almost as good as any sixth grader" he knew; Gill, who could shuffle-step like a pro. And Bex, who loved the soft rock music from two decades earlier because that's what Dana loved listening to when Bex was growing up, singing Semisonic's "Closing Time" with gusto as she riffed on her electric guitar; his eldest, who tenderheartedly watched all the classic nineties and early-aughts rom-coms and cried through all the grand gestures.

And not just the memories—the feelings were back too, submerging him like a flash flood after a desert storm. The overwhelming love, fierce and raw, gripped him so tightly it stole his breath. They—she and the kids—deserved all of his fight; they deserved all of him. Whether he made it back or not. *Even if* he never made it back.

But what if you did? Then he would have to work on being better to himself, his kids, and to their mother in tangible ways. Because how could he claim to cherish them if he didn't cherish himself?

Two days. That was all he had left to make this right. He didn't know what redemption looked like, but he knew he had to try. She deserved that. A proper farewell. A moment that honored the best of what they'd been. And she deserved him at his best.

Yes.

Where are you? I can come to your place—or if you'd rather, come here.

His fingers hovered over the keypad, hesitant. The words weren't grand, but they were real. When he hit send, it felt less like asking a question and more like tossing a lifeline into the dark, hoping it would reach her. This time, he would show up. This time, he would get it right.

Dana

Day Five/Six

Dana hopped into a cab the moment she got his text. As it crawled uptown, she stared blankly out the window, the gritty chaos of Rivington Street slowly dissolving into the curated sleekness of West Chelsea, where new glass towers fractured the skyline. Echoes of their last fight reverberated in her mind, each block bringing her closer not just to him, but to whatever truth lay beneath the wreckage. Hope and dread wrestled for control—what remains when all the artifice that binds a relationship has been stripped away?

She was just about to knock—her hands were shaking so much—when it opened. Nigel stood in the doorframe, wearing a faded Foo Fighters band shirt, his eyes freshly red. The force of her relief in seeing him in the flesh stunned her, so much so she could barely speak. Nigel, her Nigel. She started to cry again.

"I'm so sorry."

He pulled her in and shut the door behind her. Then he tentatively enclosed her in a hug. "I thought you wouldn't come."

"Nigel," she whispered, her voice cracking. Tears blurred her vision. "Words cannot . . . I'm so, so sorry." Dana buried her face in his shoulder. "For everything, but especially what I said to you yesterday. I didn't mean . . . I didn't mean . . ."

"You meant them," Nigel said. "And that's OK. You were being honest, at least. We've been tiptoeing around certain things for a while, and it had to come out."

"Yes, but not the way it all did." Dana wiped her eyes with a crumpled, soaked tissue. "God, I'm a wreck. Will you forgive me?"

Nigel gently tipped her chin up, meeting her tear-filled gaze. "Only if you forgive me too—for my part in all this. Someone very wise once told me that marriage is a two-way street. I made that wish, just like you did. So I forgive you, Dana. We got into this mess together, and we'll crawl out of it the same way. Now sit. I'll get you something to drink. What would you like?"

"A glass of water, please, and tissues."

"Coming right up. In the meantime, make yourself at home."

She admired his place while he moved around the kitchen. It pleased her to see how thoughtfully designed and beautiful the place was—at least this version of Nigel was doing well for himself in that sense. She saw the awards his campaigns had won, the trophies and plaques on one wall. Validation for his work—Nigel always craved that.

They settled on opposite ends of the couch, the silence stretching between them like a bridge not yet crossed. There was still some ground to cover before they could even begin to meet each other in the middle.

"I think . . . I think I haven't been honest with you about a lot of things, and I'd like to start now. Firstly: work."

He squeezed her hand in silent encouragement. For the first time in the longest time, Dana was opening up about an area of her life she'd always kept separate from Nigel. A kind of church-state separation, in a way, because how could someone who wasn't in health care understand everything she went through on the daily? It was impossible.

She didn't look at him as she spoke, her gaze fixed instead on the glass in her hands. Her voice was calm, almost clinical, like she was reciting facts from a file she'd long since stopped feeling connected to. The long hours. The bruising encounter with disgruntled patients and their caretakers. Frustrations with insurance companies and billing. The unpredictability of her schedules. The diseases, the illnesses, the horrors, both self-inflicted and the random she came up against every day.

"I started compartmentalizing a while ago. Just putting everything in boxes—work, home, you, the kids. It was the only way to keep going. But after a while, the boxes stopped opening. I'd come home and feel like I was still wearing someone else's skin. Like I was watching our life happen from the outside." She gave a small, hollow laugh. "I'd be in a room and I'd be in my head, just sitting and staring out at you all. Wondering how to reach you."

Nigel put his hand on hers and squeezed. "You work in the ER—I can't even imagine what that's like."

A shudder ran through her body. "You can't. And nurses—we're always there, you know? We're the primary carers for our patients, not the physicians and surgeons who get to dip in and out between consults, surgeries. It's us. And it's so overwhelmingly bad sometimes. It's not just the gunshot victims; there's just so much senseless violence around us, you know? So many preventable injuries. Especially in Baltimore, with its violent crime rate through the roof. It's like bearing witness to horror after horror up close. And then sometimes I'm at the end of a really bad day"—Dana's eyes were shiny and her voice was high—"and some kid comes in having OD'd on drugs that belonged to their parents, kids as young as Gill, toddlers only a little older than Emmie, and I'm just so—*so* done."

The screams came back first—raw, high-pitched, and unrelenting—followed by the image of a teenager staring blankly at the ceiling, unresponsive in spite of the Narcan he'd received from the first responders, as they worked frantically to save him. A toddler, limp and blue, cradled in a sobbing mother's arms, gone before they could evacuate the contents of their stomach. Dana blinked hard, but the scenes clung to her like smoke, and with them came the familiar wave of exhaustion—not just physical, but soul-deep, the kind that no sleep could fix. She couldn't stop shuddering. Nigel put his hand on Dana. "You don't sound good, Dana."

She wasn't—it was time she acknowledged that too.

Her eyes met his. "You're not wrong," Dana admitted, exhaling. "A lot of things aren't right in our old life, my job being one of them. But I don't have a choice."

"You do have a choice," Nigel said softly. "You can always take a break or take fewer shifts."

"Not in a single-income household," Dana said, a hint of accusation in her voice.

Nigel cleared his throat. "Dana, if it means you get to slow down and rest for a bit, I'll work as a receptionist or a window cleaner, whatever I have to do, if we ever get out of this nightmare," he said roughly. He took her hands in his. "I'm sorry I was selfish in that sense. You know I always took so much pride and joy from my work—too much pride, maybe. When I was let go, it really did a number on my self-confidence, but that's not an excuse. I . . . I can't let you shoulder the burden of our family's finances any longer. No matter how down or how little I felt after I was let go, I should have gotten some help after I'd had time to grieve the worst of it, instead of forcing myself to suck it up and shoulder on, which I clearly failed to do, so that I could relieve some of your burdens. I am so, so sorry."

Dana felt like someone had taken a sledgehammer to her chest. She slumped against him, her bonelessness born from something like relief.

"Thank you for offering. I—I can't tell you how much that means to me, just hearing you acknowledge how much I've been shouldering in terms of finances. And I want you to know that I see you. I see all you've done for our household and kids. That's real labor too. That's work, I know that."

"Putting finances aside, there's something else I think you need to acknowledge." He pulled back to look her in the eye. "You don't sound like you're coping with your line of work anymore. Maybe you can just request for a rotation out of the ER department. You've been working on the frontlines for a very long time. I think you're burned out, Dana."

"Burned out—" Dana tried the words on for size. "How? I've . . . I've always been in this profession . . ."

"But you're doing the night shifts more often," Nigel said. "And night shifts . . . Dana, it's not just the way it messes up your circadian rhythm, but we all know things have a way of escalating at night. You've just been taking on way more than you should."

"Burned out." Her voice cracked. "I can't believe I didn't see it. I never . . . I never wanted to, I care—"

"Dana, it's OK to be burned out. You can be burned out and still care for your job and your patients," Nigel said, and that was when something broke inside Dana and she burst into tears.

Nigel pulled her close as she sobbed into his chest. "Oh my love, I'm so, so sorry I didn't see it earlier."

"I didn't know," Dana kept repeating.

"We don't always see what's happening to us until a loved one points it out. We can become numb or inured to certain things over time, good or bad." He tightened his arms around her and drew her closer, as though he could stop her tears. Tenderly, tentatively, he pressed his lips to the top of her head. "I know I'm guilty of doing just that. I do it even with myself."

"How did we get here?" she said, "We're supposed to be the smart ones. The adults."

"You're smart," he whispered, drawing a deep lungful of her calming scent. "But we're human. We make mistakes. We misread cues, misinterpret data, have blind spots, especially in situations where things aren't clear cut."

"I've just been so angry, you know? About so many things," she confessed. "I've been so, so tired."

"I'm sorry I wasn't there for you in that sense," he said softly.

"No," Dana said, looking into his eyes. "But neither was I. I see that now." She exhaled, a shuddery, tight noise that pierced Nigel's heart. "I see a lot of things now, here."

She bit her lip, clearly steeling herself for the question she wanted to ask next. "In all the chaos of trying to get you to remember—and then racing to fix everything—I never actually asked: What made you make *your* wish in the first place?"

Nigel's face was grim but determined. "It's unpleasant, Dana. You're not going to like what I'm going to say."

Hard conversations were seldom pleasant, but they needed to occur. Dana took a deep breath. "I know."

He told her about how he'd been feeling worthless and aimless for some time, that he'd felt like an afterthought in their marriage, that she never gave him anything after she was done at work—understandable, but brutal to hear it being put starkly—that even though he could understand it from an intellectual, logical standpoint, he was having a hard time dealing with it emotionally. "I've been missing you for a long time," he said. "But it didn't seem like you missed me at all. I thought you couldn't care less about me."

His voice roughened. Dana glanced down at her lap and steeled herself, knowing that the worst was yet to come.

He told her about what happened after the dinner with Selvi, in her living room. Dana's stomach twisted as he admitted his attraction to Selvi—her kindness, her consideration, her admiration—and how in a moment of weakness, he thought she was into him. "And I almost kissed her . . . if she hadn't stopped me," he said, his voice low.

Dana flinched. *Almost.* Funny how much weight that word carried. "What happened to us?" she asked, almost rhetorically.

"Way too much." He caught the look on her face. "I want to be clear—I'm not justifying my actions at all." He dropped his gaze. "And you? Have you ever . . . have you ever cheated or come close to it? Physically or emotionally?"

"No," Dana said. "To be honest, I just didn't have the energy or time, maybe."

"What about that Yomi guy?" he asked roughly. "You think you could . . . you could be interested, if you make it back?"

"No," Dana said with conviction. "I think he's actually a really cynical guy. When he talked about how he saw peer counseling as a stepping stone to something else—I could never be with someone that cynical about the world. I prefer my men a little more hopeful, to balance me out."

Nigel half smiled. "That makes me feel better, actually."

She buried her face in his shoulder. "A lot of hard truths this morning," she said softly.

"Some of them were long overdue," Nigel responded. "If we'd been a bit more in touch with our emotions, if we'd communicated better, maybe we could have avoided this."

"I've been unfair to you too," Dana said. "You've had it pretty rough, but you held the household together so well. Thank you, Nigel."

"You're more than welcome, Dana," Nigel said a little unsteadily. "And thank you for carrying such a heavy load too."

They sat in silence, but it was a friendlier silence. A hopeful one.

"Do you think we'll ever be OK again?" Dana asked.

"No," Nigel said, then smiled faintly. "Actually, thanks to this whole misadventure, I think we'll be better than OK if we ever make it back together. We'll be fine."

"*Fine* sounds pretty good," Dana said, a glimmer of hope in her voice.

Nigel stood. "Hold that thought. I'm getting us a drink."

"Alcohol?"

"Tea. I think we'd do well to stay away from any kind of drugs. I don't think we need any more help making bad decisions."

This time, their laughter, undercut with mild hysteria, was real.

—ʍ—

The tea was hot and sugary. "Tetley?" Dana asked, fishing out the tea bag.

"You heathen. Yorkshire Gold, only the best for the damned."

She snort-laughed. "Ah, the banter is back. Who knew it only took us being at death's door to rediscover our spark." She stirred her tea and gulped it down, making a face as she did—Tetley or Yorkshire Gold, she thought they tasted like wet feet. But one made small sacrifices where one could. "What do we do next?" she asked.

"We enjoy our last days together and go out with a bang, celebrate your birthday in style. I'll reserve a room for us to spend our last night together, somewhere fancy."

Dana raised an eyebrow. "How fancy?"

"Where reviewers say things like *opulence* and *magnificence* and *presidential*."

"Sounds expensive," Dana said.

"See, I don't know if you've heard of this twentieth-century invention called a credit card—"

"Yes, the reason why American household debt is at—oh my God, is this how I sound all the time?"

"Yes, and it's necessary, but just once, just tonight, why not?" he said, grinning. "That's our motto for the next forty-eight hours." He clasped her hands and squeezed. "If this is the end, I want to go out laughing while snorting caviar."

"But you *hate* caviar."

"It's the principle of it. And then, when we're bored of our fancy hotel room, we'll go out in New York, have the dream date you've always wanted in the city."

She put a hand on his. "I'm in, although I have one small request."

"Name it."

"Can I please, please take a nap before we leave your apartment? I'm kind of exhausted. I hardly slept the last two nights."

"Just a nap?" Nigel said, eyes on her mouth. "Alone?"

A thrilling notion, that Nigel had other plans that involved them being naked, surfaced before she quickly squashed it. That would complicate things. "Yes," she said, pushing it aside. "Sleep sounds heavenly."

"All right," he said, sounding disappointed. "Can I join you, though?"

"For the nap?"

"Yup."

"And by *nap* you do mean *just* napping?"

"Just the usual understanding of the word, yes." Nigel's lips quirked. "See the thing is, I haven't had a proper night's sleep in four days."

Nigel

Day Six

They fell asleep within seconds of hitting Nigel's bed with nary an erotic overture, until Nigel woke up around 1 p.m. with his arms around her wearing only one of his old T-shirts and her panties. Then his thoughts quickly shifted to unplatonic grounds.

He caught himself (and his breath), forcing himself to think of deeply unsexy thoughts involving tax returns. With some difficulty, he managed to return to safer ground. Whoa. He hadn't felt like this, this almost overwhelming desire for Dana, in a while—a really, really long while, in fact.

Maybe because he hadn't really felt good about himself for a long, long while too.

Funny thing, desire was. When you were young and in love, in the first flush of it, you thought it would never fade. You delighted in the press of your bodies, the taste of your lover; you could not get enough. Then you start making a life with them and the rush becomes the daily drip, and you realize that passion all too often has limits. Your excitement can be boxed and put away in attics, and your person can become a stranger, unknowable, unlovable. You discover that desire is mutable, your feelings are mutable. And you can grow to dislike or even hate the person you were once in love with.

He had not always liked Dana in the last two years, and that was why he'd had a hard time even undressing in front of his wife. Because having sex is an act of letting go, and as you get older, you become more selective about who you want to be vulnerable with. You knew that letting someone see you at your most vulnerable is a privilege. Not an act of impulse. And when you're married to that person, you better like the person you're exposing personal real estate to.

When Dana started emotionally withdrawing from him, the sex immediately became a problem. He found that he could only get into the act if he had time to think about the old Dana—hence why the scheduling of sex was a good thing. He would luxuriate in Past Dana, resurrecting her in his memories, in order to connect with the current one, the silent, shuttered one who saw him as an item on her checklist. How could she, and her feelings, have changed so much? He couldn't understand it—he'd been there every day, hadn't he? He'd been there since the beginning.

Maybe the problem was somewhere along the way they'd stopped choosing to love these changes, to stop seeing each other underneath the new layers they wore: Dana with her unresolved PTSD, exacerbated by the crush of pandemic work; Nigel with his deep sadness at losing a core part of his identity.

The PTSD seemed obvious now, in the clarity of this world. Neither of them had had the language or awareness to identify and name it then, which seemed especially shocking considering Dana's professional experience and training. Yet there was some truth to the adage that health care professionals were notoriously bad at self-diagnosing, especially when it came to the state of their own mental health.

And Nigel could now admit that he had been depressed. Losing his job had gutted him in ways he hadn't fully wrapped his mind around, not just because he'd genuinely loved his job. He had grown up in a household where the value of a man was directly linked to his financial contributions. No matter how good he'd been as a stay-at-home dad, how much pleasure he derived from that, it couldn't compensate for his feelings of inadequacy at being made redundant.

He'd tried telling himself that embracing the Main Parent Life as a man was the evolved, modern thing to do, but the truth was harder to swallow. The shame of not contributing financially—of not meeting the expectations ingrained in him—ran deeper than he'd realized.

That was the thing about love—it didn't exist in a vacuum. It was messy, contextual, and fragile, sustained only by intention and effort. Real love, the kind that went beyond the fiery passion you saw in a lot of the romances marketed to young people these days, took *work*. Respect. Understanding. Tolerance. Compromise. Sacrifice. All the building blocks, the work that took to *maintain* a healthy relationship. Something he really understood now.

So much of the goodwill and health had drained out of his and Dana's relationship, so much damage had been done over the last two years because they hadn't done the work to maintain the relationship. Nigel wasn't going to kid himself: He knew they weren't going to be able to undo all that and magically restore their relationship in the remaining time they had with each other—but that was not the point.

The point was to keep showing up for each other no matter how bad things got. Even if they didn't know what was going to happen next. To choose each other, every day, until they could no longer do so.

For better or for worse.

He propped himself up and leaned over to wake her from her curled-up position, but then he saw that her shoulders were heaving and her face—the visible side—was scrunched, as if caught in the grip of a terrible dream; she was crying silently. "Hey," he said softly.

She turned around and proved him right—she'd been pretending to sleep, or she'd woken up midway and had been weeping. He realized she was clutching the Polaroid—the one with what remained of their family, Bex and him—in her hand.

"Hey," she said. She wiped her eyes away hurriedly, as though she didn't want to infect his mood.

"What's wrong?" he asked, stroking her arm without even thinking about it. She stiffened at his initial touch, then relaxed.

"I was just thinking about"—she swallowed and averted her eyes—"about the kids. I miss them so much and I worry about them."

Nigel stilled. He'd been thinking about them too. Their children—bright, laughing, real—that he would never see again. His fists clenched beside him. Dana reached for him and they held each other for comfort.

She broke their somber reverie by sitting up, determination written into her features. "We aren't going down without a fight, Nigel. We're going to plead our case tomorrow, offer them some other type of sacrifice, and who knows, maybe the guardians will have pity on us and let us both return."

Nigel pasted a smile on his face, even though her plan sounded flimsy to him. The guardians didn't strike him as beings with a lot of compassion. "They are supposed to be chaotically neutral, right?"

Dana made a frustrated noise. "So are you saying we should just give up and lie here?"

"No," Nigel said. *Unless,* he thought, *the lying down leads to other activities. Naked ones that involve Dana and me.*

Nigel sighed. Would that it hadn't taken so long for them to get to this stage during their marriage vacation.

"Regardless, we owe it to each other and our children to try to make the best of this time away from them and enjoy each other's company, don't you think?"

"A monumental task in light of my impending termination," Nigel quipped, also sitting up. "But I'll try my best."

For a moment, her expression cracked, raw and unguarded, before she pulled herself back together. "Nigel. You don't have to—"

"Of course I have to," he said roughly. "There's no question about it. If it comes down to one of us returning, you have to return, no matter what. So yes, worse comes to worst, I expire in less than two days."

There was a dark hum of silence, then Dana shook her head and muttered, "No, I'm not crying again. I won't."

"Good," Nigel said. "Because I can't cry anymore either."

"So tell me—what do *you* want to do?" Dana said, keeping her tone light.

It was hard not to let his thoughts lead him down dangerous paths, especially when Dana was this physically close.

"Let's check in for our night at The Plaza. I know that was your dream hotel if we ever visited New York together." He congratulated himself on thinking of this—he'd made the booking online just before joining her in bed.

"What?" Dana said, her eyes wide. "*The* actual Plaza?"

"Yup."

Dana's squeal of excitement made him smile. He hadn't seen her lose it like this before. Nigel started packing. "Come on, we need to celebrate your fortieth in style."

"Have you ever stayed at The Plaza Hotel?" she wanted to know.

"No, but I'm glad my first time will be with you." *And my last,* he didn't add. He didn't have to—she shot him a stricken look she couldn't quite hide. "Our last birthday celebration together," Dana said softly, her eyes bright with tears.

Nigel put down the T-shirt he was holding and drew her close. He took her right hand and kissed her fingers. "We're going to have a nice time today and tomorrow. I've got it all planned out. We'll go shopping for your birthday present, and then we're going to have a fantastic dinner and then—" He cleared his throat, reddening. "We'll live it up in the room I booked at The Plaza."

"But . . . but at the end of tomorrow—"

"Please," he said softly, "don't worry about whatever comes next. Let's just have a beautiful evening and day tomorrow and give it our best shot. If we convince the guardians to let us head back together, then great. If we don't . . . well, I want you to go out there and live your best life . . . back home. I'd want that for you."

"But I would have lost you, and you'd have lost us," she whispered, her voice cracking as she looked away.

"Hey, didn't the guardian say I won't remember a thing?" But somehow Nigel did not believe he could ever forget Dana or his children. "And as for you, maybe after a respectable period of mourning, you'll be able to find someone new—as long as it's not that douchebag Spanish teacher you dated before me, Juan-Pedro."

Dana's head snapped back to him, her expression fierce. "How can you even joke about this? I don't want anyone else," she said, indignant.

"You say that now. Give it two years . . ."

"Are you saying that's how long it would take for you to find someone else if you were in my place?" she said with only a tiny catch in her voice.

"Dana. Be real. I'd never be able to replace you," Nigel said quietly.

"I'd give anything—well, almost anything, no more deals with supernatural beings for me—to go back to how we were," she said fervently. "Even when we were barely present for each other, I'd take that."

"Me too," Nigel said. "But if I get a do-over in our real world together, I'd be more present. I'd take more time to enjoy you. To enjoy us." He paused, then leaned in, deciding to go for it. "To do . . . this."

He brushed his lips against her nose, testing the water. She let him, then she drew back. Still holding herself apart from him.

No matter, he was going all in.

"I think you're the best thing that ever happened to me, Dana Smiley," he told her. "Now come on, let's get dressed and have the best date of our lives."

—~—

Nigel stood outside Dana's room, tugging at the sleeves of his blazer and feeling foolish. Even at his corporate job, he eschewed the blazer look (advertising was forgiving in that way), but he figured that this Dana would appreciate it. He'd never made much effort in his previous life, he realized with some remorse, even when they went out on the rare coffee date—it was always whatever was at hand that wasn't too wrinkled and wasn't too spit-stained by Emmie. While he'd always told himself it was because they weren't going somewhere fancy, he wouldn't have to make the effort, the truth was, he'd given up somewhere along the way. He'd gotten too comfortable not showing up for his wife.

When the guest room door opened, Dana stood before him in a pretty blue-and-cream floral sundress, a brown cropped jacket, and white sneakers. Her hair was loose and slightly windswept, like she'd been posing for a lifestyle brand campaign right before he knocked. She looked good, if not for the puffiness of her eyes that her makeup couldn't completely hide.

"You look amazing," he said sincerely.

Dana looked down at her clothes. "I'm glad I brought suitably stylish clothes for our staycation in my getaway bag to your place—although to be honest, everything of New Dana's is pretty stylish. She has a top-tier wardrobe."

"You OK?" Nigel asked, referring to her red eyes.

She held up their family photo and Nigel saw that Gill was gone. It was only Nigel and her and Bex standing in front of their home now. "It's my only photo of the kids," she said in a level voice that fooled no one.

He impulsively pulled her in for a hug. "We'll be back with them soon, don't worry," Nigel promised fervently, his own heart twisting. He was all in now—he wanted to go back.

He put on his best *go get 'em, tiger!* smile. "Let's work on breaking the spell, OK?"

"OK," she said, the tiniest hitch in her voice.

"Good. Now let's rewind and try again. Hey, honey, ready for our date? You look great."

"And look at you, Mr. Fancy Pants. Did you raid some high school debate team's closet?"

"They wish, this is fine Italian wool," he said, brushing imaginary lint off his shoulder. "Shall we skedaddle?"

Dana raised an eyebrow. "Not until you tell me what the plan is. I want to be dressed appropriately."

"We're just hanging out, doing some fun, low-intensity activities. I want them to be a surprise."

Her nose wrinkled—she wasn't a fan of surprises. "Will the vibes be casual or fancy?"

"Upscale casual. What you're wearing is fine."

"Anything requiring swimwear?"

"Nope. Do I look like I'd submerge this hair in chlorinated water by choice? Now come! Let's enjoy a fun day out as two incredibly attractive, emotionally stable adults."

Dana snorted. "Emotionally stable? Bold claim, Cheng."

"So you admit I'm *incredibly* attractive?"

Dana pursed her lips and shook her head with a smile.

He held out his hand like a gentleman in an old movie. "Come on, I promise I won't make you regret this."

She stared at his hand for a moment, then grabbed her bag and brushed past him. "Let's not get ahead of ourselves."

The first part of his surprise was the suite at The Plaza Hotel—she'd only been expecting a room. Dana's surprised delight at the reception desk made Nigel's day.

"Nigel, a suite? That's too much! We can't afford that."

"We can, in this world, remember? You're *Dr.* Dana Smiley, and I'm Nigel Bradshaw-Cheng, CMO."

She flushed. "Well then—"

When Dana tried to pay for her half, he plucked the card out of her hands and broke the card in front of the startled receptionist's eyes. "Don't be silly," he murmured. "If I'm going to be terminated, let me at least buy you a vacation." He slid his credit card across the counter to the receptionist. "I must admit, it's lovely having a good credit score in this world."

"Damn it, I should have asked for that—for them to pay off our mortgage in our real world," Dana joked.

"I doubt she would have been able to do that—they're guardians, not fairy godmothers." He frowned as a thought crossed his mind. "Come to think of it—why are we gendering these beings? They're just putting on skin suits as disguises. Underneath it all, they probably don't even have genitalia."

The redheaded receptionist's bright smile wavered at their curious conversation before she hurriedly dialed it back up when Dana pointed at Nigel. "Charge everything to him," Dana said somberly.

The elevator doors slid open, revealing the opulent hallway leading to their suite at The Plaza. Dana was momentarily speechless as they stepped inside their room. The suite was gilded perfection—velvet drapes, tall windows framing a partial view of Central Park.

Nigel flopped onto the king-size bed with a groan of satisfaction. "Well, this is definitely opulent."

Dana spun slowly in the center of the room, letting herself soak in the sheer absurdity of the luxury. "I feel like we've won the lottery. Who are we?"

"People living like it's their last"—he checked his watch—"thirty hours on earth."

But she missed his quip, having left the room to inspect the other chambers—it was a big suite. There was a squeal from the bathroom. Dana rushed out, her eyes wide. "Nigel, the freaking fixtures are *made of gold.*"

"Technically, my love, they are gold-plated."

She was back in the bathroom. He could hear her running the taps. "Oh my God, the tub has clawed feet!"

Nigel went to the windows. He could, as promised by the room category, see a partial view of Central Park. He took in the view of the city he would have once given anything to live in, and found he only wanted to be back in Baltimore with his children and Dana.

One more night, one more day left.

Nigel cleared his throat to dispel the lump in it. He could still hear Dana gushing over the painted tiles in the bathroom. "Get changed, we have activities to do."

—∞—

First stop: a long brunch at a buzzy café in Greenwich Village, the kind of place with an actual line for oat milk lattes and a flamingo-patterned designer-wallpapered feature wall bracketed by tall potted palms that practically screamed *selfie wall*. Dana eyed the menu with deep mistrust while Nigel stood confidently at the counter. "This menu is incomprehensible. There are ingredients here I've never encountered in my natural world."

"Like what?"

"Hemp flour. Ashwagandha powder. Aquafubu."

"Aquafaba."

She made a face. "Do you even know what half of these are?"

Nigel was glad for a chance to show off. "Yes, actually, I do." He proceeded to explain what each one was.

"Impressive."

"I bake in our world."

"Baking too?" She shook her head in wonder, wondering how she'd missed that. "When did you . . . What do you bake?"

"A couple of months ago. Nothing fancy, just simple shortbreads, cakes, et cetera."

"Impressive," she said.

"It's stress relieving, and I'm trying to be vegan."

She traced her fingers over the raised lettering of the menu. "Trying to be vegan is bullshit. You're either vegan or you're not."

He chuckled despite himself. "Do you want me to order?"

She nodded, looking relieved. "Yes, please."

"Are you still pro-dairy or are you OK with a nut milk?"

She opened her mouth, and before she could answer, he intoned in a surprisingly good mimicry of her, "It's not a milk if it comes from a nut."

"Ah, glad to know some things are constant." She laughed, easing into the situation.

He ordered their coffees, OJs, muffins, and sandwiches and paid, watching Dana as she walked around the café trying to pick out an optimal seat for her favorite outdoor pastime: people-watching. There was something incredibly comforting in knowing what the other person you were with was going to do next, that predictability that oiled a couple's interactions.

All the same, he was aware that even though he knew the core of her, things had changed between them, change that didn't just flow with the fact that there were two versions of them inhabiting a body. They had been living like ships passing in the night for almost a year in their past life. In a way, this Dana was both a stranger and the most familiar person he knew, just as he was to her.

He brought their order to the table. They finished their sandwiches and then got started on the muffins.

"This is nice," she said, taking a bite out of the hemp-flour muffin he'd gotten for them as dessert.

"You don't like it," he said, clocking the slight hesitancy in the way she ate the muffin.

"It's . . . surprising," she said helpfully. "I like surprises."

"Do you?"

"Nope. But I'm trying to."

We're trying. We're all trying. That was how relationships should go, Nigel thought. You keep trying even as you are buffeted by change. Because change will happen in life, whether you like it or not, and relationships must adapt to them or risk stagnation and ultimately death. And to love each other the same way? You couldn't relate to each other the same way year over year, much less love each other in exactly the same way no matter what. It just wasn't feasible. The way you loved someone could change, and that was natural and good.

"This is . . . nice. I haven't had a chance to go to a café with you in ages, or just sit anywhere and have a chat," she said. "Work just kind of overwhelmed me."

"Listen, I've got another surprise for you," he said.

"Oh yeah?"

"Here," Nigel said, placing his gift on the table in front of them, a little embarrassed by how invested he was in her approval.

She wrenched her gaze from the couple she was watching and dropped her eyes to the table. She let out a surprised but pleased "Oh!" Nigel had sketched the photo of the five of them and framed it.

Her eyes teared up. "Th-thanks. This is the best gift I've ever received."

It was incredible, her smile. "Honestly, it took me like half an hour, before I joined you in bed. I didn't even try to zhuzh my jawline. And I repurposed an old picture frame. In case—in case you make it back with something from this timeline."

"I love it," she said emphatically. "I tried to scan the original photo, even took a photo of it—" She stopped, too overwhelmed to continue.

"I'm glad you like it."

They looked down at their food with embarrassed smiles, surprisingly shy.

Dana put down her fork, a blissful smile on her face. "That was great. What's next?"

"We go to the Whitney," he said. He was determined that the date should proceed as planned—that was to say, to perfection. He would romance the crap out of Dana Smiley.

Dana

Day Six

It started to drizzle a few blocks from the café. *Ah, April in New York City,* Dana thought, tugging her coat tighter as a gust of wind swept past. The chill carried the metallic scent of rain and concrete, a smell she always associated with early spring in the city. Nigel had brought a tiny pocket umbrella that offered just enough cover for the top halves of their bodies, though her canvas sneakers were already uncomfortably damp by the time they reached the Whitney.

The Whitney Museum loomed sleek and gray, its angular edges softened by the drizzle from the pewter sky. A line of umbrellas and raincoats stretched from the entrance down the block—the Biennial had just launched a couple of weeks ago, and the turnout was predictably clamorous. But Nigel stepped confidently ahead and flashed his phone screen to the attendant, who nodded and waved them through the side entrance.

Dana raised an eyebrow as they stepped into the lobby, shaking the water off their shoulders. "How did you get us slots on such short notice?"

Nigel hesitated, then gave her a crooked smile.

"Full transparency, please," she pressed, catching the flicker of something unreadable in his eyes.

He colored slightly. "Full transparency: I've—well, New Nigel anyway—has been a Friend of the Whitney for a few years. I'd actually pre-booked the Biennial slots months ago."

She blinked. "Months ago?"

"Yeah," he said, scratching the back of his neck. "I'd been meaning to bring a date. Obviously back then I didn't know it'd be you."

He caught the import of his words and reddened. There was a beat of silence as they stood there, the lobby warm and bright around them, Nigel shuffling his feet and looking nervous. *Let him stew,* Dana thought.

Finally she decided to let him off the hook. "Oh my Lord, you brought me to another woman's date," she teased, breaking into a huge grin.

"Well, technically, it was an open booking," Nigel said, looking relieved.

"It's OK," Dana said. "I'd rather have the truth than some pretty lie. So don't be afraid to tell it to me like it is. We used to be like that, remember? Speaking without fear of censure."

Nigel nodded, thoughtful. "I remember those days."

They were soon milling in the atrium, figuring out their museum game plan.

"Why this exhibition?" Dana asked. "Manhattan is chockablock with museums, even within this two-mile radius."

"I'll let you hazard a guess," Nigel said, passing her a brochure about the exhibition.

"*Even Better Than the Real Thing*," Dana read out loud. "How apt," she said dryly.

Nigel smiled. "You'll like it, I promise."

The air hummed with the low, insistent buzz of conversation, punctuated by the occasional murmur of appreciation from a visitor and the click of a camera or phone. They moved through the galleries, pausing here and there to study a particularly striking painting or installation. Even with the crowd control, the galleries were uncomfortably packed. Sometimes Dana would think she saw a face in the crowd that she recognized, but before she could put a name to it, the person would turn out to be a stranger or blend into the masses.

At one point, they reached a room that stopped both of them in their tracks. "Wow," Nigel said, gazing at the hanging sheets of acrylic paintings by Suzanne Jackson, hands in his pockets, rocking slightly on his heels. The artist had composed each "painting" from the inconsequential detritus of life, so that you could see mesh, raw silk, cloth, shredded mail, even pistachio shells suspended in an acrylic medium and hung up like gauzy, fantastical sails, through which one could view the other visitors moving through the gossamer sheets like ghosts. As though the quotidian messes of a life were worthy of preservation.

You couldn't help thinking about your own relationships, your own life, and wondering if there was something lovely left in the chaos that you would like to hold on to, to hold up and admire. To say: *Let's keep this. Let's keep that.*

"Wow," Dana echoed. She had always loved art, even though everyone who knew them both thought of Nigel as the more artistic-leaning person in their couple by virtue of his profession; she wished, in her previous world, that she'd insisted on bringing more art into her life—to sculpt or even paint as a way to relax, not discard it as though it hadn't once been a fundamental aspect of her life.

Their other favorites: large sheets of unfixed photographic film that would develop as the exhibition progressed, by Lotus L. Kang; Harmony Hammond's austere, layered mixed-medium paintings that spoke of wounds and healing.

Everywhere she turned, she was confronted by questions: *Is this how you want to be remembered? Is this how you want to remember? Who do you want to remember and who do you want to be remembered by?*

They went through all the floors of the museum, taking their time to pick their way through the pieces, separating, coming back, and then at some point not coming back, lost to each other.

Nigel found her loitering in the gift shop, ruminating on a pair of crystal troll earrings, trying to ground her thoughts and emotions. She was glad when he suggested they leave.

"How was the exhibition? Was it good for you?"

She nodded. "It was eye-opening, to say the least."

"What did you take from the Biennial?" Nigel asked.

"Legacy. Especially some of the film selections, like the one with the Chilean artist walking through a jungle dragging a glossy blue bolt of cloth behind them by a rushing stream in a landscape that's threatened by destruction . . . it just made me think about how we want to be remembered, and whether it even matters. Sorry, I wish I could be more poetic about my critique."

"You don't have to impress me," Nigel said lightly. He grasped her fingers and brought them to his lips. "You already are."

"What did you take out of the visit?" Dana turned the question back to him.

"Transformation. Reinvention," Nigel said, after a thoughtful pause. "A lot of the pieces were about taking pieces of something broken, or at least things people would view as being trash, and making something new out of it."

Dana said, "Sounds like you're describing us."

"Yes, I guess there are some parallels, here and there."

There were indeed, Dana thought. Yes, they were broken; yes, they were mired in brokenness, but there was beauty still to be salvaged. There was still good in them to be admired.

She was quiet. "I'll be honest, I thought the museum would help me take my mind off things, but instead it's only dredged up more questions."

"I'm sorry. That was not my intention—to add to your mental load," Nigel said.

"I know," she said. "But that isn't always bad." Sitting with discomfort—sorting through her feelings, her past, and what came next in her personal life—was a skill she'd long lacked. But this experience had forced her to confront that gap for the first time. She wasn't turning or backing away from the challenge, not anymore. She was going to welcome it. *Let that be something good that comes out of this week, even as I lose this man.*

She forced a smile on her face for his benefit. "Come on, I'm hungry."

Nigel

Day Six

After that, they went back to the suite and changed into their dinner clothes, Nigel in an actual suit and Dana in a soft gray jacket, sleeveless ankle-length black dress, and black pumps she had impulse-bought at a boutique near the Whitney, and headed to the iconic Michelin three-star fine-dining restaurant in Midtown, Le Comptoir; Dana had wanted to dine there since she'd heard Taylor Swift loved it.

Now Dana sat across from Nigel, scrolling through the prix fixe menu with an intensity that suggested she was barely coming to terms with the price of the wild-caught cod.

"This place is ridiculous," Dana whispered as soon as the waiter had taken their orders. Her gaze darted around the elegant, low-lit room. "I feel like I should apologize for not being famous."

Nigel said, sotto voce, "I'm pretty sure our waiter is not French but is putting on a French accent."

"Comes with the job description—*must be able to speak with pretentious French accent.*"

They giggled before Dana shushed him. "I really don't want him to cough elegantly into my food before serving it to me."

Nigel chuckled. "You're right." He gestured at the space around them. "So, did I do all right? Do you feel pampered? I am, after all, making up for three years of anniversary dinners spent at the local Italian restaurant in our suburb, where parsley is a vegetable, not an afterthought."

"Yes," Dana said with satisfaction. "I do feel pampered."

The waiter was back with the amuse-bouche and a round of champagne.

"Promise me something, though?"

"Anything," Dana said, her eyes taking in the elegantly plated morsel of scallop that had just been placed in front of her with a flourish.

"Don't stop me if I end up eating street hot dogs on the way home. You know, just in case I don't like the food."

The waiter's shocked intake of breath was almost worth it.

As soon as the waiter left, Nigel giggled at Dana's expression. "What? I was just testing him to see if he was really human or something out of a live-action *Ratatouille*."

Dana rested her chin on her hand, her expression softening. "You know," she said, "I used to dream about eating at a place like this, back when I was a nursing student eating ramen—and I guess even now in our real life, with our tight purse strings."

"I told you, I wasn't dating you for your money, but you wouldn't listen."

"What were you dating me for, then?"

Nigel made a show of looking around him before leaning over and whispering, "Your childbearing hips."

Dana's shocked giggle made several heads whip in her direction with displeasure.

"You are impossible," she said, shaking her head. "But I like it. I like this, how light we are."

In spite of everything.

Nigel raised his glass, clinking it gently against hers. "Here's to us," he said. Because in spite of everything, he was choosing to have fun with her; in spite of everything, he was choosing laughter and lightness.

"To us," Dana echoed, her eyes locking with his in a way that made him forget the prices on the menu—almost.

—ꟿ—

Their final stop was Grand Central Terminal. The cavernous main hall was nearly empty at this hour, its starry ceiling glowing softly above them. Nigel took Dana's hand and pulled her into a slow dance, humming "Closing Time."

"No music?" she teased.

"Who needs it when you've got me?" he said, spinning her gently.

For a moment, it felt like the rest of the world disappeared, and it was just the two of them in the heart of New York, dancing to the rhythm of their laughter and the echoes of their footsteps.

He brought her to the gallery below the main concourse, in front of the Oyster Bar & Restaurant, and made her stand in a corner facing the wall. "Close your eyes and don't turn around."

"Oh God," Dana muttered.

He ran across the other side of the room and then whispered, "I want to kiss you."

Then he ran back to her. Dana was smiling. "I take it you heard that."

"Yeah, I did. Cute science experiment."

"You're cute." Their eyes met and a warm spark blossomed in his chest.

"Anyway, the phenomenon is called *telegraphing*. It's something to do with the curved dome and sound waves. Even if the hall had been packed with people, if you were in the right spot, you would have heard every single word as if I had been standing next to you."

She sidled up to him, all mock coyness and mischief. "Or you could just stand next to me and tell me."

"Tell you what?"

"What you said you wanted to do to me," she said in a low voice.

Nigel's heart hammered in response, but he didn't want to make the wrong move and shatter the evening's cadence, so he drew her close and held her instead, relishing the warmth of her skin. He started to sing "Closing Time," and they began to sway in time to the music. He was still whispering the chorus as he spun her around and around the gallery, telling her he wanted her to be the one to bring him home.

"Really?" she said, stopping mid-spin and looking up at him, all seriousness and glinting intention.

"Always," he said. It felt right to kiss her just then, so he did.

—w—

By the time they returned to The Plaza, they were both giddy and exhausted, wrung dry of emotion. They collapsed onto the bed in their suite, still fully dressed.

"Did I do good?" Nigel asked, his voice heavy with sleep.

"Yes, yes you did," Dana agreed, her hand finding his.

He waited till she had fallen asleep and pulled out the Polaroid from the drawer next to their bed. As the clock struck midnight, the smiling image of Bex disappeared—and now Dana was all that was left on the Polaroid.

Nigel

Day Seven

Nigel woke with a jolt, nerves prickling like static beneath his skin. For a moment, he didn't move. His hand rested on the empty stretch of sheet beside him where Dana had been just hours before, warm and curled into his chest like she belonged there. Today was their last day together in this strange, beautiful, borrowed world. It could be the last day of his life, full stop.

Ticktock.

He sat up slowly, taking in the elegant suite of The Plaza with a kind of grim reverence. His mind tried to rebel against the calm around him. The thick, expensive silence. The understated luxury. The woman he had loved—and lost, and maybe was losing again—still asleep just feet away on the edge of the expansive king. He forced himself to stay in the moment. If he let the panic win, he'd lose the little time they had left. This was it. His final day with Dana. He had to make it count.

Ticktock.

He put on a brave face and inched over. "Wake up, Dee," he said, nuzzling her shoulder. She grinned sleepily and didn't seem to mind, so Nigel pressed his lips on hers and gave her a chaste (but hopeful) kiss. She protested and tried to push him away with a drowsy smile. "If you think you're coming anywhere near me before brushing your teeth, you're dead wrong. You know my thoughts on morning breath."

"What's a little morning breath between old marrieds," Nigel said, puckering his lips out like a comic-book fish and honing in.

She chuckled and batted his face away with a playful swat. "Plus, I've got sleep in my eyes and a rat's nest for hair."

"No," he said, drawing back with exaggerated disgust. "*Quelle horreur,* madame!"

He didn't mind either way—he would have kissed her no matter what.

She struggled to sit up, still dressed in his oversize T-shirt, the neckline slipping down to expose one perfect, tawny shoulder. Nigel forced himself to keep his gaze strictly above her clavicles. "So what do you have planned for us today?" she said, attempting levity. She would have gotten away with it too, if not for the slight crack at the end of the sentence.

She's putting on a brave face too.

"Free and easy, a picnic in Central Park, late lunch somewhere cool." He tucked a strand of hair behind her ear. "Basically, I just want to spend quality, uninterrupted private time with you. No crowds. Just us."

Dana's smile softened, genuine and without hesitation. "That sounds perfect." She stretched, letting the fabric of his shirt ride up to the soft expanse of her stomach and the top of black boxer shorts. "I'll go take a shower."

Nigel cleared his throat and looked determinedly at the wall as she got out of bed, lest he sully the tender moment by ogling her like a caveman. He would be a gentleman to the end, doing only what she wanted and giving her anything she asked for, because no matter what, she deserved a perfect last day with him.

But hearing her shower proved too tempting. He made himself leave the bedroom and wait in the living room, his thoughts fixed firmly on tax returns.

She came out of the bedroom fresh-faced and pretty in a red-and-white gingham off-shoulder top, wide-legged dark jeans, and heeled boots—she looked incredible, way out of his league. He suddenly felt shy, as he had so many years ago before their first date at another park, another lifetime ago.

"You look great," she said, noticing his silence.

He exhaled, smiling with effort. "This old getup?" He was wearing jeans, a white T-shirt, and a checked shirt. "You look like you just stepped out of a feel-good film. Like *10 Things I Hate About You*."

"Guess that makes you my charming-but-traumatized co-lead."

He chuckled, trying to keep things light. "We'll get rave reviews."

He held out his arm and she took it.

Ticktock.

Dana

Day Seven

On the way to Central Park, they stopped by a gourmet deli Nigel had scoped out earlier while she waited outside, trying not to cry. He bought sandwiches, sparkling water, and champagne that came with a free cold sleeve and packed them into a wicker picnic basket along with the soft cashmere sweater he'd brought for her in case the weather turned.

As they wandered through Central Park hand in hand, Dana oohed and aahed over landmarks she recognized from films, especially the Bethesda Terrace, which had been featured in a *John Wick* movie (Dana was not-so-secretly in love with Keanu Reeves—and so was Nigel). She could tell Nigel was putting on a brave front for her, but the way his hand would tighten around hers whenever there was unexpected movement or sound in their vicinity told her the truth of his mental state.

He needs a distraction, Dana thought. She flushed. She had a good idea of what could be a good distraction: The trouble was, she wasn't sure if she could give that to him.

Ever since they had spent the night sleeping side by side, Dana felt like she was constantly dodging his gaze. She feared her face might betray the tangle of emotions she couldn't untangle for herself. Desire and resentment. Longing and weariness. They all lived there, just beneath the surface, a tangled ball of conflicting emotions clamoring to escape.

It wasn't the idea of intimacy that scared her—it was the aftermath. The wrecking kind of intimacy they used to share when they were a team wasn't just physical; it was a portal through which they reflected the hidden depths of their soul at each other—no artifice. That was why their acts of intimacy these days were so efficient and ritualistic—they were reducing it to the physical to protect each other from what lay under the protective film, a plunge into something deeper, messier, more honest than she could bear to face these days. She was already hanging on by a thread, emotionally.

And now here, as they mended their connection to each other, Dana wondered what would happen if they got honest with each other during sex—if they committed wholeheartedly. If the dam broke and what lay beneath was too much for either of them, it would break them on their precious last day.

Because if she was being honest—she was afraid of what lay at the bottom of the well of her soul once they removed the cover.

They found a bench near the Conservatory Garden, under the filtered light of a tree still blooming with early-spring blossoms, pink and frothy, and sat down. The garden was quite empty for a weekday, but it could be the fact that it had rained the night before and now the ground was slightly squelchy.

Nigel passed her a sandwich and they began to eat silently, watching the park goers.

A family of ducks popped out of a bush nearby, surprising Nigel so much he dropped his sandwich onto the damp grass. He scrambled for it as the ducks hurried by, quacking accusatorily, but it was too late. Mud covered the bread.

"I'll share," Dana said, passing him her half-eaten pastrami and rye, extra mustard.

He chuckled. "I'd never thought I'd live to see the day that Dana Smiley would share her food with me."

"What are you talking about? During our first date, I gave you a bite of my sandwich too."

"You remembered," Nigel said, looking pleased.

"Of course I do," Dana said. "I dashed out after my shift to meet you at Middle Branch, and you got us sandwiches from Lenny's like I asked you to."

And I was too nervous to eat. Just like she was now. *I wanted to impress you.*

They sat in silence for a moment, the easy kind where no words were needed. Dana shut her eyes and let the sun drench her skin and Central Park life buzz around her. It felt good to be out in the warmth with Nigel; she could almost forget this was the end of a cursed week.

A tear pricked her eye and she knuckled it away, determined to let Nigel have a pleasant send-off. He deserved that, and more.

"Everything OK?" he said, sliding a glance at her.

"Just the wind," she said brightly, tamping down the fear. "I'm hungry, what else have you got for me in that bag of food?"

Nigel picked out a sandwich from the paper bag. "Another pastrami and rye, but of course."

"And what did you get for yourself?" Dana always took a bite of his food—it drove him crazy in the early days of their relationship.

"Pastrami and rye," he said with a grin.

"Oh no," Dana said, disappointed.

"Just kidding." He fished his out and waved it in front of her. "I got us a Reuben with extra sauerkraut, just the way you like it." That was her second favorite sandwich.

She laughed. "Man, you're really going all out."

"If only I'd known how easy it would be to win you over back in the day, I would not have spent so much money on all those fine-dining joints."

"I don't know, I did save your life."

"You did," he said, his eyes lingering on hers. "You did."

Dana bit her lip and was on the verge of saying more when he abruptly got up from the bench and began walking toward a patch of sun-drenched grass nearby. "Come on, let's find a spot in the sun and eat."

They made a spot in the sunshine without further ado, Dana smoothing out the blue-and-white picnic blanket and Nigel unpacking the basket. Something in the atmosphere between them had changed; the energy felt charged, combustible, slightly dangerous. They were hesitant to get too close to each other. They sat at opposite ends of the blanket and ate in silence for a moment, the only sounds around them the rustling of leaves and the distant hum of city life.

Tell him how you feel, come on. It's your last chance.

What's the point? It'll just make it harder for us both when it's over.

Sometimes it was easier to say nothing. Easier to just let things be. Keep the status quo going.

No, I need to start telling him how I feel, even if the conversation is difficult.

She finished her sandwich and leaned back, staring up at the sky. Beside her, Nigel did the same.

"Sandwich for your thoughts."

She turned to him and smiled. "In a way, I guess I'm grateful that at least I got to experience life in New York and spend two perfect days together with you, even if the price we paid for this one vacation was absurdly high."

"I won't lie," Nigel said, his brave facade cracking at last, "it's a little extreme. I could have done with less peril to our children and less losing of my life to get here, you know?" He held his hands up. "And let it be noted that I am *not* blaming you."

"I know," Dana said. Her throat tightened; she was really struggling now. "I keep wishing . . . I keep thinking, if only we'd taken more time off together. Like even a staycation at the local Marriott, you know? And just really talked, every day. Real check-ins that had nothing to do with household admin or logistics. Maybe we could have caught ourselves before the spiral. Mabe we could have avoided . . . we could have avoided all of this." Her voice cracked, the guilt rising again.

"I know," Nigel said, just as hoarsely. "I did have something planned. For your birthday. Booked it and everything."

"Really?" She was inexplicably touched. Nigel didn't really do surprises. He liked to meticulously consult her on plans to eliminate risk, then execute them to perfection. "What was it?"

He ducked his head, embarrassed. "This farm-stay cabin thing—apple picking, rustic fireplace, the works." He gave a crooked smile. "We'd have made love in the evenings, watched bad cable in the mornings. It would've been cheesy and perfect."

Dana looked at him then, really looked, surprise in every syllable. "I thought you had nothing planned. You didn't even seem to like being in the same room as me."

"I kept waiting for the right moment to tell you," he said. "But I think I missed a lot of them."

If only, if only—the theme song for this week.

"That would have been an amazing way to celebrate my fortieth," Dana whispered. "Almost as good as when I rented out that Viet-Chinese restaurant's private room for a birthday karaoke."

"You wish," Nigel said, trying to be flippant. It almost worked. He put his face in his hands, a sob escaping him. "Goddamn it, I told myself I wouldn't cry."

Dana felt something inside her crack wide open. Seeing him break down—Nigel, the embodiment of British reserve, who had always held it together even when she was falling apart—shattered what little composure she had left. She pulled him into a fierce embrace, holding him like she could anchor them both.

Her own tears fell unchecked as he rocked against her, weeping. The snowdrifts were melting, the ground underneath ugly and barren after a hard winter. And so what? In time, life would tumble out of the ground, new green. How was it any different when it came to them? They had dashed themselves against the rock and come apart. They'd seen each other at their worst this week. They'd said things to each other that could never be unsaid. Truthful, hurtful things. They had revealed the rotten core of their marriage to light. And so that was how life was. The good, the bad, and the ugly. For better or for worse. What was she afraid of? Losing control? Maybe that was exactly what she needed to do with Nigel—loosen the tight reins she'd held over this part of her life before they calcified and killed them.

"Why the hell shouldn't you cry?" she whispered. "You should be allowed to feel anything. Do anything. Say anything. Whatever . . . whatever it is you want, so long as it's within my power, I'll help you fulfill it."

He pulled back slightly, and for a moment, she saw all of him: the anxiety, the exhaustion, the heartbreak—and the love. Then, despite the tears and the streak of snot on his upper lip, a glimmer of mischief flickered in his brown eyes.

"Anything?" he said, raising an eyebrow.

"Yeah," she said, blushing. *Don't get any ideas, he's probably just setting us up to go to a fight club next.*

"All right, woman," Nigel said, sitting back on his elbows and considering her. "I'll recalibrate my plans for later. In the meantime—" He reached into the picnic basket for the bottle of champagne he'd bought at the gourmet supermarket and made a face. "It's gotten a little warm even with the cold sleeve, but it should be drinkable."

"Champagne is always drinkable." She hesitated, rethinking her statement. "Well, almost always."

He popped the bottle open and poured it into their plastic stemware. They drank the glasses silently.

"Thank you," Dana said, her voice soft, almost shy. "For today. I didn't realize how much I needed this."

Nigel clinked his glass against hers. "A park date seems a little slapdash, but I'm glad you approve."

"It's the thought that counts," she replied, tucking her legs under her as she turned toward him, her knees brushing against his. "I never really realized how much I missed this—just us, just being present with no distractions." Her fingers found his, intertwining with his, squeezing tightly. Had his hands always felt this good? Maybe. She squeezed them again.

"Well, good," he said, his voice a little rougher than usual, the weight of his words hanging in the air between them. "Because I want to spend the rest of this day with you like this. Just you and me. No distractions."

"Well, you've got me," she said, leaning in closer to him. "What's next on the agenda? A museum? Introduction to jujitsu? Wine tasting?"

Ask me to go back to the hotel with you.

Nigel's gaze sharpened. He dipped his head close to her and murmured, "To be honest, I was kind of hoping we'd revisit the whole Maintenance Shag thing—maybe bump it up by a week." He pressed a kiss to the pulse near her mouth and worked his way down her neck, each touch sending tingling waves of pleasure radiating outward.

"That is," he murmured, lips brushing skin, "if it's not . . . too much of a hassle to reschedule."

"I . . . I guess I could be convinced to schedule it tonight," she said, flushing.

Nigel's breathing was uneven and shallow. He brushed a strand of hair out of her eyes. "How about now?"

Nigel

Day Seven

They couldn't get a car fast enough: Both of them tried booking one on two different apps, giggling. Now they were in the car that Dana had found on an app and her hands were stroking him over the fabric of his jeans. Now they were giggling as they stumbled into the lobby, Nigel walking behind her with her tote bag positioned strategically over his crotch. Now they were in their golden suite with the partial view over Central Park. He was pulling off her top before the heavy door closed. His plaid shirt took more time to unbutton because he was running his hands over her body, trying to peel off a bra whose hooks would not cooperate. He let her take it off while he gently pulled the hair tie out of her wavy hair and let it tumble over her shoulders.

Dana uncrossed her arms hesitantly, almost as though she were doing it for the first time. She was beautiful.

"Wow," he said quietly, taking her in with his eyes in a way that made her blush.

He lifted her and put her onto the massive bed and they kissed in a tangle of limbs. None of this felt like their scheduled lovemaking. They took their time even though they both wanted to go faster. They were both hungrily in the moment, reveling in the way they felt under each caress, each whispered direction, each move. They were present and wanted to be present for each other; they existed only to please each other, to receive pleasure. There was no one else in that world but them.

—෴—

He traced a finger down her back—she'd always liked when he did that—and relished the small shiver of pleasure he elicited from her. She nuzzled into his chest, her breath bringing up goose bumps on his skin. *How could you have forgotten this?* It was unthinkable. He must have hit his head on concrete or something, coming here.

It's the right time, he decided. "Dana?"

"Yeah," she said, her voice slow with impending sleep.

"There's something I wanted to bring up," he said, still tracing his finger across her back. He could feel her tense beside him. "I know it's hard, but what you said really stuck with me, and I wanted to address it."

She sat up and turned to him, her face wearing that guarded look he knew well. But there was a willingness to listen in the soft incline of her face.

"A few days ago, when I asked you if you had been unhappy with our life, you deflected and said it didn't matter. That family is what is important." He hesitated when she dropped her gaze and flattened her lips, but made himself push on. "But it does matter, Dana."

He waited till her eyes met his. "I wasn't unhappy because I didn't have a job, Dana. I was unhappy because I felt like you were no longer happy with everything—including me. Your happiness is important to me, Dana. And it should have mattered more to you. Promise me this: No matter where life takes you, no matter what happens, you'll love yourself a little more. You'll look after yourself. Because the way you treat yourself—it means everything to me."

Dana's tears started to fall silently onto the bedspread.

"I'm so, so sorry, Nigel," Dana said simply. "I wish I could have done it all over again, the last two years, really."

"Stop," Nigel said. "I'm banning us from using the word *wish*. Forever."

Dana laughed. "OK."

He dropped his head and gave her butterfly kisses along her neck and collarbone that made her heart flutter. She shut her eyes when his mouth found hers. Whatever came after this—whatever storm waited on the other side—none of it mattered. Not now.

All he wanted was for her to stay here, with him, in this one unburdened moment. To let herself feel joy without apology. To forget, just for a while, how much she carried.

It wasn't for him: It was the smallest kindness she owed herself.

Dana

Day Seven

They put on their matching bathrobes and called room service to send up another magnum of champagne and caviar, as well as Dana's special order: a medium-rare steak and extra fries—because why not?

Dana sighed and set down her spoon after her third mouthful of Osetra caviar. "I want to say this is the life, but it isn't, really."

Nigel stretched out by her feet on the bed and downed another glass of champagne. "Speak for yourself. I just had a fine, sexy time with an amazing woman, and now I'm drinking top-shelf vintage champagne. I'd say I'm pretty lucky."

His tone was flippant, but his eyes were serious. Trust Nigel to find the light side of anything.

Dana's watch beeped—it was 11 p.m. Almost showtime. She had a plan up her sleeve, but she couldn't let Nigel know.

"Dana, why do you have a weird look in your eyes?"

Think fast. "Indigestion," she said. It was gratifying to see him chuckle—they had had so few lighthearted moments lately. "Nigel, do you believe in God?" She herself was agnostic, but now she couldn't stop thinking about what happened after death.

"I guess?" Nigel replied, giving her a curious look. "I mean, at least from a Christian perspective. There was this altar call at a church when

I was fifteen and visiting my aunts in Australia and—" He shook his head. "Wait, how is this relevant again?"

"It's just . . . in case the guardians misrepresented the facts to us again and what they mean by you staying behind means you getting killed and you get sent to some horrific place where you suffer for an eternity."

"Honey, you're not making me feel better."

Dana's lips wobbled. "I'm just so worried." Her filter was gone, eroded by her sense of urgency.

"Aw, Dee," Nigel said, reaching out for her. He pulled her close and hugged her tightly. "Don't cry. We don't know anything for sure. Look, don't worry about me. I don't believe in the afterlife—not if you and the kids aren't with me."

Now *his* lips were wobbling.

"I love you," she said, her voice steady despite the tightness in her chest. "And I'm sorry."

"I love you too," Nigel said. "And I'm really, really sorry."

He pulled her to him and they kissed tenderly—until it wasn't. The bathrobes just didn't hold up their end of the bargain of enrobing, and Dana didn't help. "Technically we have fifty-three minutes left," Nigel reasoned, his breath hitching. "And I'm assuming you can't get pregnant from what we do here."

"Such sexy talk," Dana said.

When they were finally spent, catching their breaths in the quiet aftermath, Dana murmured, "I'm sorry I wasted so much time not doing this with you. And now it's too late."

He chuckled and kissed her forehead, his lips lingering. "For what it's worth, I think we more than made up for the last two years. If the last twelve hours are any indication."

Dana moved to wash up and slip on one of Nigel's shirts and a pair of boxers, as did he. Being naked in front of a supernatural being felt disrespectful—or just plain wrong. He even shaved in the washroom.

Ten minutes before midnight, the guardian and her colleague reappeared, this time abandoning any pretense of humanoid forms. They emerged as shifting masses of smoke, eyes glowing amber, trailing the distinct scent of camphor and eucalyptus.

"Hello, Nigel and Dana," the guardians said in unison as the smoke began separating into two distinct forms.

"You smell like Vicks VapoRub," Dana said by way of greeting. "It's almost comforting, if you weren't here to—I don't know—tear us apart and ruin our lives."

The guardian and her protégé exchanged glances—or the suggestion of glances. "I sense . . . some animosity."

"No shit," Nigel said. "Wouldn't you be angry if you were about to be ripped away from everyone you love? I thought you were supposed to be chaotic neutral, but you are definitely not nice."

"*Nice* is subjective," the first guardian replied with a slight edge in its voice—Dana recognized it as the woman she had met in the parking lot.

"Besides, you won't remember," the younger guardian added.

"But I will," Dana said softly. "And so will the kids. Doesn't that break the parameters of my wish—to return without my real world impacted by what we did here?"

"We said 'no lasting consequences,'" the younger guardian said. "Death doesn't last."

Dana's eyes welled. "You are eternal beings"—she didn't add *heartless*, although she thought it—"and don't see death the way we do." She placed a hand over her heart. "Because it marks us here, for those that survive." She touched her temple, trembling. "And here. For the ones left behind."

"You have a point," the other guardian said. "But a wish is a wish, and there's no way out of this."

"But there is," Dana and Nigel said at the same time.

They turned and looked at each other. "Oh no, you don't," Nigel said. "Listen to me—I've got it figured out."

"No, *you* don't," Dana exclaimed. "*I* do." Her face had hardened with resolve. She turned toward the guardians, who were watching in silence.

"It's simple," she said, her voice high and strained. "Please—for the love of all that's good—save him. Take me instead of Nigel. This is *my* fault. I-if you take me, you would still fulfill the parameters of our wishes because *I* would cease to exist. There'd be no life left to affect." She blinked, tears catching in her lashes. "That way, Nigel can continue to live."

"No, I don't want that," Nigel said, his voice cracking as he stepped forward in front of Dana, as though he could shield her from herself. "*I* don't accept her interpretation. I won't."

"It works," Dana said, pushing him away and pointing to her chest. "Trust me, I've worked it out. Take me instead."

"Absolutely not," Nigel said, his face twisted in grief. "Dana, the kids need you more. I've had a good two years with them. It's your turn now. They need *you*."

"I won't let you make that choice for me. The kids need you . . . you're the hands-on, patient parent. You once stayed up two nights in a row to finish Bex's science project—I would have just let her fail so she'd learn from it." She turned back to the guardians. "And he once dashed onto a road to save a hedgehog stranded in the middle. I would've driven off."

"Really?" Nigel said, side-eyeing her.

"I wouldn't, but I needed to illustrate my point."

"Which is?" the older guardian asked.

Nigel shook his head forcefully. "Let me take the fall. Dana should stay. She is the love of my life and I want her to live."

They were at an impasse, Dana knew. She had a plan C, and she was ready to launch it if they failed.

That's why she had ordered the steak.

She gripped the edge of the dining table behind her, positioning herself to act when the moment came. It would not be easy, but there was nothing she wouldn't do—couldn't do—to save this family.

Blood had opened the portal in both their cases. Hence, it stood to reason that if she went ahead with her wild plan—

I love you, and I'm sorry, Dana telegraphed to Nigel.

Nigel turned to the guardians, his face lit with passion. "What if we made a new wish?" he said, just as Dana said, "What if I don't give you the choice?"

"We are confused," the older guardian said.

"Speak for yourself," the second guardian said. "I'm half your age." Their eyes fixed on Nigel and Dana. "But you may supply clarification for the other slower one's sake."

"There's no confusion," Nigel said. He had taken out a steak knife—*her* steak knife—and the metal caught the light, trembling in his unsteady grip, even though his eyes were resolute. "I want to make a new wish. I—I wish to undo our original wishes."

"Nigel, *put that away,*" Dana said, her eyes fixed on the serrated blade, as if her will alone could lower his hand.

Nigel held the knife to his wrist. A thin band of skin whitened under the pressure. "No, I can't," he said hoarsely.

He tensed, ready for action, and then he made his move.

Nigel

Day Seven

Now.

He tried to drive the blade across his skin but found he couldn't move a muscle, no matter how hard he strained—and neither could Dana, who was frozen in mid-lunge, pure terror in her eyes. The shadows around them solidified and held them in place, like flies in old amber.

"We told you, you can't force our hand," one of the guardians—the older woman, from the sounds of it—said. "We hear your distress—it's interesting that you both had the same idea—but even if you sacrifice yourself, you can't *undo* your wishes. What is set in motion cannot be reversed. So don't get any bad ideas."

There was a gentle breeze, and suddenly they could move again. Dana ran to him and he hugged her. "Oh, Nigel," she said, sobbing freely into his chest. "How *dare* you steal my idea?"

In response, he kissed her nose. "Great minds," he said simply to her shaky chuckle. It had been a stretch, but he'd had to try.

The smoke solidified into two human forms—an older woman and the one who had come to Nigel's "rescue" at the accident, both of them wearing gray robes.

The older one held out a hand. "Now please. It is time—"

You can't rewrite history, but what if you can make a follow-up wish?

An idea struck him. "Wait. Let me speak with you alone," Nigel said. "Just for a moment. Please. A private audience."

"Why would you need a private audience?" Dana asked, grabbing his arm. "Anything you want to discuss can be done here, freely."

"Not on this matter," Nigel said softly. He fixed his eyes on the guardians, not wanting his wife's fear to sway his resolve.

The guardians glanced at each other, unreadable.

"He has the right to ask," the older one murmured.

"Very well," said the other. "Come."

In the space between spaces, all was still. The air shimmered, silent. Nigel stood before the psychopomps, Dana obscured by a veil of shimmering energy.

"I'm not asking you to undo a wish," Nigel said quietly. "I—I know the rules. So I'm making a new one that respects existing boundaries—that is, if you'll allow it." He drew a steadying breath. "And I'm prepared . . . I'm prepared to offer a sacrifice for another chance."

The guardians exchanged a look. "You broke more rules than Dana did, by seeking her out after we expressly forbade further contact, binding your new timelines even more closely together in contravention of your old wishes. Thus your sacrifice must proportionally match the revised stakes."

He bowed his head. "It will be," he whispered.

What he was about to ask of them, of himself—would cost more than his life. After all, a life, no matter how precious, was finite—whereas this involved the eternal. His only qualm was this: He had lied to Dana, somewhat—he did believe in God and the afterlife. As soon as he'd heard that he might die, his convictions had clarified. But a perfect eternity without them felt remote and intangible to him, as did a fiery death as promised in the Book. He was human and limited, and he thought of his family first. He hoped she would forgive him. He hoped God would.

The guardians said nothing, merely observing him. Willing him to speak without their interference.

"I . . . I'm pledging myself. Not my life, which as you know is fleeting on earth—but my soul." Nigel's voice cracked. "When my time on this earth ends, it's yours. I pledge it in service to you for as long as you need it. For eternity."

Shocked expressions flitted over their normally placid faces. "That is . . . that is a big sacrifice," the younger guardian said, clearly discomfited. "That's eternity. What does a mortal understand of eternity? You do not know what you ask. We cannot accept wishes that are open-ended like that, even if we could accept souls as offerings."

"And we can't," the older one added. "That is not our purpose, Nigel."

"Then put a goddamn number on it," Nigel said, desperate now. "My soul—or my service, in the undead realm, for fifty—a hundred years. Call it a kind of blood offering, only more powerful."

The younger one's voice gentled. "We are an order of beings that have existed since before your kind began. We are not in need of . . . human servitude."

"Please." The word tumbled out of Nigel. "You can . . . I don't know, loan me out, put me in cold storage then, whatever is fair. I just want a chance to rejoin my family in my real life. *Please.*"

The guardians turned to each other, heads bowed, and conferred in their strange tongue. Every second that passed without a verdict felt interminable. Nigel's head buzzed with fear—he had to shut his eyes in order not to faint with terror.

Finally they spoke: "All right, Nigel."

Nigel's eyes flew open. "You accept my terms?" He wasn't sure if he felt relief, elation, terror, or dread—every one of those emotions was working its way through his system.

They nodded. "In a sense, yes," the younger one said. "We are giving you a chance to return to your original timeline *after* the accident."

Nigel's relief escaped in an audible hiss. Elation threatened to overwhelm him. He would see his family—and Dana!—again. But then the guardians interrupted his relief.

"You must understand," the older guardian continued, "that if you fail to wake up, we will claim your soul—as pledged, for whatever purpose we deem fit in our service—without further ado. You won't have a fallback world—or life. Nothing. You will not pass through again."

Nigel nodded. "I accept that," he said with more bravery than he felt.

The other stepped forward. "Then you must offer your covenant, as always."

Nigel took the steak knife and pricked his thumb with the tip of it. Blood welled. He held it out and then the blood disappeared, licked by an invisible force.

"It is done," the younger one said softly.

The shimmery barrier disappeared. Dana ran to him. "W-what did you do? What happened?"

"I made a deal," Nigel said.

"Not another deal," Dana whispered, her face ashen.

"It's a good one," Nigel said quickly, glossing over the edges. "I don't die. Not physically. In either world—as long as I make my way back."

Dana's eyes filled with tears. "How is that supposed to comfort me? 'If' you make your way back? Nigel, that's not a plan—it's a gamble." She stepped closer, voice sharpening. "Tell me everything, Nigel Bradshaw-Cheng."

He swallowed hard. Right now, she was more terrifying than any unknowable cosmic consequence.

"I asked them to let me fight for it," he said. "To earn my way back. If I can't wake up in the real world . . . then they get my soul." He hesitated. "Temporarily," he added, too fast. He wasn't sure if they'd agreed to fifty years or a hundred—but either way, now that he was saying it out loud, both sounded ominously long.

Also, he conceded silently, in retrospect, he probably wasn't a great negotiator if the next jump between figures was double-fold.

"Tempo—" Her voice failed her. Her face leached of color. "Nigel," she said at last, "Why?"

"I had to try. For you. For the kids."

She broke down then and threw herself at him. "You *idiot*. What did you do that for? You could have stayed here. You could have had a life."

He kissed her forehead, his stomach in knots even as his head felt clearer and more resolute than it had at the start of the day. "It isn't a life if it's without you and the kids."

The clock struck midnight. The first of the bells. The guardians murmured to each other in a tongue not made for humans. "It's time, Dana and Nigel."

They clasped each other, shuddering. "I'm sorry we couldn't find our way back together," Dana whispered. "I love you."

"I love you too," Nigel murmured. "So much."

The guardians stopped conferring.

"The portal has been opened by your new blood and new vow, Nigel," the younger one said. "You may both return."

"If your will is strong enough to find the thread of your true life, the soul will remain yours. But should you fail . . ." It trailed off.

Dana kissed his nose, her eyes somber—he could tell she was putting on a brave front for his sake. "He won't."

The air thrummed. The world around them was growing dim and her form was fading—their time was up. "I'll find my way back to you, Dana," he promised her, hoping she could hear him. "Whatever it takes."

And then—the light in his world went out.

Dana

Day Seven

I can't believe he did that. She didn't know the details of what he'd pledged, but she could tell it had *not* been well negotiated. Nigel wasn't exactly detail-oriented—he was the big-picture guy. The dreamer. The impulsive one.

Whatever it was, it couldn't be good—especially since it involved his soul.

Nigel had made an impossible, terrible deal for the slimmest of chances to be together. She would have laughed if she weren't so close to tears.

Because she wished she had thought of doing that first.

Silly, brave man.

One of the guardians was waving its arms around as Dana and Nigel exchanged parting words. She held on to him and drew him close. Her world shimmered, the edges of the room dissolving like ink in water. Her heart sank as the hotel room faded into nothingness—and with it, Nigel. "Nigel?" she cried out, reaching desperately into the darkness to find her husband, but her hands grasped at empty air.

Darkness engulfed her and she had the sensation that she was falling. Then, as suddenly as it started, it ended.

Dana hit the ground with a hard thud, pain flaring in her tailbone. She groaned, blinking rapidly as her vision adjusted to the dim, familiar surroundings. The white porch of her home. She scanned the street and yard, her heart pounding, alert for any unfamiliar changes in her surroundings. Her eyes landed on the mailbox, its crooked wooden post still leaning slightly to the left from when Nigel had backed into it last winter. The blinking porch lights that she had been meaning to fix for days but hadn't gotten around to. Everything looked the same.

From the raised window by the porch, she caught the sound of familiar voices and laughter coming from the back of the house. Her children.

Her phone buzzed on the floor next to her. She twisted to check the time and date.

It was just past midnight on April 7, the night she left, and once again Dana Smiley was back home.

She stood up and made her way to the front door, her heart in her throat.

Dana

Reset

This is it. This is the moment of truth.

Dana stood on her porch, her heart thudding with dread and anticipation and her fists clenched. She felt nauseated and slower than normal. Everything *looked* the same, felt the same, even *smelled* the same. The porch still had its planter pots of gardenias and pansies, subtly perfuming the evening with their sweet fragrance, and the second step still squeaked when she put her weight on it. Their lovely olive-green front door's vintage brass knocker, salvaged from a yard sale, had the same reassuring heft and patina. But she didn't know what she would find once she quietly unlocked the front door to her home.

She stepped into the low-lit hall and automatically made her way to the kitchen, toward the sound of young-throated, happy chatter—no adult voices here. Given the hour, the dinner with Shobana and Bex must be over, and the kids were up uncharacteristically late.

"Mom!"

Dana turned toward the voice, her heart nearly bursting with joy at the sight before her: Bex, Gill, and little Emmie—clinging to Gill's back like a tiny knapsack, half asleep, her arms looped around his neck while his hands held her securely. And Moped, who must've been napping by the back door, came skittering in at Bex's call, a blur of fur and frantic barking. They stood there in the kitchen—whole, safe, a little rumpled from play, but unmistakably all right.

She was back in the right timeline.

You're forgetting something, a little voice whispered, but Dana brushed it aside. She was too eager to see her children again.

She paused to take in the moment, tears in her throat, so grateful for her second chance that she almost couldn't bring herself to take another step into that kitchen, toward reclaiming her space with her family. But then Emmie woke up and reached out to her from Gill's back. "Mama," she said, smiling, and Dana felt a huge weight lift off her as she scooped her child into her arms. She almost didn't let it affect her when Emmie started struggling after a few seconds and ran back to her brother. Almost.

"Have you eaten?" Bex asked, gesturing to the remains of what she now knew was Nigel's homemade Bolognese in a covered pot. "There's leftovers—Dad left it for you."

Dana couldn't trust herself to speak. She shook her head and leaned over to kiss her cheek. "I'm not hungry, but thank you." She was drinking them all in, her beautiful family who she had kept herself away from for too long.

"Didn't you have a shift? Aren't you hungry?" Gill asked, worried.

"Nope," Dana said. Then without another word, she hugged her son.

She knew, on a deeper, more fundamental level, that she would have to sit with her children—really sit with them—and begin the slow, patient work of undoing the damage her sustained emotional absence had caused over the past year or so. She would make it up to them, one PTA meeting, one home-cooked meal, one honest, hard-won conversation at a time. She would make time now, whatever it took, even if it meant the family would have to cut back somewhere.

Dana surfaced for air from the hug with Bex. "Come here," she said, beckoning to Gill and Emmie to join her and Bex. They drew close. Dana hugged them tightly, breathing in their familiar, individual scents: Bex—citrus oil and musk; Gill—sweat, cardamom, and something faintly hormonal; Emmie—soft butter and powder. Even Moped leaped in with a volley of off-pitch barks. Her world felt righted again. The deep dive and the explanations could wait until tomorrow. They were safe—they were home.

When they finally pulled apart, Moped bounded away to explore some corner of the house. But Nigel didn't appear.

An uneasy feeling blossomed in the pit of her stomach.

"Where's Dad?" For some reason, when she thought of Nigel, her head was woolly, her thoughts jumbled.

"I don't know," Bex said, stifling a yawn and rubbing her eyes. "He left over an hour ago to drive Shobana and Shobs's mom home because their car wouldn't start." She stretched and added, "Man, I feel like I've been hit by a truck. I'm exhausted and so stuffed after that meal."

"Yeah, me too," Gill said. Emmie was already half drowsing where she stood. It was, after all, a school night.

"Can I—can I take her?" Dana asked, gesturing to Emmie.

"Sure, Mom," Gill asked, arching an eyebrow at her. "I mean, I'm just a placeholder for you, you know?"

She didn't think that was quite true, but she'd take it.

Dana gathered Emmie into her arms and carried her to bed, the little girl's head nestled against her shoulder, warm and sweet with sleep. Bex and Gill trailed behind, ribbing each other about crushes and other teen things. *This. I missed all of this.* The guilt, the remorse, the regret, came hand in hand, and Dana let herself sit with those emotions—better this than to numb herself the way she had for so long. Because they weren't the end of it. There was joy to come. And contentment and hope. The renewal after a loss. All part of being human, and growing from a lesson.

She was choosing to sit and stay in her discomfort, and learn and grow from it.

Later, in the quiet dark, with Emmie curled beside her, an arm flung over Dana's chest, Dana started to cry softly. She knew she had been given an enormous gift—a once-in-a-lifetime chance to reframe her life and to make right previous wrongs where she could. She didn't know what tomorrow would bring—what she'd have to sacrifice to make things right—but in that moment, wrapped around her child's gentle weight, she was very glad she'd met that old woman in the parking lot.

—∾—

When Dana awoke, light was streaming through the wooden blinds in the bedroom. Her mouth and eyes were as dry as new cotton and her head was pounding. Disoriented, she sat up. There was a split second of panic when the events of the week before came back to her. She calmed down when she saw Emmie still lying beside her on her bed. Voices and the occasional bark drifted up from the kitchen downstairs—the other kids and dog were up.

And—she cast her eye around the room, something like fear waking up in the pit of her stomach—Nigel had not come home. *Where is he?*

That nagging, uneasy feeling was back again, but she still couldn't grasp what she was missing.

Her attention was drawn to an insistent buzzing noise. Her phone. Shit. Sixteen missed calls. *Shit.* Her phone must have been accidentally put on silent.

She dived for it and picked up. "Dana Smiley," she said hoarsely.

"Dana?" A thin, reedy voice crackled with strange static; Dana recognized it as belonging to Liz Worsham, her nursing colleague. "Dana, it's Liz. I don't want you to panic, but—"

She told Dana about Nigel's accident, and goose bumps broke out over Dana's arms. Déjà vu, and something else—fear, as everything that had happened in the other universe resolidified in her memory.

She and Nigel had reverted to the night of the accident, and there'd been no change to that trajectory.

Her stomach lurched and her veins sang with ice—given her years in the ER, the fragility of the human body, and the failings of the health care system, she was conditioned to expect the worst-case scenario. Catastrophe felt like muscle memory.

She moved quickly but carefully, gently rousing Emmie from sleep and carrying her downstairs. She broke the news as calmly as she could manage, trying not to alarm the kids. “We have to go to the hospital. It’s Dad. He’s been brought in. I don’t know much more than that.” Her voice trembled despite her efforts to stay steady.

“Don’t panic, Mom,” Gill said quietly. “We’re here.”

She grabbed her keys from the hook and headed to the driveway, where the SUV waited like a lifeline. Dana had never been more grateful to see a car.

“Let’s go see your dad,” she said, and opened the door.

Dana

Reset

The SUV was, of course, out of gas. Dana quickly refueled with an emergency can of gas that Nigel kept in the garage—thank God for his reliability. She'd always forgotten that part of him. Nigel the Reliable.

Nigel the Brave.

Nigel the Hurt. Nigel the Human.

"Is Dad going to be OK?" Gill asked.

"I hope so, honey," she said tightly.

Dana's skin prickled as she walked her kids down the hallway to the ICU, to the room where Nigel lay unconscious—his face mottled with bruises, a gash in his hairline now neatly stapled shut, his head partly wrapped in gauze. He was surrounded by a web of IV lines, monitors, and the quiet menace of the ventilator, its mechanical hiss punctuating the sterile quiet of his room.

Diffuse cerebral edema. That was what the neurosurgeon—Dr. Fred Mann, someone Dana didn't know—had called it. Swelling in the brain. Trauma-induced.

The surgeon pulled Dana aside in a quiet nook farther down the hallway. "We've placed him in a medically induced coma to reduce metabolic demand on his brain," Dr. Mann explained. "He's otherwise stable, which is encouraging."

Dana, fluent in the language of critical care, translated automatically: The coma was protective, temporary. A controlled state of suspension to give his brain a fighting chance.

"But you should know," Dr. Mann continued, gently but without sugarcoating, "we lost him briefly in the OR. He went into cardiac arrest during the craniotomy. We managed to resuscitate him after a minute and forty seconds of compressions."

Dana's breath caught.

"He's still young, and he came in with decent vitals. That's in his favor. But I won't lie—it was touch and go for a while. We'll begin to taper the sedatives in the next twenty-four to forty-eight hours to assess neurological function."

She thanked him and joined the kids by the window, where they watched their father with tears coming down their faces, and Dana couldn't blame them. He looked so frail lying there. So human.

"Papa," Emmie said. She started to wail, giving a voice to Dana's pain. She pressed her face into Gill's thigh and held him close. Bex turned to Dana and clung on to her, sobbing into her shoulder. Dana bit her lip and automatically arranged her face in an expressionless mask. She was terrified, panicky, and her legs were in danger of giving out. Yet you would never have been able to tell from the line of her posture. That was the point of her training, and old habits died hard.

How do you do it? Nigel's voice piped up. It was something they had discussed before, back in their suite at The Plaza on their last night in their other life. *How did you, such an empathetic person, last so long in this job?*

I didn't, clearly, she responded to Nigel in her head, the last piece of the puzzle falling into place. This place, her job, had been slowly erasing her. *I was falling apart from all the things I can't unsee. I'm a burned-out old bitch.*

Then you're my *burned-out old bitch,* he had said in response.

"Oh fuck—" She excused herself and walked around a corner to find a quiet spot to freak out, her fist shoved in her mouth. She was dry-heaving and couldn't stop. She was crying and couldn't stop.

Someone placed a gentle hand on her shoulder. Bex. "Mom, hey, it's OK, we're here."

Gill hugged her from the back. "Yeah, Mom, don't be sad without us. Be sad *with* us."

"I don't know how," she sobbed, the words catching in her throat. For so long, she'd been alone with a father who taught her that emotions were a weakness. Then came the job, where composure was currency. She'd been praised for her professionalism—Dana the Unshakable. Put her in an ER and she could handle anything: a drunk driver who'd slammed into a lamppost while celebrating a promotion, a teenager dying of an opioid overdose, a mother bleeding out from a gunshot wound. She was the calm in the storm. Dana the Superwoman.

But now, in this waiting room, with the sterile walls pressing in and her children watching her for cues on what was to come, that title felt like a burden instead of a badge. Unshakable. As if she'd ever had the luxury of falling apart. As if being strong hadn't also meant being alone. She had worn that strength like armor for so long she hadn't realized how heavy it had become—how it had kept people out, even the ones she loved most.

What good was composure now, when the man she'd built a life with lay unconscious in a hospital bed, suspended between worlds? What good was being unshakable when her family had been shaking under the weight of her controlled detachment for months, maybe years?

She wasn't unshakable. She had found her limit.

"Mom," Bex said, squeezing her shoulder and rubbing her back as Dana wept against the wall. "Mom."

"We're here," Gill reminded her. "You're not alone."

She hugged them; she wasn't alone, and she wouldn't let them be.

—ᴡ—

They tried very hard to fix him.

He was still in the ICU nine days after his accident; scans showed the swelling had subsided, his brain activity was healthy, and the doctors had determined that he could breathe with minimal ventilator support. They started tapering off his sedation in stages while monitoring his vitals, hoping for signs that he was returning to them, but Nigel didn't wake up.

Two weeks passed.

The doctors told her to keep visiting Nigel, to speak to him so he could find his way back to her. So she did. She also reached out to the hospital's in-house counselor, who had contacted her to see if she needed help when she first heard of Nigel's accident, and finally conceded that yes, she did need mental health support, for Nigel and other things in her past.

She and the kids decorated his hospital room with photos of the family and some of Emmie's best finger paintings. Tommy Foo and his family visited and brought him flowers, fat, nodding yellow daffodils and tulips.

A month passed.

She took reduced shifts, keen to not burn out, and made sure to spend an hour with him every day with the kids. Bex and Gill would regale him with stories of school life, and Emmie babbled in somewhat comprehensible phrases at her dad. Tommy Foo (ever a pillar of support and geniality) would take the kids back, his wife, Valerie, would sometimes stop by with food for Dana so she wouldn't have to eat "nutrient-dead" hospital food; with this support system in place, she was able to spend a couple more hours with Nigel, staying by his side, reading and watching over him when she grew weary, chatting at him when she wasn't.

"You know," she told Nigel, stroking his face, "the Foos are kind of awesome. I don't know why you used to bitch about them so much. Was it because you were jealous? It's the hot tub, isn't it? And how perfect their lives looked."

She leaned over, adopting a conspiratorial tone. "Last night, I saw Tommy walk out of the house covered in oatmeal—at least I hope it's oatmeal—spattered pajamas, which is unusual for him, since he's always in, like, expensive polos and suits, and he basically just sat on the stoop of his porch and stared at his driveway for twenty minutes.

Not that I was staring at him the whole time, mind you. But I thought he didn't look so good. We always just assume other people are holding it together, when they could be falling apart, and I just think it's high time we stop expecting perfection in our home and marital lives, and that we normalize chaos and confusion and all the 'bad' emotions we're told to keep in check, to keep hidden."

She sighed, feeling defeated. Some days were harder than others. Some days—like today—even looking at him hurt. "Anyway, all things considered, even in icky pajama pants, Tommy Foo is, like, really hot. He's legit Marvel Action Hero material."

Only the soft beeps and his gentle ventilated breaths greeted this statement. She had hoped that would annoy him out of his state, but it didn't work. Not even when she made herself some Yorkshire Gold with the hot water from her flask and told him it was Tetley.

Some days, the only emotion she was strong enough to sustain was anger. "I just got you back, Nigel. I just got you back. Why won't you just open your eyes?"

Some days, when she was at her lowest, she resorted to emotional blackmail.

"Seriously? Still? After this year? And everything we've gone through financially? This hospital stay will ruin us, you know? That's like, the less romantic aspect of it. Because if you never wake up, I'll probably need to get therapy, and that's just another very expensive expense on top of the whole hospitalization bill."

Her eyes welled up again and she pressed the heel of her palm against her hot forehead. "I'm sorry, you know that's not important. I just miss you, OK? You big lunk."

"Why don't you try some music," Andrea, the nurse on shift, suggested on one of her rounds, sometime around week five after his accident. "Some people react well to that."

She did just that: She brought him some music courtesy of a Bluetooth speaker and Spotify playlist.

"You should remember this," she told him, giving his ribs a light poke.

The Bluetooth had a tinny sound quality that distorted her and Nigel's favorite romantic song, Whitney Houston's "I Will Always Love You." But Dana sang along in her husky contralto voice and made it her own.

Please wake up, Nigel, please wake up.

When the song was done, Dana leaned over and kissed Nigel softly on the lips. "I hate to say this," she murmured, "but I'll see you tomorrow. You better make more of an effort." She tossed her items into her tote bag with barely a thought and stood up, ready to leave.

Then she heard a weak, raspy "Dee."

Her heart skipped. She whipped her head around, hoping and dreading all at once.

Nigel blinked at her, lifting a hand slowly for a half wave. His voice was barely above a whisper. "Miss me?"

Dana's heart squeezed. She carefully wrapped her arms around his body, pressing her face into the softness of him as tears welled up. "Are you kidding me? Of course! I was so worried, so scared."

Nigel poked a couple of fingers through her hair, brushing it clumsily, trying to offer some comfort despite his weakness; he was always trying to comfort her, her Nigel.

"Sorry," he said.

"Don't be," she whispered, straightening up, wiping her eyes. "You're back now. That's all that matters."

He winced slightly, his voice coming out with difficulty. "I had a really weird dream before you woke me up."

Dana tilted her head, curiosity piqued. "Oh? What kind of dream?"

He grimaced. "I kept getting chased around by my high school biology teacher, who wanted to hit me with a badminton racket. And then halfway through, she turned into my mom. It was . . . weird."

Dana snorted despite herself, wiping the last of her tears away. "That's definitely one way to face your fears."

"Dana," Nigel said quietly.

"Yeah?"

"Thank you for saving me."

"You remember everything?"

Nigel nodded. "Yeah. And some of New Nigel's memories too." He flashed her his crooked smile. "I'm looking forward to applying some of the lessons from his bedroom to ours."

Incorrigible Nigel is back. "At least some good came out of that debacle."

He laughed. "But honey, we've really got to stop meeting like this," he said, gesturing around.

"No more hospitals," Dana agreed, giving a huff of laughter.

A young nurse with her hair in a low bun—Sally—poked her head inside and smiled, pleased to see Nigel awake. She paged Nigel's doctor and came back. "By the way, your parents just arrived. Would you like to see them?"

Nigel nodded. "Yes please." Nigel's parents were nice but very, very old, and had boarded a plane from Heathrow that morning, since his dad had just recovered from a hip replacement not long ago and couldn't fly when they first heard the news.

Dana handed Sally a slip of paper with a phone number scrawled on it. "And could you call Valerie Foo for me, please? She has the kids, and I'd imagine they'd want to see their dad."

Sally nodded and ducked out.

Nigel gave a soft chuckle and shook his head at her. "Man, it's good to be back."

She felt the old defensiveness creep in and forced it back down. "I'm sorry, I'm basically planning your schedule for you. Are you even up to receiving visitors?"

He clasped her hand and nodded. "Absolutely. Besides, it's not like I can go anywhere, anyway," he said, gesturing at the lines and machines surrounding him. Nigel the Joker.

He grew serious. "Not that I'd want to, even if I could. I think we've done enough traveling this year, wouldn't you say?"

She gave a theatrical shudder. "I'd be very happy to not go anywhere else with you."

"Well, maybe just that staycation I originally planned for your birthday. I'd still like to celebrate your fortieth in style at that luxury experiential farm I was talking about."

"Where I'll have to pick the vegetables for my own dinner?"

"You know it."

She chuckled. "OK, maybe just that one."

She kissed his temples, which were just beginning to gray. He wasn't perfect, and neither was she. But they were each other's for a reason.

They had started this journey together with a promise: for better or for worse. Had pledged to answer life's great questions together:

What do you want?

A life with you. All the lives with you.

Who do you want to journey this life with?

You, my dear.

As you are. As you will be.

Acknowledgments

This has been one of the hardest books I've ever had to write, in part because I drafted and redrafted it throughout 2024 and 2025—an incredibly challenging period for me, both personally and professionally. During that time, I was working full-time in humanitarian diplomacy, often grappling with the growing, even blatant, disregard for the very laws meant to monitor hostilities and conflicts. It was—and remains—a sobering experience to witness the erosion of principles that, by now, should be beyond dispute. My mental health was deeply affected, and I imagine I'm not the only author who felt this way: How do you write about hope and rediscovering love in a time as heavy as this, when it feels like we should be mourning the greater losses unfolding around us?

A good friend then challenged me: *Why not?* Isn't that the role of fiction—to help us find our own way back to hope, and love, in our lives? Who among us hasn't asked, in some form, *What next? How can I go on?*

So I did just that. I set my mind to explore what happens *after* the happily-ever-after, or at least the promise of it—in the context of an ordinary millennial couple. Any long-term couple will tell you: Love is a journey, not a fairy tale. I wanted to dig into the raw, unvarnished reality that comes after the storybook ending, when the afterglow fades and real life—the drudgery, the doubts, the distance—starts to seep in, especially when life gets rough. How do we keep love alive while trying not to fall apart ourselves? Where does love go when we are lost? What happens when we can't even connect with ourselves, let alone our loved ones? I hope that you will find this story an inherently hopeful one, as I intended it to be.

To my editors Selena and Carissa, copyeditor Tara, proofreader Kellie, Karah (and everyone at Amazon who helped), and book wizard Andrea—thank you for guiding this book exactly where it needed to go. I'm deeply proud of what we've achieved together. Amazon Publishing—especially Selena—was endlessly patient with me as I missed deadline after deadline (which, I promise, is not how I usually operate, as my agent can attest—this *is* book four, after all). I truly couldn't have done this without you.

To my agent, Katelyn Detweiler—thank you for navigating the roller coaster that was 2024–2025 with me. I'm so lucky to have you in my corner. And yes—fine—thank you, Jesse, for leading me to Katelyn in the first place.

To my family—my siblings, my parents and in-laws, the Hos and the Wohl-Schneiders—thank you for your unwavering love and patience, for feeding me, and for taking care of the kids when I needed time to write or just breathe. Your support has been my foundation. And as always—thank you, Ying Wei, for the extra medical expertise (any mistakes are mine, not his).

To Oli, for persevering when I get hangry, and for being a patient and good partner. To Sophie and Henry, thank you for cheering me up always—you are the best part of my every day.

To my friends—both in real life and online—you know who you are. Thank you for being there, always. Special shout-outs to Marissa, for all the HHs (and everything else), and to Laura, for new beginnings in an old friendship. And thanks to Club Med Asia for taking care of my kids while I write when I'm supposed to be on holiday in beautiful destinations around Asia.

And last but not least—to every reader, every bookseller, every reviewer who chooses to read my books: Thank you for supporting my work. I'm so glad you're Team Ho. Let's go!

About the Author

Photo © Marvin Kho

Lauren Ho is the author of *Bite Me, Royce Taslim*; *Lucie Yi Is Not a Romantic*; and *Last Tang Standing*. She is a former legal counsel turned author whose writing explores the messy, heartfelt, and often humorous realities of modern life. Originally from Malaysia, she has lived across Europe and now resides in Singapore with her family. When she's not writing multi-genre fiction for both adults and children, Lauren can be found watching (and occasionally performing) stand-up comedy, belting out karaoke, or hunting down the perfect bite. For more information, visit www.hellolaurenho.com and follow her at @HelloLaurenHo.